FANG

VOLUME 6

Edited by Ashe Valisca

FANG Volume 6

Production copyright FurPlanet Productions © 2015
Cover artwork copyright © 2015 by Mehndi

Published by FurPlanet Productions
Dallas, Texas
www.FurPlanet.com

Print ISBN 978-1-61450-240-1

Printed in the United States of America
First Edition Trade Paperback June 2015

BAD DOG BOOKS

Table of Contents

Introduction   11
    by Ashe Valisca
Ashes   13
    by Slip-Wolf
Inspiration   45
    by Whyte Yoté
The Gallant Endeavour   67
    by Tym Greene
Initiation   113
    by Kyell Gold
Moral Folly   129
    by Miriam Curzon
Summoning   155
    by Tym Greene
Tithes   171
    by Chris "Sparf" Williams
While the Wind Shook the Barley   207
    by NightEyes DaySpring
About the Authors   245
About the Editor   249
About the Artist   249

Introduction

by Ashe Valisca

Putting together an anthology is a complicated beast. Part of it is finding harmony within the stories; another part is working with authors to encourage growth while not harming their personal styles; and the final piece is being able to let go of the manuscript in its final form. I am proud of this collection and I am happy to have worked with each and every author here.

With the theme of this year's collection being Victorian Romance I may have painted my writers into a corner, but all of them have risen to the challenge to create engaging and moving stories. This was an era of change, an era of complexity, and an era of sexual exploration. Society existed in a state of extremes from the stark prudishness to the rampant consumption of "adult materials".

This anthology has explored many different parts of what would be called "indecency". Not only are these stories set in an era they are, each in their own way, commentaries following the adage, *'The more things change; the more they stay the same,'* it can be startling to realize how little has actually changed in the past century.

So in this collection you will find the price of love and betrayal; the primal translated to the erotic and emotional; how far one man will go for love and the strength of his pride; the thrill of research and exploration; the cost of obsession; the corruption of the world and the price of love; and a tale of true love.

For my partner in life, who steadily bears my heart aloft the stormiest seas.

Ashes

by Slip-Wolf

The gaslights off the moor haunted our flight like distant furies. Too closely did they resemble the lamps of our pursuers, closing in on us. I went first with our pilfered file, attacking the manacle binding my swollen ankle with frantic sweeps. Barstowe kept watch, his black ears drooping and his dark nose quivering at the sounds and scents that drifted through the mists. I had to hurry so as to stand watch when it was his turn.

"You almost through?" He asked in his gravelly cockney. "I thought I 'eard the horn blow. We've little time."

"We should have fled to town and done this indoors." My south-Victorian lilt crept under my stiffened lip, reminding me that the Queen's English was the tone of whispers. Just over the rise, the whole of London was listening.

Disapproval dripped from the half-hound's sigh. "Oh Nathanial, do you want us dragged back by our whiskers? People'd notice two men in leg-irons no matter how careful they be, 'specially after the constabulary get to town and—"

A dull bellow reached us from the Thames and dragged shards of ice down our spines. The prison ship's horn sounded once, then again, mourning a shortage of damned cargo.

Barstowe whispered a curse. "Lets go." He dropped to his knees in the loamy ground.

"I'm not finished."

"I can do it faster."

I passed over the metal file and sat upon a felled tree. He raised my calf in his dark paw, caressing the grey fur over my muscles as he guided my foot between his thighs and went to work, panting as he worked the file up and down. His loose ears fluttered as he struggled. There was no sound from either the foul ship off the distant shore or the damp outskirts of London a few hills over. Just the harsh wheeze of the file on the iron cuff, and then the cool air on my ankle when it fell away was shocking in its relief.

Barstowe took a breath, leaning forward so I could see under the loose prison garb on his back. Just one of the scars under his black fur showed its pale whiteness on his narrow back. Then up came the blue eyes under that sweating brow. "I hear them." Barstowe said, and so could I - shouts in the distance.

"Switch! Quickly!" I tried to keep my voice down.

The next set of barking shouts grew in definition.

"There's no time." Barstowe stood and the heavy manacle still about his leg hobbled him as he stood straight. "You've got to go, Nate. Go now." His resignation cut me deeply. I picked up the dropped file and my teeth chattered as though in winter's grip. The urge to surrender came and then fled like a wraith; replaced with an anger that welled within me. The demons of our wooden hell were close at hand, but my revenge was somewhere under a cold roof in London.

* * *

It was just another moment on the most miserable of days when my weary eyes set on Nathanial for the first time. We were on the wagons that took us towards the Thames, where a prison ship awaited near overflowing with England's surplus scum, vagrants, debtors, and fiends that could not be wedged within the packed walls of Newgate. The fox and I, stirring among the stink of the many crammed into our cart, caught one another's eyes and traded our despair. I still felt the stings from my whipping, done in a closed court where my screams sang back at me off cold stone walls. The queer grey fox had pain in his eyes, but not the slump of a lashed back. He sat in silence 'tween a cursing cat and a gibbering weasel, whose complaints about sodding useless lawyers magnified the miserable din. The gentle-fox's manicured claws were starting to blunt and the once stately trim of his fur was now matted. He was a man of lost means whose expectations had dimmed. Or, as the fury in his eyes led me to suspect, had been *made* to dim.

It was a short ride to the banks from which runner boats took us onto the York's hard bulk, a decommissioned, mast-less warship whose guts had been scraped bare and walled-in for packing in lawbreakers. We were shoved in a cell together with three others; it was then that I first understood what burned the fox. The winking snicker of the bulldog and the rat soldiers running the deck, the spittle at our feet, the nickname they gave him. "Grey daisy", they said, "Have a dandy dance with your new mates", they said.

But there was no shame in his dirtied white cheeks. The fox foully reminded me of my last honest profession as a chimney sweep before my meager fortunes turned. He had a landowner's arrogance. At first I wanted little to do with him, stealing looks his way and wondering what that beautiful grey fur would look like as the months of sea-salt and cold worked its way deeply inward. Would he feel himself become anonymous as his new world scratched at him? Would he break all at once or crumble slowly like rot?

In short order we five traded names. Nathanial would only give his first name grudging like he were gabbing at lackeys unworthy to hear his high-born surname. One of our cell-mates muttered about bunking with a bugger, and brought up the first stirrings of violent intent. Such was how pecking order came about in our cell.

Most others saw the fox's scrapping anger, ignored the badger's barbs and stayed silent, kept to quiet miseries that awaited us in the uncountable days until the York belched us back to the carts that would bring us to a proper prison.

Fate set to make things worse. A little later as the upper cells crowded we were all moved. Iron-hobbled feet dragging on the planks and we found ourselves alone, just us two in a moonless wooden cell two decks down. I had silently hoped to be put in with anyone else, save the rabbit who coughed with the phlegm of consumption, but there we were, just Nathanial and I. It was small enough to turn and stand next to our stacked bunks and nothing more, listening to the moans and complaints of other unwilling pairs.

As the first night bore on and our bread and water went down, the first of our secrets came out in whispers turned hisses. The dandy was reluctant to talk to someone as low in the social orders as I. He spoke to me as the men who'd paid me to dust out their chimneys had in a life I was fast forgetting. I was a pitiful curiosity under yet another crusty aristocratic nose. And his questions to me were cutting.

"But did you steal, Barstowe? That is the simple question."

I snorted at him with all due ire. My cockney affectations made the contempt sound stronger. "A'fore you ask me that Nathanial, my good sir, perhaps you should ask the questions the magistrate wouldn't. How can a 'sweep run out of work if he's a hard worker? A simple question answered by two more. How many fires do the city folk need lit in the heights o' summer. How many fires light in the belly of a starving dog? Tell me Nathanial, do you think I had other choices?"

"You chose to steal, therefore you put yourself here." He said with smug certainty, and I wished the badger had knocked his teeth loose.

"And what did you choose, then? If yeh look down upon one such as I, then tell me what put you 'ere? I'm no fool. A few acts against public decency wouldn"t drop a gent so low, not one of such high noble character." I almost spat that last bit at him. He was spoiling for a fight and the thin air was bringing me round to the same. I counted the fox's teeth when he growled. A scuffle happening somewhere else had guards shouting for some worthless sense of order.

There was a moment I was sure he'd rush me an' draw blood. I was ready to mar that pretty, angular face of his. Instead the words broke through a hardened dyke. "I chose to trust." Nathaniel snapped under a hackled crown. "I chose to love and to trust. And I was betrayed; thoroughly and viciously betrayed by the object of both."

That took the wind out of my sails. My claws fell to their sides and I held myself in short order. It was awhile afore we spoke again, staring off at different planks that shaped our tiny world. In the silence that followed Nathaniel's outburst, we weren't quite enemies anymore.

* * *

The file was still hot in my teeth, and I breathed around it as I stumbled on with Barstowe leaning upon one shoulder. His manacled leg clanged loudly when it struck a rock and I prayed the sound wouldn't carry. My own now free trap had sunk to the bottom of a shallow bog, where it was hopefully lost. We both breathed raggedly as the darkness bore down. Our eyes and noses were adapting in haste to the day's loss, but so were the natural tools of our relentless pursuers.

"You shoulda left me." Barstowe grunted.

"I'll hear none of that." I scolded, taking the file in my other paw for a moment. "Be silent."

I nearly tripped on a creeping root. Ahead, I could see the accumulation of London's nighttime glow cresting the hill beyond. The farms were closely clustered together at this point. Anyone out for a night-time stroll or conducting late-night agricultural business would easily spot us now. I smelled the drifting sweetness of roasted mutton and my mouth started to water. The moment's distraction nearly resulted in my dropping of the file. We needed time and space in which to stop, rest, and remove Barstowe's confining brace. But where? Soon there would be constables knocking on farmer's doors and then sending word deep into the looming sprawl of London itself. Escaped convicts were in flight.

My tail shook as though fighting off a chill. My grey fur would catch glints of moonlight if the fog were to part and my panting was frightfully loud. Barstowe, with his black fur and lean reserve, seemed made for these stealthy exertions, and would have been the quicker of us without his manacle. Under my supporting arm I could feel the muscles under his ragged prisoner's garb moving fluidly.

"We can't go much farther this way." He said with resignation.

"I know." Could we steal into one of the barns, take a family hostage if need be? I realized that such a gambit was beyond the pale for both of us. I'd only ever known one person with such a lack of scruples, and he took his hostages with the power of lies alone. Anger at the memory of that personage quickened my pace and despite not knowing its cause, Barstowe matched my vigor. Ahead, I could see the ruin of a small cottage, reduced to ashen bones by a long spent fire, and that sight, combined with my memory of the man whom I hated with all my heart brought me my answer.

"One mile. The outskirts of the city holds our sanctuary." I declared.

"Into London? Are you sure?" Barstowe was more than a little dubious.

"Trust me. It is a part of the city that London itself wants to forget. I'm the only one who never will."

* * *

Weeks passed and our wooden stinking world went up and down. Storms were the only occurrence that broke our boredom. Maintenance of the York was in its unwilling cargo's care. We were brought out to scrub the decks, polish fittings that hadn't been removed when she'd been taken off the battle line, and replace planks as they rotted. Nearly a dozen ships like her drifted off England's shores in the haze, endless work for we condemned and each was falling apart bit by bit.

I watched the Nathanial struggle to work at the deck's grit, nearly biting his tongue with the wheezes that came out of him. He was learning to be stronger, I gave him that. This came despite that fact that he'd suffered rarely before coming here due to his priggish pedigree, which made me jealous. After being dragged from a chimney with stolen food in my paws, I'd been able to afford no lawyer to speak of, so my punishment was no surprise. I'd met the whipping post with gritted teeth, grateful my crimes had not bought me to the noose. Nathanial had only one scar on his shoulder which I spotted when we changed for the wash cart, taken when jawing against one of his jailers. As with most things, he was tight lipped and unwilling to speak about it. When the fox got his second scar a few days into our stay on the York, it was nearly his last.

Food was the basest fare as one would expect. To get us to exercise as they meagerly d stocked our bellies, the guards marched us one group of cells at a time up to the deck where it was served and eaten in small bowls at a short range of mess planks. We dozen shuffled slowly, the manacles on our left feet preventing more than a labored trudge. In the line to be fed I was parted from Nathanial by a guard who held me back to check a looseness in my hobbler.

A greasy pelted otter filled the space between us and my keen ears picked out his first words.

"You're a catch, you."

Nathanial shuffled towards the bowls and stew pot, vended by a dull-eyed buck who chewed at his own lip. Nathan ignored the otter who was all but nuzzling his shoulder. No one save myself standing behind them both could hear.

"I'd pay twice a deuce hog to get a Margery with a tail like that." The otter gibbered in a tone that I fast took for naked lust.

Nathan turned his muzzle back, just slightly and one eye gave a baleful look. "I don't know what that means." He said levelly.

The otter coughed a laugh and I could guess from the wrinkle of Nathanial's foxy nose what his breath smelled like. "Oh I see. You're a right demure confirmed bachelor, yeah?""

"That is none of your business."

"I'm making it me business. I likes the square-rigged high society types like you, always playing so coy with the slow wags. You're looking for a topper, don"t tell me fibs."

Nathan's ears lowered and mine went back. The batmen who watched our sad line either ignored what was making or decided they could do with a bit of show. I'd been here no longer than Nathan, but I knew from reading dispositions my whole life that the otter"s airs were getting hot.

"Leave off or you're going to wind up in what passes for a salt box in this crate," I hissed.

The otter made a show of eyeballing me as the line moved again. "I've got no eyes for your Nancy, blackie. You'd best leave off yourself. Will be a long slog in the cage and I could use a cottaging before its nothing but cinderblocks around me, an' so could he." The otter turned back to face Nathanial, who presented his back with shoulder's hunched in instinctive caution. "There's too few chances to mix and mend when we move about. I could show this wanting toff the best moments of his life."

I didn't see the otter's paw reach out but I knew what he'd grabbed on by Nathanial's reaction. The fox made a proper squeak and spun around, clanging the empty gruel bowl he'd taken across the otter's muzzle. The otter choked out a curse, swiped at his head with thick claws and went straight for Nathanial's throat.

The fox was quick to react, but not as strong. The guard's barked for order at a remove and the shouts were deafening. The bowl clattered to the deck as the squat and muscular otter brought Nathanial down, with no end of obscenities.

It was not my fight, nor my concern. The arrogant fox who had spent his days sneering on me as his lesser had come upon the worst of prison's stabs and was now seeing his mistakes through bulging eyes that wanted to escape his skull. The ship's constabulary still did not step up. They wanted to play this out, see if the incident could unload two bodies off their overcrowded, planked hell. Their truncheons were out but still.

I'll never know why I dropped to all fours and grabbed Nathanial's bowl, the man who thought me a simple wag. I turned it over, brought back my paw and introduced it to the back of the otter's skull with the speed of a devil. His head jerked back and he grunted once, his tongue unable to collect sense. He toppled limply to the deck and Nathanial's freed throat drew the breath of the drowning.

The batboys were upon us then and a truncheon cracked at my shoulder. A second one hovered menacingly above me and I heard Nathanial rasp out a plea. "He saved...he saved-" he had no breath to make sense and it didn't matter. The second batmen's blow found my brow. The mess deck of the York swam through a molasses of ungodly colors as my muzzle struck the wood and on came the dark.

I came to much later, flat on my bunk. The meager lamplight showed me the shadowy shape of a vulpine in vigil above me. "Are you alright?" Nathanial asked.

I could feel the waters under the boat through the beating cage of my skull. "No," I answered truthfully. "I'm right knackered."

A damp cloth touched my head, cool and soothing. I heard it return to a bucket. I was thirsty enough to drink whatever was in that bucket bone dry. "You saved me," Nathanial said again, and I could hear the rough going of the words through his swollen throat. Those strong otter's paws had made their mark.

I cleared my throat. "I'd miss our talkings on stations in life," I said, and immediately realized I'd stung him with those words, even if they were deserved. "How long's it been?"

"A pair of days. Do you remember waking?"

I didn't. That was a worry, but I must have had some time about. The bed didn't smell of piss and I wasn't hungry. I remembered strange dreams and it came to me that I"d mutely seen to my basic needs. I had been two days without sense.

"Can you sit up?"

I did so carefully. Rather the boat righted itself around me as I shook off spider's webs that clung to my mind. I was still for a long time. "I'll be fine,"" I said long before I was sure of such.

More silence passed. Neighbors moaned and boards creaked under officer's paws. "Thank you," Nathanial said at long last, as though he was ripping the words from somewhere deep and hard to find. "That tosser was crushing my throat and I was going to perish." The next words from his mouth seemed to spill out woefully. "I will ever be in your debt.""

I said nothing, only blinked and listened to him keep on.

"I have been remiss with you Barstowe. Seriously and horribly remiss. I only wish I could repay you in some way. I have not any possession left to give to you and have not even the currency of character that one should pay to a fellow in the same situation."

"Life paid you a bad turn and you have fallen with the rest of us. Foul moods are to be expected."

"But not accepted. You have borne my shameful conduct with admirable restraint. I had thought you were acquiescing to the pretensions of my station -" Nathanial studied the deck under their feet, "of my former station."

"No. It wasn't differences in us that kept me bearing your ire, sir. Nothing o' the sort at all. Nor was I afraid of the consequences of putting you level.""

"Then why? Why put up with the whining of a humbled mandrake in a hole such as this?"

I rested my bare back, as I had been stripped to the waist, against the wood of the wall that split us from the next cell, where snoring was apt to saw through the hull itself. We were crowded together and yet completely alone, the chief horror of prison that one almost never comes to terms with 'till the bars are all around you. There was nowhere to run to.

"I kept silent because of what matches us in all this mess. I'm like you, Nathan. Not in crown's conviction or contempt for those who have harmed us in life. I"m what you are."

The fox was confused.

Of all the times to lose *his* wits. I sighed with a saint's patience. "I'm a bloody mandrake like you."

The stunned look of surprise was amusing, even while I was still tonguing for loose teeth. Another lover of men, all this time, sharing his cell, enduring his presumptuous barbs. He picked words, threw them away, scrounged for more. I filled in the silence. "I didn't like you much when we met. Still not sure on that account, truth be told, but that wasn't what kept me quiet."

"You didn't want to have the same treatment as I did." Nathan supplied in a voice so low he nearly seemed out of breath.

"I didn't want worse." I told him plainly. "Even afore coming on this boat, to this fate, I worked in a menial job where integrity is the only currency you bring with you. A sweep wouldn't fear exposure of a liking for the other boys because of the jabs and jests you'd get as a man slippin' in and out of tight, hot, dirty places. In the dirt, yet so often above the world, I've heard all the best curses. No, Nathan, even as I stood in the docket for the food I'd nicked to live on and inwardly yearned after the imagined company of the handsome and slender prosecutor who was seeking to burn me, I knew that my thefts in addition to the buggery charge would have finished in the price of a worn rope for the kingdom and nothing more. We would have no chats, civil or otherwise. Silence has literally bought me my life."

"I…beg your forgiveness." Nathan said, almost mumbling, still shocked. "I wish I could repay you for what you've endured on my behalf, and in the act of saving me from my arrogance." I could see his dirty white tail tip coming through the space of his legs as his abjection came to sour completeness.

Nathan's eyes glinted in the light of the hanging wick outside the cell. All was quiet and for the first time I was aware that it was night outside our floating prison. A moonbeam striped the deck that ran between the cells. "How can I thank you?"" His paw reached out slowly and fell to my shoulder. "How will you let me?"

I didn't know the fullness of the fox's mind as his claws touched me like I were ashes that could fall apart at any moment. I kept away a shudder. We both were a mess; filthy, swimming in the layers of our own musk, yet the stirrings that visited me in the silence of night with my nose giving taunts to my loins visited me in strength just then. The fox ran a tender finger down my collar bone and chest, claws tracing my wiry body like a road on a map. I could see the ruff of his neck, his bruises hidden by the dirtied white bib of his fur. I could imagine how far down that milky waterfall toppled and what lay at its end.

The fox, lusting after my body in kind or overcome with guilt or who knew what, slid his paw down my belly and stopped at the string that held my issued breeches tight. "The otter was right." The fox said, as much to himself as me. ""We have little chance left to satisfy what needs we have." His eyes were milky with sorrow for both of us. "I've heard that Newgate prison is a horrible place. Isolated cells small enough to be tombs, menial pointless work meant to break us. They have winches in walls that the condemned turn for hours on end, attached to nothing but boxes of sand. Droning sermons in chapels where we sit in total isolation. People fighting in squalor over single rays of light. We have too little life left to us, Barstowe." His once furious eyes were taken by the grip of fear and I could see his desperation. "Let me thank you."

He drew my tie-string and coaxed me to lift, slipping the breeches down and away. The pink crown of manhood stood sheathed over my jewel sack. The warmth that bled out into me when his claws gently touched it was painfully wonderful, like the first sip of cold fresh water into a parched soul. "Let me thank you." Nathan said again, his breath beginning to catch.

He hunched down, difficult in the confines of our cell and his whiskers touched my thighs. His nose took in the fiery grime of nearly twenty years of chimney soot, drawn down to my hide and bound to my person as twined as my blood. He breathed on me, alternating hot and cool drafts upon my shaft as my manhood crept out. My thighs parted all on their own. His tongue pressed forward. Wet found wet and the boat seemed to roil again as his essence touched mine. The stars came out in my vision and I had to say the word that came to me through breathless lips. "Stop."

The fox pulled back, his mouth agape. His expression was almost pained in its confusion.

"I mean it." I said, biting back a sigh.

He nearly fell back and slumped against the wooden wall, nearly rattling the boards. "You don't like me."

"That's not it." I shook my head. "That's not why."

He worked the juices in his mouth as he waited for an answer. I couldn't see his arousal, but I could smell it clear as day. So many scents on this deck, one more of a blessed sort wouldn't stand out too soon. "I won't do it here, Nathanial. One last grasp at joy don't suit me, and if you have any pride left, it won't suit you neither. It would just make us meek and willing for the coming of our long, slow end." Though it made my head swim with lust and pain in harsh drams, I had to lean forward to whisper. "We're getting out of here. Somehow, before they ship us back ashore and send us to rot in Newgate, we're leaving this boat. I don't deserve for my life to be over and neither do you I expect, not if what you tell me about that place is true."

"The prison itself isn't what I fear most." Nathan said, and a darkness moved in over his shock. "I have scores to settle."

I blinked. I had nearly forgotten that about him. Lust was the smaller whip driving this fox. "If that's what gets you sharp, than by all means good sir." I smiled and offered my paw. "Barstowe Pottersdam."

The fox's warm pad took it and squeezed in a way that was firm but genteel. "Nathanial Lynchair."

Where lust lost control of us, camaraderie burgeoned fast. Having finally cast off the last of his noble pretensions and my own distrust of others finally sloughing away, we came to find small bits of common ground. As time marched on and the wound deep inside him festered, Nathan brought himself, in a fitful night where storms raged above our purgatory, to tell me of the man who'd betrayed him and consigned him to misery.

* * *

I first met my former partner, Luc Winnaker in business, both of us bachelors, wealthy, and with families' influential in many circles. Luc's flourished as well-situated property holders in various quarters of London, while my parents shipped tea and other goods from their plantation in India.

My courtship with Luc had been the slow affair of moving continents as females in and out of our respective species came and went in a sort of aimless sport. We had both long known without candor that we had little interest in the opposite sex, but it was Luc's guard which fell first. I came to him with a business proposition for a carriage network to operate from London to Bristol and join the two arteries of commerce together. I entered his study unannounced to discover it was Luc's own artery of commerce that was employed in a rodent rent boy over the Victorian chaise. To say I was dumbstruck would woefully understate things.

I had Luc's fate in my very paws. The Winnaker's were a hard-line protestant family with links to all the levels of government, many legal professionals, and of course the clergy, the highest level of influence one could have outside the royal family. The Winnaker"s held influence in every place that one could erect a church, a business, or a tenement house and could merely snap their fingers to see a property erected or a derelict removed. In their connections to the church, this extended to anyone who they saw as an enemy. Luc's wants, his very needs, were contrary to everything his family stood for and could be used to take them all down. We were only newly friends, and I could have had the cowering kitten in my pocket.

But my heart bled for his predicament and I offered my hand in understanding. With a thrill I professed my own leanings of the heart. Thus our partnership quickly grew secretly to encompass new worlds both intellectual and amorous. We secretly professed our love while publicly maintaining distance and the business we built together with the matched portions of their family fortunes grew our public stature in short order.

This was not to persist. For while I kept our mutual secret in confidence for obvious reasons, Luc was inclined to try new heights of experimentation, fraternizing with the campiest animals ever to romp from ball-to-ball. I should have taken him aside, urged restraint, but I loved to see him happy. In the end I was left to wonder, long after the dust had settled, when our secret was uncovered, and by whom.

But not who acted against us.

A letter came in Luc's hand-writing offering rendezvous at the Adelphi theatre for a special private engagement, and I obligingly wore my finest to meet his partner and paramour. The box was dark when I entered and the white cat's fur was bare, far above the ermine dramatists crooning below. When I disrobed as the letter sent to me instructed, ready for a game of amiable pinning, I was surprised by the sudden and rude arrival of no less than four constables who viciously grabbed and hauled me away. I was able to look back to see how Luc fared against their assault, but the naked feline dragged into the light, tail wrapped demurely around himself, wasn't Luc at all.

Such was just the first act in my betrayal. I was denied contact with my family and my lawyer was bought away from me. Friends abandoned me one by one as the scandal broke and letters to Luc were intercepted. These letters were thrown down before me in the gaol by a solitary visitor, Manfred Winnaker, the family patriarch.

Words were short, accusations thrown liberally. He claimed I had corrupted his son, brought Luc down the path to spiritual ruin and that I would take the whole family down in my wake. And so, with all correspondence intercepted and the law arrayed firmly against the mandrake pussy-willow who tried to destroy a noble boy, a choice was given me. Either accept the meager penalty for buggery of a fine and two years in jail, or go down for theft of carriage company funds and be relegated to Newgate prison for a dozen years.

There was to be no doubt that I could be proven guilty, and no shame was felt on my aggressor's part for the necessary framing of my character. Documents had been forged to the effect of his charge. I had no means of recourse. So with no hope, fearful nights spent among cutthroats and completely cut-off from my waylaid lover, I surrendered to Winnaker"s whims, confessed and pled guilty. My trial was short, full of hellfire sermonizing and skewering of character that reduced me to a carbuncle on London's immaculate face.

But it did not end there. On the morning following the worst night of my life, in which I'd been soundly beaten in prison for being a dandelion and a rogue and then left weeping for the warm embrace of my stolen lover, they finally tore my world in two. The magistrate summoned me back to court, and a new charge was handed down, that of the threatened embezzlement. And who should have signed the affidavit attesting to my falsified crimes but one upstanding victimized member of high society named Luc Winnaker.

The trial was set in time for the letter from my parents in India to finally arrive and disown me without even a request for clarity. My father had long been distant, and worried at how reputation would affect his desire for Royal matriculation of the family. My mother was taken by religious dictates. Had they found out about my proclivities more discreetly…it became useless to even speculate. Paid witnesses marched before the court attesting to my morally bereft and self-serving character. But when Luc took the stand and sobbed under oath on my irrepressible appetites and threatening aspect, it was finally too much to bear. I was dragged to the holding carts under the crack of the gavel, senseless with my own damning screams.

* * *

So did Nathanial tell it; flatly as a fox whose tears were forever wrung dry.

I had already shared my simple-enough tale with Nathan, and he was unsurprised at the degree to which a few stolen trinkets could be used to make an example of me in the docket. How they snorted and laughed at my wretched appeals, how the observers dock could barely restrain their glee when the flogging and confinement were both thrown upon me. They didn't have public whippings anymore, though I did spend a day afterwards in the stocks among other pickpockets and vagrants, one a mere nine years of age. I studied the pebbles on the ground for hours, ignoring the barbs of passers-by and saw those rocks for weeks after in my sleep.

All we two wanted was to find reasons to trade kindness, but experience had smartened us. We minded our actions with discipline, avoiding the barbs and scraps and even each other in the instances where whispers might collect about us. We sought nothing in each other's company save re-assuring words and stilled our carnal furies quietly as monks in a sacristy. It was wise not to fulfill what drove us. Caught in any act, we'd be beaten and separated.

Our plans depended on timing and patience. Small distractions, access to the keys that gained the upper deck, knowledge of where the guards roamed. I had never been a mariner, but on many a night, sliding down the chimney on a long job I would look up the dark shaft of brick and grime above and try to guess my orientation within the chimney by the squared lid of stars above. Here now, I knew where the York was along the Thames even if the lights on shore gave no clue, and where she was allowed to drift. Distant lights through the murk revealed we were a mere five miles outside of London itself.

Food was rationed and portions hidden, hard tack that would stay edible for our flight. A file was stolen from the tool locker on the mid deck during a distraction in our exercise, along with a small piece of metal taken from the upper decks. We could never saw through our bonds before they'd be inspected and such evidence was sought to locate the missing file. Not to worry. It had other uses to us for the time. A guard was made to drop his key, and I was ready to pick it up with a greased kerchief and return it quick lest I get a beating. Its mark on the kerchief grease was used as a shape from which to slowly file a metal strip down over days and days. It was a fragile, rough dupe we made, but it only needed to work once. And on the night when we timed ourselves against the rounds, broke our filed key in the cell door, counted all twenty six steps to the vacant gunwale and felt the cold embrace of the filthy Thames, we felt a joyous abandon in the knowledge that we could truly escape from the horrors intended for us.

Swimming to shore with the drag of our weights nearly proved our undoing, and exhaustion had us face down on the wet mud of shore for precious minutes. In flight, we were discovered gone sooner than intended. Then came the York's klaxon, hungry for her missing souls.

* * *

Barstowe was panting viciously when we arrived, his manacled leg now concealed in flotsam to resemble a rough splint around an imagined injury. We scarcely managed avoiding attention through the small collections of beggars and vagabonds that liver-spotted London's East outskirts. Fortunately I knew that sanctuary was close at hand.

The hovel I brought us to had once been a two story range of inexpensive apartments for labor-class families following the expulsion of lesser folk from central London for grander building projects. The rotten structure had succumbed to the stresses of two harsh winters and had collapsed a few months before my incarceration.

Only two rooms remained under the rubble, bolstered by a lone chimney which still reached for the sky. The rest of the deceased building was slowly collapsing until such time as the land could be sold at a better rate than the neighborhood warranted. I was one of only two people who knew of the standing chambers in the condemned calamity, open to the sky in parts. I knew my way through the twisted rubble, and soon Barstowe lay next to me on the wooden floor in the small den where only months ago, some family with barely pennies to rub together were robbed by the splintering of shoddy beams of their only shelter. A single empty candlestick stood on the fireplace mantel, the only trace left of the people who'd been chased out with dust on their coats. Many families hadn't been as lucky from the stories I'd heard. And the survivors could afford no lawyers.

What a perfect place to muse over the impending fate of the Winnaker family, who had stolen my life away as they had so many others.

Barstowe was at the point of exhaustion and I filed away at his manacle with sore fingers. Stolen trousers and shirts from a farmer's laundry line awaited us in a nearby pile once free of the York's dank uniforms, but the manacle was the priority. The black hound"s leg was released soon enough and I marveled at the bare patches of bloodied skin that the tightly clasped bond had left behind. I threw the iron into the empty fireplace and watched disturbed soot settle around it.

"You sure we'll have no visitors?" If Barstowe felt pain from his leg he hid it well.

"This place is condemned, much to my former partner's chagrin. His father charged a swindle for these apartments after paying a pittance to erect them."

Barstowe sighed, seeking a change in subject as we chewed the hard tack we'd smuggled with sour faces. "How do you feel as a free fox?"

"Famished. I would so love a good port and a flake-pastried kidney pie."

"A gatter fer me. Cold, malty with a tall head. The food next to it would be a trifle by comparison. Would be nothing finer." Barstowe turned his head and regarded me. "Someday soon we'll have that. When we're clear of here."

There was a suggestion in his earlier question that he didn't state aloud. We finished our meal and lay on the cool floor boards for a time, close enough to feel one another's heat. He was taciturn in breaking the lingering silence. ""Can you leave this be? Just forget about him?"

The hope in his voice stung me, but not strong enough to weaken that same resolve that drove our escape. I responded with utmost certainty. "In this or any moment, I can't. What future I had I lost because of him."

Barstowe raised himself up on one arm and leaned over me, startlingly sudden in his contact. We were muzzle to muzzle for a space. "You gained a different life Nathan, one you would never have suspected. Be honest with yourself. Were you a bachelor, secure in wealth and pedigree and such, would you turn your eyes on some sooty sod what cleaned your chimney for you?""

My silence was painful as I struggled for an answer. Barstowe's presence in that moment brought a comfort that seemed a lost part of myself. But would I ever have known so much as his name had fate not forced us into that same wooden box on the York?

Barstowe could see my struggle. "You have a life stolen back from those who tried to take it from you. And it's a life you never expected, which is a gift of sorts. We all have slights paid us by this world and we can't avenge them all. Shouldn't you enjoy what freedoms we've taken back for ourselves, especially since we don't know if we"ll be keeping them for long?"

The black half-hound's dark eyes sought understanding in mine, and despite tiredness and anxiety, my heart fluttered for the pain I saw there. Words could not settle what was in my breast, so without preamble, I leaned over and kissed him. Barstowe met it without surprise, our lips sliding around one another's and our tongues courting gaily through the cage of our teeth. Breath passed between us in slow washes, hot summer breezes that belonged only to us. For as long as I could hold that moment with the man I decided then and there I loved, I wouldn't have to dodge his questions or lie to him.

When our lips parted at last and discussion was forgotten, the great dog fully straddled me. I felt the warm center in my breeches rising to meet his, brushing one another through the damp togs that needed discarding. I slipped mine down and away, tossing both parts of the prison garment into the fireplace with Barstowe's manacle and he rose momentarily to do likewise.

I was now free to gaze in better light upon the worn but proud frame of the hound who would never have been any part of my past life. Beautiful as he was, I could see that his exhaustions mirrored mine, and he had the same desire for proper respite from our pains. Deep within me churned yearnings for the trappings of station I'd lost. The hot bath I could have been drawing now, the delectable repasts on brass platters, the pipe smoke swirling to the cornices crowning my parlor. All these boons were even now being enjoyed by the worthless cheat who had stolen my life away and betrayed me with poisoned promises.

Barstowe saw the anger in my eyes. His sigh was pained. "Even now, right here, anger has a hook in you, don't it? You need to forget your scars, master Nathaniel. Learn to bury them like the rest of us do." He said this to me as though I were a cub, and I found the rough timber of his voice soothing despite myself. "This world has many cuts to make. You can get over each of them, keep those who would spit on you from seeing their marks." With those words he leaned and touched the ashen floor of the fireplace next to us. His dark fingers came away granulated with soot. Wordlessly, still warmly astride me, Barstowe gently touched at the scar on my forehead. The wound made by the otter, on our first night of the détente that grew between us, was still raw through my fur. He traced the scar once, and his digit returned to the soot anew. His next caress reached behind my shoulder to the truncheon's injury caused before we'd even made acquaintance on the prison lorry an eternity ago. "Don't let the bastards see you bleed Nathan, any o" them. Don't give them that."

I felt a tremble in my limbs with each touch and with shaky fingers I blindly reached over the fireplace lip. My dark paw returned even blacker. I watched my hound's chest rise and fall above me, then began to trace his scars and scrapes, much as on the night I first desired him. A hard lifetime was there, badges of ill treatment and years of hard labor, every mistake having its consequence. The soot was lost in his dark fur, but I could just see the faded remains of those scars covered by my passage underneath.

"That's better." His growling cockney, once a mark of lower-class breeding was positively melodious to my reformed ears, my very soul lightened by his rich timbre. My auspicious breeding, my berth in London society, my many possessions and petty distractions, all were worthless against the anointment of Barstowe's reassuring touch. I wanted to bask in his handsome imperfections, all the marks of his stalwart character.

Our members touched, rubbing together with growing warmth and I stole a glance at the shining pink eye that gazed back at me from the sheathing that retreated from it. So mesmerized was I by the sight that I almost didn't hear his next words. "You can leave him behind Nathan, all of it." He dipped his finger in the inkwell of ash and reached down between his own legs to where the purses of our manhood nearly touched. Ash traced in a line on my testicles and I moaned deep in my throat as his sac touched mine and rubbed the dark mark between us. "To hell with our pains. Let's you and I find something else."

Unable to restrain myself, I took one last sample of soot and raked it in wings across the unseen scars on Barstowe's broad back, furrows like planters rows left by the whip that tried to take his dignity and failed. He took a deep breath, shivering at my finger's caress and without a further word, raised himself, sliding forward, his wet member erect and soft sac dangling like a black pearl over my abdomen.

His black tail swept coolly across my bare thighs. I guided my own staff with sooty digits to a fully upright stance, aligning to the rich portal creeping above. He descended, and with a pucker of heat I pushed through and was enveloped in splendid warmth. Barstowe's muzzle canted back in a throaty, almost lupine growl towards the broken beams above as he settled low around me. My own limbs had fallen loosely to the floor and it was a dizzying moment of bliss before I regained possession of myself. I reached out and carefully grasped the hound's swelled member, massaging it with ashen fingers as he raised himself and descended again like the waves below Dover's cliffs, taking me in with a warm embrace that retreated and renewed as I flushed within him. I responded in kind, ministering to the hound's pink male flesh with worshipping strokes that streaked soot all across his stiff manhood.

At the join, our mutual heat increased and small sounds of glee pressed the back of Barstowe's teeth as he gazed down at me with fiery, wanting eyes. Mine were no less insistent as we rejoined our efforts and Barstowe bucked upon my pillar like a carriage rider in flight. Ecstatic in that moment, ridden like a steed while I handled my lover like a votive object, we were able to finally leave our accumulated pains in the soot of that hovel, forget all that threatened us beyond these crumbling walls.

Capture would mean life in Newgate and the lash for both of us, but I didn't care. I was at peace with the world's pitiless barbs and thrilled to the joys we smartly stole back from it. My hot expansion within the hound ran out of room as pleasure took me to the seat of heaven itself. I felt my potency release with all that I held back in those long weeks since he brought me the first glimmer of hope.

With a buck of his hips, he released his own milk in quick spurts upon my white chest, growling a low song in his throat. I could barely see him through the stars that danced in my eyes. It was a blissful slice of time before my swelling subsided and he was able to slip away, leaving my member to cool next to his. Barstowe placed his arm across my heaving chest and his paw traced the spot above my heart with soot, mixing seed into my fur along with it. It was a badge I was content to wear.

Our eyes found one another's as we lay. He spoke in a whisper. "We can still get away from London. You can forget about Winnaker and start a new life elsewhere."

The smell of soot upon him was strangely comforting and I turned his words over. I had love here, the kind of love I'd assumed lost. There were places we could go. I had made a business of knowing the fastest routes from here to any shore in the south. There we could find boats, new lives in Europe. Paris was beautiful in the summer.

But as the lightness in my heart receded and the summer heat stilled my rapture, I fell to the pragmatism of our situation. We had no money, no friends, no prospects. We would have to smuggle and steal our way out of this country. I had nothing to draw upon to help us.

The Winnakers, before condemning me to the deepest hole they could find, had made sure of that. I thought of Luc's feline face, sobbing in the docket as he sold me off, a memory burned forever into my cold inner soul. The anger that had kept me going for months returned anew. I would only need it a little longer. "We will need funds and provisions to get us to freedom. I know of only one place where we can obtain them."

Barstowe lay his muzzle on my chest and I could feel his breath brush against my lips. "Where, Nathan? After tonight they'll already be looking for us. We have little time, you an' I."

"Where nobody would expect to find us," I said, and the mix of sadness and dejection that crept to Barstowe's face when he realized what I was on about was sour indeed. ""It is in the den of he who stole it all from me."

* * *

There was naught to be done. Nathaniel would not be talked out of his hunt. I could see in his eyes why it was impossible. On rich and poor I'd seen that look, the absolute moral certainty that wrath lay ahead for one who deserved it and the world would know no right from wrong till the score was settled. I saw that in the grey fox's eyes, a living angry spirit who would haunt every space he entered until his living demon was felled low.

And so, morose though I was, we planned. After changing into the clothes we'd stolen off a Londoner's line and buried our discarded prison rags under the collapsed room's debris, we decided upon Nathaniel's entrance into the Winnaker family home. The estate doors would be locked, leaving only one way in. We argued some particulars, but I won that fight, seeing as my expertise was called upon.

But the biggest issue, I lost. It was he who'd go in and I who'd keep watch. That was for certain.

Time was against us. When word spread among members of Nathaniel's former gilded set that he'd escaped…

Hungry, but determined, Nathan led the way, both of us walking separately in our stolen clothes so as to avoid suspicion through increasingly more wealthy gas-lit lanes of London. Despite the wildly split fortunes of the place we left and the place we sought, we only had to creep a few miles, hot and hungry again. Nathaniel was driven as though a blaze were burning London behind us, eyes fixed on his purpose ahead.

The estate was squat behind its locked gates and mortared walls, but Nathan didn't let that stop him. He was over the wall in a flash, as though the constabulary were right atop us. And when I struggled over with him and saw the small garden that sat in the grand house's lee, I felt a wave of dizziness. Tiredness was catching us both.

"Last chance, Nathan. We can still turn away."

Nathan gazed across well-kept garden, a miniature paradise kept tidy from the squalor of the streets beyond. His jaw was set. "This won't take long."

"They will hunt us down for the rest of our lives," I said firmly.

"They already shall. But I won't let them have you again, I promise. Mark me one hour. If I don't return, I bid you to go. Find a fox not consumed by anger as I am and imagine me when you show him affection."

I said nothing, the matter settled. Sentimentality would only slow him down. Having accepted what was to transpire, I wondered idly what he would nab of value on the way out, but had not the gall to ask.

Scaling the two stories was easier than expected, as the ivy clung tight and the brickwork had many holds. We were both atop the roof, crouching in the shadow of one of its chimneys, muscles aching. "This chimney leads to the bedroom. The cat never once used it in summer," Nathaniel muttered, unable to bring himself to speak his name.

I peered down, allowing my eyes to adjust to the tiny square of ghostly light below from the room with an open window. "Quite tight, no creosote lumps. Flue's a brick-and-half square. These were the kind they now set cubs to, them that didn't know proper fittings. As long as you don't bring your knees to your chest you won't get stuck, except…" I peered further. "No, the shaft tightens as you go down, I can see the shortened brick lengths and the rough mortaring. Your clothes will catch on that and you'll be stuck." I felt a slight quiet sense of triumph when I said what needed saying. "You'll have to abandon this Nathaniel."

"I'm not letting justice be thwarted by tight passage."

I sighed at his pure pigheadedness. "If your clothes catch and you get stuck, what will they make of you when they catch you? Assuming they don't just make a mind to burn you out?"

We stared across each other over the descent to Nathaniel's revenge, roof-top gargoyles at an impasse.

* * *

I slid down into the depths as Barstowe instructed, knees and claws employed carefully and back flat against the wall. My ears had barely passed from sight before my naked fur was already covered in soot. I went cautiously, breathed slowly, careful not to choke on the black dust that thoroughly coated me, and as the square of moonlit brick below grew larger and the faint stars above grew further, it was all I could do not to wheeze. Silence was essential.

I made the barest of noise when my blackened paws touched the warm stone, the cat's fireplace long cleaned out and unused. Only the soot set deep in his chimney clung to my body, around my trunk, under my arms and drifting off my thick bushy tail as I crept forward to stand proudly on the floorboards of Luc's bedroom.

My heart beat with ferocity in my chest. I had come as death, an ash-stained avenging angel, coated in the miasma of my betrayal. Under the sheets, lightly snoring and unaware, the white muzzle of the cat I had loved stirred comfortably.

A fire-tending kit stood by, wrought exquisitely in iron. I took the fire poker from it. It was a firm weight in my paw as I hefted it high, took creeping steps forward and covered the cat's mouth with a sooty paw. He breathed in the ashen muck and awoke with a choking cough. His green eyes fluttered open, he saw a black wraith bearing the instrument of demise above him, my white teeth gleaming viciously in the light of the moon through his window. I pressed down firmly on his scream.

"Silence you wretch!" I hissed with ungodly vehemence, "Or I will stove your deceiving head in."

He gulped and choked, his pink paw pads fleeing the cover of blankets to take a posture of meek, warding submission. "Please, oh please." I felt him beg through my paw.

"Say not a word louder than a whisper or I will finish you." I waved the poker with menace as I lifted my paw away, leaving a villainous dash of black on Luc's muzzle and chin.

"Please bring me no harm. I am a man of means and can accommodate anything you should want of me."

A stab of anger snarled through me as he spoke those words. I fought to keep spittle from forming at my darkened mouth as I pressed my paw against his night-clothed chest. "A man of desperation has no means at all, especially when a soulless, heartless coward has conspired to take all his wealth away. But you already knew that, didn't you Luc Winnaker?"

My copper eyes shone from the dark nightmare of my stained fur and recognition found Luc with cold horror that folded his ears like the sails of a drowning ship. "Nathanial? Oh God, is that actually you, Nathan? How is it that you come to be here, in this state?"

"Why aren't I locked away in the filthy cages of Newgate? Is that your first question for me, you heartless beast?" I pressed harder on his chest and circled the firepoker's tip like a feral buzzard. I wanted nothing more than to kill him that instant. But my anger had led me too far. I demanded an explanation for the full extent of his injustices. "Have you no other questions for the man who loved you with all his heart, supported you in all your passions and sought to share a life with you? Have you any explanation for the sheer depths into which you cast me?"

"Oh Nathan, oh my dear," he gasped as he scrabbled the mud of his tired mind for words to calm me. "I didn't seek to ruin you. Oh please don't think that. It was my father who-"

I struck him. Not with the poker, which would have knocked him beyond sense and been the first step to his end, but backhanded with the paw that I had pressed against his chest. The slap rang loudly in the dark room. He gasped, his whiskers bent and a bead of blood welling at one nostril.

"It was your name on the affidavit that sealed my fate!" I growled. "It was you who railed against me in the witness dock as a baseless sensate who endangered our business and brought your family to ruin!" I was shouting now, but I did not care. Let Luc's servants and footmen stumble in here upon us. At that moment I would happily kill them too. "It was *I* who placed deflections against *your* incautious conduct Luc, which always endangered our secrets. It was your risks that led to our exposure. How dare you deflect responsibility?"

Luc had tears in his eyes as he gazed up at me from his soft pillow. "Yes Nathan, it was I who took dangerous risks, but those days are over for me and always will be. My father-"

"Deflect blame to him once more and feel this come down upon your skull!"

"You'll wake him!" Luc set to sobs, his paws quivering against his chest. "He is in the next room. Please, you'll wake him."

"So the cad comes to stay with the traitor. I suppose I should meet the old devil whose machinations weighed so heavily against me, settle two accounts tonight!"

"He isn't visiting Nathan. He resides here. Ever since my... shames were learned of, he has always lived here. This house belongs to him Nathan. It always did.""

The poker was growing heavy in my grip and I lowered it just slightly when his words registered through the pounding of blood in my ears. "What?"

"My every move, my every dealing, my every social interaction is policed by him, Nathan. Oh if only you knew his fury, saw the scars he beat upon me when I had done as he ordered and betrayed you and then got me alone with my mother away on holiday. That poker you wield even now, Nathan, look on its shaft. There are two others like it in this house."" With a shaky arm, Luc pushed down the sleeve of his night shirt and spread his fur for Nathan to see. The pinkish lane of a scar under the fur had faded, but remained. "There are dozens Nathan, all where none can see. Not my business associates, nor the woman I am now promised to marry. Dozens of scars earned on the way out of my sinful, slovenly conduct, to become the man my father knows I am destined to be. I have saved myself from all you have wrought me."

I gazed in shock down at the cat lying in those bedclothes, in the very room in which so many candlelit games had warmed us on so many nights. It was a barren place now, all gaiety stripped away. My jaws parted in shock. "Saved from all I wrought you? What lies have you told yourself?"

Luc broke like a dam in that moment, tears washing in streaks down his face, his last threads of composure lost in knots of despair. "What you did to my heart was cruel. You made me a weakling and everyone knew it! Father and mother knew it and it nearly destroyed my entire family."

"Damn you! Our love was a weakness? You felt every pang of the heart that I did, every joy in every moment we joined together. If you ever hated me it was because I was a self-made man and you were but a product of your hated father's money. He ruined you long before we ever met and taught you to see all your strengths as your weaknesses so you would never be independent of him, never! So you would never feel a thing he didn't want you to feel. I gave you *real* love and you betrayed me for that gift!"

"That wasn't real Nathan, even if it felt that way. Part of love is duty, duty to the family trust and preserving the family line." Luc spoke the words in a sobbing monotone as though forced to remember them by rote. "Such is the only real true love," Luc dully gazed around the stillness of the bedroom, at the angular furnishings and the conservative dress that awaited him come the morning, "and whosoever betrays that has no place in this family, or in this house."

I saw the defeated look in his eyes, set in a stony soul, and at once my fury resettled itself like the debris of a fallen tenement block being cleared away. The man I had loved was not within this bed. I brandished the poker and took a step back. "Remove your bedclothes." I snapped at him.

Luc's eyes widened.

I had the poker up high before he could utter another word. "You will do it or I will finish what I first came to do. Hurry. Time is short." I was biting back tears at what warred in my breast. I could not see straight through my desire to rain blows upon him.

Shakily, with trepidation, Luc rose from his bed and did what he was told. The night-clothes slipped over and off his body, exposing the same white fur I'd caressed and held close on countless nights. He shivered as he dropped the linens, his tail between his legs, his male sex a pink dot far receded in a sheath topping his small sac.

"Climb atop the bed." I ordered him, fighting back tears.

A low moan escaped him and his pleading eyes sought mine. Despite our mutual weeping, I was firm. My free paw coaxed my manhood forth with effort. Soot streaked it in swirls. "Do it while you still have time."

Shaking fearfully, the cat climbed atop his bed and, understanding my mind, turned himself away from me. I used the poker to guide his legs apart and then coax his tail up high. The pale circle of his anus hung before me.

Quickly, without the slightest sensation of lust, kept stiff only by pure resolve, I stepped forward and pressed against him, feeling the resistance of his hole to my lance's advance. I held there, on the precipice of entry for several moments, remembering all the times we had joined this way in celebration, all tarnished memories torn asunder. My wetness created a slickness against the dark star in his fur's white sky. I heard Luc gasp with surprise at the touch, and heard the smallest, desirous whimper escape from him as he held perfectly still for what would come next.

"My musk is now on you," I said flatly. "That buys your silence."

I stepped away from him, and walked across the floor to the fireplace, hanging the poker back where I found it. "You would betray me again to your father, of that I have no doubt. But then he would smell my musk upon you, and I would rail to all who would listen at how passionately we reacquainted."

Luc's tail fell, and the look on his face when he turned back to me, naked and fearful and painfully aroused, was tragically heartbreaking and gratifying all at once.

"Of course, he would convince the public you were violated, but then your father would get you alone again." I rattled the poker before releasing it and turned once more to gaze upon the pathetic form of Luc Winnaker, consigned to his smothering wealth and enslaving comforts, sobbing on the bed with his legs still spread and the sheets clutched by blunt claws before a wet muzzle. "This is truly the worst of prisons," I observed piteously. "Unfortunately, it seems you have condemned yourself to a life sentence. Goodbye."

I felt almost weightless when I crept back up the chimney towards the stars above to where my love awaited me. I took no wealth from the room below, and I didn't want to. Barstowe and I would steal up north, take up residence, find work, perhaps even sail for France where more quarter could be found for those like us. Life would not be easy, but we would be together. The last of the fog had faded and the stars were a crystalline spread above me. When at last I cleared into the night air, even more coated with soot than before, I saw my stolen clothes resting on the rooftop.

Barstowe was nowhere to be seen.

I wanted to call out for him, but feared how my voice would carry. An hour certainly could not have passed. He had to be about the residence somewhere, keeping watch. It took several moments of searching the darkness before I saw him, down in the garden. My heart froze in my chest.

He was surrounded by canines, rodents and mustelids, all constables in brass-buttoned coats, moving in with truncheons deployed and ears flat in preparation for a fight. Barstowe's look of desperation moved from man to man as they closed in. Then his hard eyes crept up and saw me. There was something in the resigned sadness there, a spark of something he had but an instant to share that tore me in two.

"Come on, you ugly bastards!" He kicked dirt at the nearest. "It was I that killed that cat, who looked down on my sort all his sorry stinking life. What"re you gonna do now that another o' your gilded masters has gone to the dust? Have at me you bastards!" Barstowe rushed a corgi, and they were all upon him, burying him in blows, kicks, punches and strikes. I had no time to dress, none to climb down from my high vantage. I could only leap from the roof in time to assist, perhaps land atop one or two of them. "Get clear o' me! Don't be a fool!"" I heard him shout, knowing my mind to intervene. "There ain't no chance to-" A knock to the head stilled his words and the arrestors quickly set to binding his limbs.

I hurried down from the roof as they carted him off, nearly plummeting to certain injury. I avoided the constables knocking frantically at the estate's door as I struggled into my clothes and slipped away. I tried to follow, trace the arrestor's path, feeling my lover grow more distant from me moment by moment as the prisoner's wagon turned a distant corner. I was sobbing when I finally ran out of breath, coughing into the cobblestones, my tears accepted by a layer of grime.

My hound had bought me this, for my own vengeful hubris he'd paid the greatest price. I wandered alone for hours down the hollow shells of empty streets, unmindful that I was still a criminal at large who could be collected at any moment. In my brazen misery, Barstowe's sacrifice fixed in my mind, I could not enjoy one single breath of free air, no matter how dearly my love had paid for it.

"There ain't a chance." I heard him shout, over and over again.

With despair creeping around me in London's hot fog, I refused to listen.

* * *

Weeks later find me where I need to be, staring at a wall that my heart itself could tear through had it limbs to do so. Barstowe is within, his sentence set and sealed. Whether at the whipping post or being prepared for the noose I do not know, but I won't leave him to face either.

God knows by now that stealing from fate is what we two are best at.

I place a paw on the rough stones below the weighted rope I have thrown and prepare myself for the madness my heart has led me too. Barstowe will want to beat me senseless when all this is over and I look forward to an angry kiss at the very least when I find him in there, overcoming just one set of overwhelming but ultimately irrelevant odds to follow. He should know as I do, that no prison can hold him and none can keep me out. Not while I draw breath.

As sure as he and I love one another, this dark, monstrosity before me has a chimney or two.

For Tym, my forever boyfriend, whose love of all things Victorian helped immensely with the writing of this story. And, as always, to my constant readers, whose support is a rock when my muse and motivation get all sandy.

Inspiration

by Whyte Yoté

I stood, my muzzle agape, clutching my valise to my chest. "You can't be serious."

The otter porter, who couldn't be a shade over fifteen, shuffled his patent-leather shoes on the deep pile of carpet that lined my private Pullman car from wall to wall. A dark vermilion, it wouldn't have been my first choice if I'd had my druthers, all angry and not complimentary to my russet fur at all. Emerald. Emerald would have sufficed nicely.

"My apologies, sir," stuttered the otter without quite meeting my eyes. I couldn't direct all of my irateness toward him, though. Not really. He worked for Union Pacific, sure, but the orders did not originate from him. He was merely tasked with delivering them. "Because we are within the town limits, sir, we must put you up in accommodations other than the train. It may take several days for the local smithy to forge new parts." He seemed genuinely sorry, which did little to assuage the irksome nature of the situation.

I kept my ears down just for show. Looking around the car—extravagant silks in one corner, a trunk full of lace over in another, over a thousand dollars worth of material—I wondered how in blazes I would transport my cargo to the nearest safe or strongbox.

"What am I supposed to do with all this?" I asked the otter, spreading my arms to indicate the textiles surrounding us. "These are some of the finest fabrics in the Orient. I had to go to San Francisco to get them. I can't leave them here alone."

The otter boy followed my gesture, but the way he looked at my precious findings indicated he knew little about the value of fine things. His uniform was wool with brass hardware, hot and likely itchy, and I could see where the hem had been lengthened by simply adding a few inches of material to cover his longer torso. How barbaric.

"You registered your cargo with the purser, sir?" He was quite obsequious for his age; I could tell he'd either been brought up on the trains or trained well.

"Yes, they have a record of everything. I would have taken photographic evidence, but Matthew Brady was unavailable."

"Sir?"

"Brady? Photographed President Lincoln? And that little war we just had five or so years ago?" I was about to affect a huff when the boy's muzzle tightened, his whiskers trembling.

"With all due respect, sir," he offered quietly but assuredly, "my big brother fought for the North. He lost a leg, but he didn't die. I'm proud of him." It took me a moment to realize he was acting defensive because of my accent. I couldn't be angry with a child standing up for his kin.

I crossed the short distance between us and placed a paw on his shoulder. He started, his stoic facade crumbled. Before he could apologize for his insubordination, I said, "I was only born and raised in Louisiana, son. I live in Chicago, and rooted for the Union the whole way through. I'm on your side." The wave of relief on his face took the edge off my irritation at the damnable railroad. "Alas. What does Union Pacific propose to secure all this? It is extremely expensive." And they were, every single bolt, but no one had to know I paid wholesale but registered their retail cost. Insurance for my traveling trouble.

"We have heavy-duty padlocks at each door, sir," the otter replied. "With several tumblers. No skeleton key. One for you, and one for the purser." I glanced ruminatively around me, recalling all the haggling I'd had to do with Orientals who I didn't understand, for a price that was likely still more than the fabric was worth. Only twenty minutes ago the conductor had walked the length of the train announcing the breakdown of some part or other, and the mid-afternoon air was already stifling.

I had little choice.

"So be it," I relented. "But I'll need my luggage brought to wherever I'm staying. Just my valise. And my suitcase." I considered. "And that one trunk. Some of these items cannot leave my sight."

Unburdened, the boy gave a curt nod, dug into his trousers pocket and produced a key. "I'll lock it personally, sir, and show you the proof. You can count on me."

"Will you be handling my bags?"

"Of course, sir."

Taking out my billfold, I took the key and placed a five-dollar bill in his upturned, webbed palm. He appeared stricken of some apoplexy before stumbling over his words.

"Thank you! Oh, sir…I can't take this much. I haven't even done anything yet."

"That's why there's another waiting upon delivery," I winked. "You're stuck here, same as I. Go see the town procuress, have yourself an evening." He was smiling, but he didn't seem to understand my gist. Not that he would be able to buy a lady for the evening at his age. Perhaps he was better off; in a few years he'd make a handsome young man for a proper woman. Or not. One never knew.

I watched after him and his thick tail as he left my coach. Definitely the workings of a gentleman, if he kept his nose clean. Working the Pullmans was a good start.

Not until he was a good ways afield did I realize he could have helped me pack the few things I'd need while stranded. Already perspiring, I doffed my topcoat and rolled up my sleeves. This was too much work for a single man, let alone a single fox.

"Blast it all to hell, why here?" I wailed at the stack of trunks, but the tufted-velvet benches and tasseled curtains (so commercial, so tacky, and so gauche) bore me neither pity nor sympathy.

* * *

As it turned out, letting the otter boy go worked in my best interest, as he sent two strapping draymen from the Sweetwater Hotel to assist me with my things. Which meant the mustang carried the trunk that held my most valuable purchases and the mule carried the trunk with my personal belongings and wardrobe, some of it tragically folded for the journey. I cringed at the thought of my good shirts and trousers suffering wrinkles, but I was buoyed by the twin sets of solid flanks flexing within their denim prisons.

A survey of the Rock Springs depot yielded the only sights worth seeing, as far as I was concerned: sturdy males, mostly hoofed, mostly shirtless, all gorgeous. Pulling carts, shoveling coal, laying track and pounding spikes. Oh, how I wished I were one of those spikes. The dusty air was acrid with musk, multiplied by the heat, and I took out the cheap paper fan I'd bought in Chinatown earlier that week and tried to keep myself cool, but to no avail.

"Sir." The otter lad came up beside me. "The locks are ready for your inspection."

"Those men know where they're going, I trust?" I couldn't keep the worry from my voice. To them I was just some dandy fox from Illinois with an attitude and too much money. Some of the fabric in those trunks cost more than either would make in a year or more, I was quite certain.

The otter smiled down his blunt nose at me. His whiskers lifted and twitched below warm, green eyes. I idly wondered if he'd bedded anyone in his short life, then shook the thought from my head. San Francisco had been a boon in the business sense, but a bust in romance. "They have explicit instructions, sir. If you would follow me?"

He led me to both doors of the Pullman car, showed me the thick ornate padlocks on each and used both his key and mine to demonstrate their facility. I feigned satisfaction because I tended toward neuroticism when it involved my trade as haute-couture maven, especially when large sums of money exchanged paws. After thanking the boy for his attention to my concerns, I followed him out of the depot and into the town proper.

Town, however, was a generous endowment. It owed its existence to the Union Pacific Railroad, a local coal mine and mill, and little else. My feet kicked up dust all over my fur and spats;no amount of high-stepping would keep them clean. As we crossed Main Street on a diagonal, I took stock of what the town offered: the Sweetwater Hotel, a general store, a druggist on the corner to my right, a barber, a brothel and numerous saloons.

I inwardly hoped the hotel had a bar of its own so I would not be required to mingle with the local tradesmen; all that bulk in one place would set my eye to wandering, and the repercussions might not be as friendly outside of a major metropolis. Putting a finger to the top of my muzzle, I felt the nodule where a well-placed blow by an offended gentleman had once broken the bone.

Oh, but how this had been a lonely trip.

Thankfully, the Sweetwater was just a couple blocks away from the depot. Looking up and shading my face, I could see the three-story building up on the left. I shuddered to think how the place looked before the benefit of the Golden Spike and its attendant traffic. Judging by the rugged nature of the locals, I doubted they even knew what a stereopticon was, much less what it did. If I took mine out, I might be excoriated as a warlock, for all I knew.

I kept my gaze on the otter's swaying tail and let it mesmerize me, not due to its owner but from its incessant, rhythmic motion. Water would feel like splashing heaven on my face after this long, trying day.

"Heave!" a voice bellowed to my right. "Ho! Heave…ho! Put your backs to it, men!" I looked up in the direction whence it originated. My jaw fell wide open: eight draymen—three bighorns, two Clydesdales, a wild mustang, a bison, and a black bull—were pulling the crippled locomotive of my train from the yard to the smithy, presumably on the other end of town, along a section of track laid down the center of the wide thoroughfare of C Street. One of the Clydesdales was shouting encouragement to the rest, and down to a man they grunted and perspired and dug their hooves into the rail bed at the rate of a foot per second, if that. All were fine specimens, clad in various pants with nary a shirt to be seen.

And that bull - he was…magnificent. He was big and black and shining with foam, and he didn't belong here. Not that he wasn't suited to his task, but that he stood out from the rest of the men. His coat iridesced through its layer of dust, while the pair of cut-off jeans he wore concealed nothing. I was agog, standing stock still in the middle of the packed-dirt street as there was no sidewalk, and I did not care. I had seven-plus feet of Michelangelic sculpture straining against his ropes not far from me and I was rapidly becoming indecent.

"Sir? Is something the matter?" the otter asked me with a tug to my sleeve, his voice a league away. "Sir. You had better stop that."

"Pardon?" I looked at him, licking the inside of my bone-dry mouth. He cast his eyes downward, then back up to mine, and I felt my paw squeezing where a gentleman should never squeeze in public. Heat, hotter than the day, traveled up my neck and set my hackles on edge. "Oh, my dear. I'm so sorry, my boy. I'm a heathen." I tore my eyes from the bull and cleared my throat. "Please. Show me to my room."

We passed the bell desk, as the railroad had taken care of those details already, and mounted the stairs to the second floor. At the end of the hallway stood the hoofers who'd carried my luggage, one on each side of the door, arms crossed. They made way for the otter, who produced a different key and unlocked the door.

"Ain't nobody been here except us," the mule said. "Your items are secure." This duty above and beyond was impressive even to me, and I gave each one five dollars for his trouble. I could practically see the gears turning inside their heads.

"Trapper's Gulch?" the Clydesdale asked his cohort.

"Trapper's Gulch," the mule replied, sharing a toothy smile. "And a few pints to boot!" He turned to me and bowed, clearly a gesture unfamiliar to him. "Our sincerest appreciation, sir." We could still hear them hooting and hollering down the staircase after the lad had closed the door.

I clapped my paws together. "It would seem I made someone's night, wouldn't it?"

"Coupla gal-sneakers," said the otter before he fell silent, wringing his paws some. At first I thought he was embarrassed to ask for the remainder of his gratuity, but he spoke before I could oblige him. "They're beautiful, aren't they?"

"Pardon?"

"The men." His misty green eyes held mine, as if on the verge of crying. "The Western towns are full of them. I didn't want you to see trouble, so I stopped you from staring too long. If I was out of turn—"

"No, son, you weren't. I appreciate your wary eye." He suffered the same plight as me, no doubt about it. Those emerald eyes, full of longing, reminded me of my own youth. His scent changed subtly, but I brought out my billfold before he did something untoward. "Here. For keeping me in my skin."

50

He gawped at the five. "I can't possibly."

"If you don't, I'll inform your superior of your ingratitude." I smiled despite my tone, and the boy took it, folding it reverently into a breast pocket.

"Anything. You mention it."

"Fetch me that bull out there."

He paused. "Anything...but that?" We had a good laugh and I bid him adieu, silently wishing him the best of luck in case I didn't see him again. Times were changing, but slowly.

* * *

Even though my room (actually, it was a suite of rooms, as befitted my First-Class ticket) faced north, and I had opened every single window shortly after the otter's departure, the oppressive heat overpowered the benefit of shade and breeze. Though it was hardly a gentlemanly thing to do, my jacket and trousers found their way into the pitifully small closet with the rest of my personal affects, leaving me in a pair of silk drawers and a short-sleeved shirt. I felt practically naked, but I had no one to impress at the moment.

With the ambient workaday noise as my accompaniment, I knelt next to my best steamer trunk and unlocked it with a key, much less elaborate than the one supplied to me by the railroad, and surveyed my treasures: here was the silk in a wonderful shade of periwinkle with an intricate geometric pattern, there was the brocade in an endless blizzard of falling cherry blossoms, here again another silk in black with very subtle floral stitching that would make a wonderful mourning dress for the right woman.

My trip to San Francisco, though loveless, had been a smashing success. No doubt my clients back in Chicago would praise my hawkish eye, especially since the Transcontinental Railroad had turned a month-long journey into a trip just shy of three weeks. And staying in one's own personal sleeper car was infinitely better than hopping a stagecoach from Laramie to Salt Lake City. Or tramp-steaming around Tierra del Fuego. Never again.

I laid each precious, priceless bolt along one wall, my mind's-eye devising outfits as I went. The fine white coutil I had wrested from a Chinawoman's delicate paws for twice what any sane person would pay I could weave into a fine boned corset with perhaps some red lace and pearl accents. And the dresses, oh, the dresses! As soon as I set foot in Illinois again my pencils would fly. Alas, my dress-forms were back in my studio and drapery would have to wait. But I could still attempt some sketches.

But not now. It was much too hot. I didn't even dare put on the kimono I'd spied at the corner of Stockton and Jackson, for fear I would sully it. It hung in the closet on the opposite side of the room, unworn and unwrinkled. I rested on the chaise-lounge, wilted and sweating. I considered sending my superiors a telegram informing them of the delay, but unless the repair took several days the money would have been wasted and I would arrive before the message.

Closing my eyes, I listened to the din outside and shaded my brow with a forearm. I saw the fabrics floating before me, and I willed them to unwind. Suddenly I was on the streets of Chicago, fabric flowing all around me, eager to dress the wealthy cattle barons and their wives (and their mistresses) in the finest the Orient had to offer.

The dour cottons and wools turned to satin and velvet at my touch, flowing dresses of every color trimmed in fine lace and Oriental patterns. Men's suits with ivory buttons carved from the very tusks of the craftsmen themselves, accented with a bit of color here and there that told the world, "Zebulon Thibaud was here."

Zebulon Thibaud, the son of a Louisiana catfisher who left home at seventeen to pursue the art of fashion because the opportunity simply didn't exist south of the Mason-Dixon Line. That, and Southern Baptists couldn't keep a secret if their lives depended on it, unlike my clients.

In Chicago, no one cared whom one preferred as long as one fulfilled one's professional obligations. And even if they did care, they didn't let that interfere with business matters. Also, it was well known that if one went to Zebulon Thibaud for a wedding dress or debutante gown, one could rest assured that the dandy fox with the pencil mustache would never try to take advantage of their ladies. The husbands, suitors, and fathers however was a different story.

That was only once. And only because the puma came on to me in the fitting room. I never did get an accurate inseam measurement for him, but he still came out stunning.

Women in various stages of undress (purely for the purpose of addressing fit) made way for gentlemen in much the same way, starting with the puma. Aloysius something-or-other, it mattered little because his surname wasn't impressive as the size of him in my throat, driving my ears while lewdly hunching the back of my head into the mirror, his need overshadowing decorum at least for the moment.

Then a series of images, as from my stereopticon: hoofed and padded, avian and cetacean, all the males over the years I'd landed or pined for, a parade of flesh that evidently sent my paw to my groin, because I woke from my doze clutching an erection so hard it was painful. I unbuttoned the fly, a clever little addition to the drawers since they were my own creation, and brought myself out.

"Damn it all..." I had been much too busy in the city to take care of it in the week I'd been shopping. A squeeze behind my knot elicited an embarrassingly vulpine sound. I needed to calm down.

Crossing to the basin by the water closet, I poured the provided pitcher into it and splashed the contents against my face, not bothering to doff my shirt. What looked back at me resembled a drowned water rat more than a red fox. After toweling off and checking my teeth for errant scraps, I opened the door to my right—to find a bottomless chair with a bucket beneath.

I should have known, but I had been too preoccupied with securing my possessions to worry about something like indoor plumbing. I looked at the bucket with despair, imagining the indelicate position required to use it. No different from other indelicate positions I was used to, but still.

There was no toilet. There was no bathtub. There was no scented powder, even, and upon this discovery I whirled and gathered my clothes, hurried them on, and descended to the lobby.

The mole manning the desk took my mildly disguised indignation with aplomb, informing me that the Sweetwater Hotel had the finest facilities around, which did not bode well for the rest of the Wyoming Territory. Each room was supplied one pitcher of water daily, and First-Class guests like myself could order another if need be. I could use an outhouse, behind the main building, but when I rounded the corner to inspect, the odor drove me back. Additionally,

I would receive a fresh bucket each day while those rickety wooden structures were cleaned once a week—if the staff remembered.

Also mentioned were the "bathing facilities" in the basement, which turned out to be several troughs of dubiously cloudy water refreshed daily. One look at them, and the rowdy men occupying them, and I turned back up the stairs. My constitution, much less my fur, couldn't handle the shock. It would never get clean.

So just as the sun was touching the tops of the low barren hills to the west, I gathered my only bar of soap, my furbrush and a small vial of cologne designed to complement my natural scent. These I carried in my valise, now relieved of its paperwork and sketch materials. I threw on the kimono, the one piece of clean laundry that wouldn't cling to the dirt on my body, and tucked my single towel under an arm as I made my way out of the hotel via the rear.

Past the noisome outhouses, down the gently-sloping hill behind the hotel, was the river. I had spotted it earlier, while I held my nose and tried not to retch. Not knowing the source of the water, I had no clue as to its temperature, but it wasn't stagnant, which had to be better than the alternatives. Dignity be damned, I needed a good scrubbing more than I needed to adhere to decorum. In this town of ruffians and cowboys, who would care?

I picked my way down the grassy bank when it dropped off, the soft soil cool on my pads since the heat of the day had dissipated quite a bit. Colors had ceased to exist in these shadows, but my night vision allowed enough contrast for me to avoid a tumble. Once I reached the sandy bank I saw a bend to my left where the river narrowed and trees lined either side, providing at least some cover. I padded the fifty feet or so, swishing my tail to combat the soft sand between my toes. A nearby branch held the kimono, a boulder below served as a makeshift table and, soap in paw, I waded in.

Soft susurrations surrounded my ankles, then my knees as I got used to the cool, but not cold, water. It smelled different here, scrubbed clean of the town-scents around me. Not a claw-foot bathtub, nor a warm gravity-fed shower, but refreshing all the same. Wet to the waist now, I submerged the rest of me in one go, shocked but now very much awake. And as I began to scrub I hummed "Camptown Races," a favorite ditty from my youth, and imagined myself back in my room, clean, and thinking up new designs with my pencil in paw.

"Oh Susannah," I rubbed my belly, "oh don't you cry for me," I soaped up my sheath, "for I come from Looziana with a banjo on my knee."

"Alabama," someone said beside me, and I screamed two octaves above what one would expect, even from a slender fox. I also tried to cover myself, and in my haste stumbled and fell into the river, tucking my tail just in time. Sputtering and clearing my eyes, the first thing I saw was a set of thick blunt-tipped black fingers, spread to help me up. My eyes traveled up the chiseled arm to the snout and horns.

I was sure I had drowned. And Saint Peter was in fact a bull.

"Pardon me?" Past the bull's tree trunk of an arm were two grapefruits in a velvety sac. I wanted to look up, I really did. So I forced myself.

"It's Alabama, I think," he said, more of a rumble than a voice. We grasped wrists and he righted me as if I were a child's plaything, a ragdoll. "Not Louisiana."

With not a speck of clothing between us, I could only stand stiffly and hope to not go stiff. Covering myself with my paws would only draw attention. "You are correct, sir. I merely insert the state of my birth as a nod to my childhood." Only then did it occur to me that this bull was not only the same one I'd seen earlier pulling the locomotive, but he had approached me in the river on purpose. While I bathed.

How fortuitous. I minded not in the least.

"You are okay, then?" he asked in an accent I couldn't quite place, other than it was as handsome as the rest of him. Standing a full two heads taller than I, he should have been intimidating, but his docility tempered the impression somewhat.

I sluiced some water from my chest, flicking it off my fingers. "Yes, I believe so. Thank you."

"You're welcome." My my, but he was a polite one. I began to warm in places that should not be warm, but at this point I couldn't help it. His proximity was to blame. Thrusting his hand out again, he said, "Jasper de Gonsalvo." Lord help me, a foreigner. A Spaniard!

"Zebulon H. Thibaud, at your service," I said with as much flourish as any red fox can muster while naked and soaked to the skin. He about crushed my paw in his fist. "I believe I saw you pulling my crippled locomotive to the smithy earlier?"

Jasper thought, then nodded. "Yes, it was quite heavy. But Ernest is a good driver. We got it there."

"I bet you did," I added, making furtive glances at the heavy shaft swinging between his legs. I pretended the water dripping from its hooded tip was something else. I felt myself slipping free, and didn't much care. He'd not be able to see much of anything without proper night vision. "Are you down here for the same reason, then, I suppose?" I reconsidered my wording. "Cleaning up after a hard day?" He wouldn't be at the hotel, certainly.

"Every night," he said, hands on hips to crack his back. "Some of the men like to wallow in their own filth. My father taught me better." He guffawed, the sound reverberating off the trees.

I wanted to reach out and touch his stomach. Just run a claw over the peaks and valleys. He seemed friendly enough. He might be worth a try. And even if not, I wouldn't have to spend the evening alone. The bull had no shame, but no pretensions either, thinking nothing of chatting up a stranger while nude in the middle of a river. Not naïveté, not quite. Something just - natural.

"Good man," I said. "The hotel up there has inadequate facilities, so I ventured out here for some running water."

"It's peaceful," he said, almost a whisper, seeming lost in thought. "Sometimes I wander the river for an hour or two, by sound, listening once the town goes to sleep." He turned away from me, bent over (oh Lord help me) and came up with a stone, smooth and flat. He attempted to skip it, but it plunked out of sight. "I used to do it better, when my hands were smaller." That smile, chicle-white teeth in a sea of pitch. He should have a ring in his nose, I decided.

"Better than I could do," I lied, having skipped up to a dozen times in my own youth. "Say, Jasper, you seem like a fine gentleman. What say we go up to the restaurant and have a meal? I haven't eaten since noon, and you likely have the stomach catalysis of a squirrel." I tried to give him a friendly pat on the shoulder, but could only bump my fist against one of his massive pectorals. It hurt, like punching granite.

"Oh, I cannot afford a place like that. I just have some soup at one of the saloons, usually."

"I didn't ask you to pay, sir. I invited you, so there is no presumption of obligation." My tail tried to wag in a friendly way, but watered down it hardly moved. "It would be rude of you to turn me down, as well." In all actuality he could have begged off, but he didn't have to know that.

Arms crossed, posing like a piece of living art, he eventually nodded, his face brightening up as much as a black-haired face could. "Mister Zebulon H. Thibaud, I accept. My evening just got more interesting."

"That makes two of us," I replied, fighting to keep my paws from my groin.

* * *

We rinsed and dried separately, since Jasper's clothes were around the bend from my own, and climbed the riverbank together. I tried my best to keep up with the bull's massive strides, but to no avail, especially as I was picking my way carefully so as not to catch the silk kimono on stray branches. Curious as to my dress, he asked a couple questions and I answered honestly about my profession and purchase, and he seemed to accept it. I was from a big city, anyway, and things were different there.

I very much enjoyed watching the big bull's eyes (they were brown, now that I could see) widen at the prices on the menu, which were less than I was accustomed to but well above his usual fare. The restaurant had daily deliveries of refrigerated meat, so I took advantage of the luxury by ordering a chicken dish with new potatoes and green beans, while Jasper ordered the alfalfa loaf, a popular dish among the ungulates. I ordered two Sazeracs and promised the bull he'd like it once he tried it.

Anything with absinthe was good, in my opinion.

"I feel under-dressed," he said, though he now wore long trousers, an off-white cambric shirt and a brown cap balanced between his horns. It brought out his eyes. Combined with my kimono, we did receive a look from the waiter, not like I cared.

"Nonsense. I'll hear none of it," I said. "Dig in."

Between bites, the chicken was a bit chewy, but nonetheless satisfactory, we traded histories, mostly at my urging because I was trying to find a way to get him up to my room without arousing suspicion. In the meantime, I was learning much more about him than I thought I would. Normally this would bore me, but watching Jasper talk kept me in rapt attention.

One Sazerac became two.

"So, your name isn't Jasper?" I asked, dabbing my napkin at the corners of my muzzle.

"Gaspar," the bull replied. "At least, back in Seville. After my father sold his business and moved us here, he suggested I 'Americanize' my name to lessen the prejudice."

"Evil, but necessary, I suppose," I said. "I can only hear a trace of an accent, Jasper. It's as if you hadn't spent thirteen years here."

He shoveled another forkful of alfalfa loaf between his lips, full-fist, like a little boy. Adorable. "My tutors are to blame. Or to thank, depending on your opinion. People say my Spanish is perfect, as well. Of course, no one in Thermopolis speaks Spanish."

I kept hearing "Thermopylae." I had Greek gods on the brain. "And your father thought he could bring the word of Christ to the Blackfoot and Cheyenne tribes up near there?"

"Sold nearly everything we had and boarded the RMS Oceanic," he affirmed. "I was only fourteen. We were all surprised at the Indians' unwillingness to convert, though now I look back at it and wonder how Father could have convinced himself. We retreated a safe distance away, near the hot springs, and built a homestead. It's the only one in the area with electricity and geothermal heat."

"So why are you down here, pulling rail cars?" I asked, lubricated by alcohol. Just a bit. "You could be going to Harvard, by the sound of you."

Jasper shrugged the mountains of his shoulders. "I want to pay my own way."

I withered a bit at that. When I had moved from Lafayette Parish to Chicago to pursue fashion, my father had a fit. I was too far away to help with the catch over the summer. He'd thought I was abandoning him. Yet he kept wiring me money; not enough for it all, but enough to help.

This bull would never earn enough for college working like he was.

"I admire that, Jasper," I said, leaning over to put my paw on his hand. My fingers made their way around his before I could stop them. The bull stared at me for just a moment, and I swore I could see him blushing. "There aren't many men left in the world. Countless males, but very few men."

"Thank you," he said, and he squeezed my fingers before straightening up. I shifted in my seat, twirling my mustache to mask the flare of arousal. Jasper snorted. "And thank you for the meal. I am very full."

"Listen," I interjected before he could continue. If he bade me goodnight now I might never get another chance. Taking my time to fold my napkin on my plate, I composed myself as best I could. "Listen, Jasper. I—you have an amazing body."

"Er…"

"Hear me out!" I corrected, palms up. "You know I'm a designer of clothes. All of my clients are wealthy business-types, either ectomorphic beanpoles or endomorphic blobs. You…you mesomorph…I never have the opportunity to design for such mass. Your shirt and trousers are ill-fitting, no?"

The bull shifted uncomfortably, as if I'd offended him. "They're not perfect…"

"Exactly!" I exclaimed, perhaps a little louder than I had meant to. But I almost had him by the horns, and I was nothing if not a tenacious bastard. "You have turned an inconvenient stopover into an engaging conversation, and I thank you from the bottom of my intellect. I never intended to make such company, and I think it's the least I can do to, perhaps, fit you for a suit. In case you had a mind to apprentice somewhere in the business sector, and not manual labor. Because pulling trains and pushing coal won't buy you an education."

At this Jasper looked down and studied his lap. This was not the first time he had either heard it or thought it. He knew. And I meant what I said. He would get a suit, a Zebulon Thibaud original, no matter what happened.

"So what say we get a round to take up to my room and I can draw you. The art of drapery is very complex, and I haven't used my pencils in days. I have nothing but time."

Jasper drummed his fingers on the table, staring at his plate, empty but for a few scraps of stray alfalfa. He appeared to struggle with himself. "I am a proud man," he finally said. "I don't take charity. But I accept gifts with humility." His flat teeth gleamed.

"Bully!" I shouted, causing several patrons to glance our way. I did not care.

* * *

Jasper held my drink while I unlocked the door. The lantern, supplied by the hotel, dangled precariously from one of his horns to light our way. Once inside, I lit a candle from it and spread the light to the rest of the lanterns throughout the suite, closing the windows to keep out the wind and the chill, so different from the daytime heat. I had no idea the high desert was so extreme. I shivered in the loose-fitting kimono, nude as I was underneath.

Bathed in fire-glow, the suite took on a romantic air, which was not my intention but a pleasant side effect.

"Please, stand over by the chaise," I said, grabbing my glass from his hand.

"This one?" he asked, indicating the correct piece of furniture.

"Yes." Digging around in my suitcase for my pencils and watercolors, I added, "nude, of course." I almost heard him bristle. He hadn't had a problem in the river, so why should he now? I certainly had no problem with his nudity. Clothing rustled to the floor, and the scent of the room changed dramatically. Until now he'd either been masked by the river or his own garments. Now it was just his hide and nothing else.

I turned, tools in one paw and paper in the other, and held my breath to take in the sight before me: Jasper, all six-foot-plus of him, laid out like a Renaissance painting, arms out like a Vitruvian Man writ larger. This time I let myself slide out, unabashedly, underneath the kimono. If he smelled me, so be it.

"You can relax. No need to be completely formal." I saw no need to inform him I usually measured my clients with at least underclothes on. He rested his arms, which still stuck out to the side a bit. "First we measure, so I can construct a form that matches your dimensions. Then we sketch so I have a shape over which to draw the outfit. Of course, most of that takes place back in my studio in Chicago. My means are severely limited here."

"Okay," he said, clopping from one hoof to the other, probably understanding little of what I said. In my element now, and fairly inebriated, I wouldn't jeopardize the events I had set in motion. His musk was everywhere it was in my nose, on my fur, in my clothes. Croceus, he was irresistible, and he knew nothing of it.

I took out my tape measure, in its engraved-pewter case, and unrolled it to an arm's-length. Then I drained the rest of my third Sazerac to steel my nerves. "Ready?" Not waiting for an answer, I stepped behind him and slid the cloth around his middle at navel height. "Thirty-six waist."

"Is that good?" he asked. I noticed, when I came around front again, a perceptible plumping.

"Very good." I kept noticing it as I instructed him to lift each arm, then kneel for his neck. He snorted again when my now-full sheath came close to his snout. His cock twitched slightly. I perceived his discomfort in the otherwise silent room, though my sense of empathy had become somewhat dulled. Then the thought struck me like lightning. "My music box!"

Jasper stared after me, still kneeling, as I opened up my suitcase and took out a bundle of swaddling clothes from when I was a kit. I unwrapped it reverently and set the box down on a side table, opening its intricately-inlaid wood lid to reveal the brass cylinder and countless teeth. "Wait, just wait!" I whispered though he hadn't said a word, and I wound the spring. Turning, grinning like a fool at him, I flipped the lever.

"Camptown Races" began to play.

"That's why you were humming it," Jasper said, eying me warily now. I must have looked daffy at that moment.

I came back over to him, unsteady. He was noticeably turgid, muskier than ever. I trembled as I instructed him to stand, kneeling as he'd done, and ran the tape down the outside length of his leg, swaying in time to the melody.

"Doo-dah, doo-dah," I mumbled, reaching his hock. I didn't even look at the number. All I could see in my periphery was nine inches of absolution.

"Mr. Thibaud?" Jasper asked in his perfect, not-foreign accent. I heard him lick his thick lips.

I started at the hoof and got as far as the inside of his left knee before I collapsed against his leg, encircling it, smashing my cheek against the shiny black hide. "I'm sorry," I said. "I can't stand it. I can't stand you."

The music box stopped playing, replaced by a basso rumble. "Why not?"

I let go and threw the kimono over my head, sitting with my legs tucked but my need on full display. The bridge of my muzzle throbbed, my head swam. Jasper towered over me, my Colossus of Rhodes, my Helios, not a torch in his right hand but his cock, fully erect and imposing.

"I didn't realize," I began. "I mean, I saw you there in the street and thought, 'He would never, with a sodomite fox. He would sooner beat me to a bloody pulp.' But now we're here, and you're… like that…and I don't know what to do."

Jasper knelt, his manhood descending past my nose, driving me nearly insane. Even there, on the floor, he looked like he should be guarding some ancient temple. "You talked to me. Nobody here ever talks to me, unless they're giving orders. You bought me a dinner, you offered to clothe me." Oh, that accent. "Mr. Thibaud, if that's what a sodomite fox does, then I like sodomite foxes." And then he hugged me to him, tight and safe and warm and hard and leaking, and I squeaked with something like joy except much more jubilant.

Having no words, and not knowing what else to do, I took him in my paw and held him in the candlelight, hefting its bulk, feeling its aliveness. I may not have known his leanings, but they hardly mattered anymore. He didn't stop me from craning my neck, from sticking my tongue out, from licking between his foreskin and glans, from taking out all of my frustrations on the thing closest to my mouth at the time.

The bull would not hold my head. Instead, he kept his hands on his hips and—I assumed—watched me devour his maleness, one inch at a time. I was out of practice, but I quickly remembered, and I pulled on his testicles ever so gently while slathering over the rest. Then they, too, were in my mouth, one at a time, with his shaft lying lazily over either side of my head, pinning down one or the other ear, mussing everything with slick fluid. Eventually I convinced my gag reflex to retreat and only when my nose was buried in his thick pubic hair did he venture a soft bellow.

I wanted to beg him to ravish me. And I knew he would, too, if I turned around and lifted my tail for him to spit on or lick me wide open. But I also knew I was drunk, and when I was drunk I was loud, and it would not do for either of us if I made our tryst known to the Sweetwater Hotel and anyone else within earshot.

So I closed my eyes and memorized every contour of his cock, each vein and the way it curved just so to the right, the way it fit down my gullet, and imagined myself on all fours or on my back, impaled either way, asking for more even once his balls touched mine. I slapped his hand away when he reached for my rear. If he made it past my ring I would surely give us away.

"Later," I promised raggedly, and his response was to wrap his fingers around my shaft, dwarfed by them, and stroke me to a shattering climax in less than a minute. Several volleys hit my chin and the underside of his member, and I tasted myself on the next plunge. Thankfully I didn't have to warn him to be quiet; I wouldn't have been able to because then he did hold my head, grunting and lowing deep in his throat while gobs after gobs flowed over my tongue, out the sides of my mouth, and even out my nose.

I kept him in as long as I could, breathing nothing but bull. It was a place in which I was happy to be. Then he scooped me up in those arms, and kissed me, and the Rock Springs sheriff and all his deputies wouldn't be able to pry me out.

* * *

I leaned back in my chair, the cloudy Chicago day providing the perfect light by which to scrutinize my work. I transferred several pins from one side of my muzzle to the other, very delicately but automatically, like a memory. My fingers drummed across the surface of my sewing desk, the claws blunted, the pads sore and wounded by countless pinpricks.

But it was done.

The suit wrapped the form like a second skin with its broad shoulders, thick collars and tucked waist. I had dug through my entire inventory to find my finest wool, a dark grey affair sourced from the flockhouses of Ireland. It covered a collared vest of the same material, with onyx buttons, over an ivory shirt with a studded collar hidden by a smart ascot I had taken pains to match to Jasper's eyes. Trousers of the same wool hung below the form, pleated and hemmed. And, although I didn't have to, I had bought a silk top hat with a brown ribbon, and cut notches to accommodate his ears and horns.

It had taken ten days of long hours and late nights, but I had made him a promise, and I was a fox of my word. Just imagining him in the outfit put a spark in my loins.

We had eventually made love, of course, once I had sobered up and we had taken the time to properly prepare me. Once Jasper mounted my spread legs he became a gentle giant, rocking the both of us in the bed, touching the deepest parts of me before ultimately breeding me like a vixen. Or a cow. I'd never asked his preference and he'd never offered. Not that it mattered in the least.

My luck being what it was, the Rock Springs blacksmiths had worked through the night and, come morning, the locomotive had made its way back to the rest of the train under its own power. My otter seemed concerned at my sudden melancholy, but I had assured him it must have been the water or something.

Jasper had stayed through the night, keeping me warm. He had gone by the time I woke, though, for another day of labor. He'd left a note, tucked into my music box, with his mailing address in town and a simple, if cryptic message, below it: You were right. I could live with that.

My tail thrashed the air behind me as I searched for an error, some misplaced stitch or a loose thread. I'd gone over it three times, and nothing. Nothing was ever perfect, but "good enough" was as close as one could get sometimes. The bull would look just as amazing as he did with nothing at all.

I sighed, turned back to the desk and read the short, simple letter I had written to him: "Impress the hell out of them. Never give up. Send me a photograph of yourself in it. I hear Matthew Brady is available. Zebulon." My name I signed in flowing script, with my usual flourish on the Z. This I tucked in the breast pocket of the coat, next to my personal label manually sewn to the liner.

I hated to fold up such a piece of work, but it would go through the mail no other way. Making sure to follow the natural lines of each garment, I lovingly wrapped the whole kit (sans top hat) in canvas that I sewed shut and lay in a small wooden shipping box on a bed of packing straw. It might be overdone, but I had worked too hard to have it be ruined by the elements.

With broad brushstrokes, I wrote Jasper's address on the top of the box and nailed it shut. The pegboard to my right was covered in telegrams from clients who couldn't wait to see my newest procurements from the west coast. They all thought I was ill with some kind of California bug.

The bolts of Chinatown fabric lay along one wall, untouched since I had unpacked them a week ago, shortly before a coffee-fueled overnight design session. The fine ladies and gentlemen of Chicago could wait just a bit longer for their originals by Zebulon H. Thibaud.

Wrapping the box in twine, I carried it out to the street. A drayman, a palomino trussed up in leather, pulled to the curb when I waved, his hooves sparking on the cobbles. "You wanna cab?" he barked in his Chicago accent, something much less nuanced than Jasper's mild Seville.

"I do," I said.

"Where to, fox?"

I rolled my eyes. Not everyone could be like the bull. But they could at least try. Honestly. "The nearest post office, please," I said, climbing in behind the dash and settling into yet another tufted-velvet seat. So gauche.

To my own "Buttercup," who knows who he is.

The Gallant Endeavour

by *Tym Greene*

I was home, that day, when Hubert returned from the morning patrol. Though I had at first tried to make light of it, I knew I had to tell him the truth.

"The smithy is closed," I finally said, laying down the sheet I had been trying to fold. "The *Manufakturen*—the new ones—they say they're making us craftsmen obsolete."

"But I thought," protested my beloved, removing his cap, "they could only do cheap rough work, iron stoves and pans?"

"The old ones, yes." I paused, reflecting. The steam-driven, workerless *Manufakturen* had been heralded as the harbingers of a new era of wealth and plenty. That future was harder to see now that the rhetoric had faded. "But these new ones…I've heard they use difference engines to run."

"Surely they cannot—"

"Reproduce the work of a master craftsman? Hubert, the flask I gave you three years ago?" It had been a birthday present, chased silver, with entwined wheat stalks, surrounding his favorite Psalm. It had taken me four days to make. He pulled it out of his uniform's breast pocket. I could hear the slosh of the brandy within, brandy he kept "to warm blood and cool nerves."

"You know I cherish it, Tobias."

"They can do work like that—I've seen it—and faster, and the same every time." I pounded the sheet for emphasis, hurting my knuckles on the table underneath. I tried not to wince. "So I have no job. I've been replaced by gears and cogs."

He must have seen my shoulders slump, for he put his arm around them (despite being almost half a meter shorter than me). "Darling, it will be alright. You're a skilled man, and by far the best silver smith I've *ever* seen."

"Thank you," I said, trying to keep the bitterness from my voice. "That means a lot."

We undressed after that. It had been too long since we had had time together like this, utterly at leisure for the evening, and we made the most of it. I fairly carried my little police fox to our bed, where I ran my fingers over his body as though for the first time.

But when I dipped down to lip at his shaft, he pushed me aside, protesting: "No. Not yet." He crawled over beside me, hot breath on my own sheath.

He coaxed me out, seeming to marvel at my size as he always did—though I'm hardly well-endowed, especially for a horse; a more convenient mouthful. I reached down, gripping his ears like an automobile's yoke, and wondered if the other officers knew, or cared, what their colleague did at night. I had considered inviting one or two over for dinner. Perhaps more than dinner. I'd never had the courage to ask Hubert, though.

Once he had me up and hard, he pushed me away again. When I turned to look, I was presented with a rare sight: Hubert, on all fours, tail lifted invitingly. Cupping my fingers around his soft cream-colored sac, I asked, "Are you sure?"

"Quite sure, Tobias. I want to make you feel better."

It did not. Lying in bed, a quarter of an hour later, both of us were thoroughly spent. He was resting, muzzy in post-orgasmic satiety, while I watched the foamy sweat drying on my belly. It had been nice, but couldn't have lasted forever. It couldn't last at all. I had twelve marks in my pocket, wherever my trousers had ended up. Twelve marks of severance pay for a decade's work. Barely two days' wages. It would not last.

* * *

I did not see much of him after that. Not knowing how long it would take to find other employment, Hubert had spoken to his captain the very next day, and started pulling double shifts immediately.

"We're very lucky," he said before falling asleep that night. "Johan—the wolf on the night shift, you remember? He was chasing down a thief, a gypsy hare, and got bitten in the struggle. As it turns out, the hare had rabies, so now Johan does too. He's in the hospital now, and I was able to take his shift." He yawned, and I watched his tongue curling up as it always did, revealing immaculate white teeth. Then, when he rolled over and let me wrap my arms around him, he added: "I feel sorry for his wife and pups, though. The whole department is praying for them. We should too."

Despite the additional hours, however, money was still tight: it would be at least two weeks before Hubert would receive a single pfennig for the extra hours he was working. So I sat on our bed a few days later, listening to my stomach rumbling. There was no food in the house, nor money to buy it with.

And so I sat. I had scoured our flat and found almost nothing of value. We had not been in the habit of accumulating possessions, nor could we have afforded valuable trinkets, even in the better times. I knew what I had to do, but that did not make it any easier. It was this, or starve. I almost preferred the latter.

I had to pawn my tools and the small ingot of silver I had kept, just in case. Like every craftsman of my generation, and all those who had come before, my tools were my own—no matter where I worked, or for whom. They were as much mine as the knowledge in my head and the experience in my muscles.

And then I thought of Hubert. I could already see the toll eighteen hour days were taking on him. The thought of his limp whiskers and lank fur—more brown than russet now, from dust and sweat and lack of care—was enough to stand me up and walk me to my box.

Crafted by a cabinetmaker in exchange for a set of elaborate drawer pulls, it was to be a showcase of my skill. A silver plaque, engraved by me, proclaimed:

— Tobias of Gartenau —
— Master Silver Smith —
apprenticed under Georges LeNotre

The box had other inset plaques, displaying figures, patterns, monograms, and popular sayings. My eye fell on one in particular: "It's often darkest before the dawn." I had chased the Egyptian-style letters, strong and sturdy, beneath a sun, bursting through clouds; it was my family's particular charge. I held my box and remembered the planning I had put into it, thinking that by placing the symbol of my family at the front, above the clasp, they would watch over me and bring me luck. It did not seem to be working.

Within the box were, nested in purple velvet niches, all the tools of my trade. Several had been made by my father, or his father, but most were of my own design and creation. I shut the lid. It had to be done.

I put on a clean shirt, a thin black tie, and my new apron. *Thirty marks I won't see again*, I thought bitterly; I should not have bought it, especially not with how slow work had been getting. And four days later the smithy had closed. But I had to look my best, trustworthy, professional. I even went so far as to give my hooves a buffing before closing the latch on my box, lifting it by its strap, and locking our door as I headed downstairs.

The Belgian-run *confectionaire* that rented the room on the ground floor of our building smelled as delicious as ever. And, as always, I was tempted to purchase even a single piece of dark chocolate or fruited truffle to nibble while I walked. That day, however, I did not even allow myself the luxury of a glance through the plate glass windows, or a sniff at the open door.

I marched stalwartly onward, eschewing hansom and omnibus alike. The former because I could hardly afford the two-mark ride (no matter how handsome the drayman pulling it might be), and the latter because I could not justify patronizing—no matter how paltry the sum—the sort of steam-powered automaton that had stolen my own livelihood. I walked, therefore, halfway across Gartenau, thankful for the mild November chill that kept the snowdrifts crisp but did not promise more.

The city seemed as lively as ever, but as I walked I noticed the differences. Fewer draymen were in evidence, for a start, the horses who had moved the traffic of the city with the strength of their backs. There were more beggars too, and more men standing idly by, looking hungry as jackals.

I crossed Huf Straße and left the more prosperous commercial district for seedier environs. My destination would not be in the "proper" part of town. The idlers had changed, now wearing—men and women alike—fancier garments. Though on a second glance, I could tell that the clothes were old, dowdy pieces in last year's fashion, re-cut to reveal what was legal to reveal, and accentuate what must remain covered. A too-lean fox saw my gaze and sidled up to me. He gave me a winning smile that did not quite reach his eyes.

"I could use a warm man right now, a strong man. You look plenty strong." He glanced—too obviously—at the front of my apron. "And I bet you could use a light little 'snack,'" he struck a sultry pose, "to sate your appetites and not fill you up too much. Only two marks for half an hour."

"No." I turned away, barely managing to toss a "no, thank you" over my shoulder as I rounded the corner. The kit could hardly have been over fifteen, and yet he was selling himself on the streets. Hubert had told me about such children: abandoned or sold by families who didn't care, they sold themselves again and again, as often as possible. Then they gave most of that black money to pimps and procuresses, who provided only the barest of essentials in return.

Apart from a few thin-stretched charity organizations, there was no help for them. That's what Hubert had said, at least.

A few more streets and I was beneath the three gold-ish balls of Josef Issacson's shop. The polar bear looked up at me as the door dingled open. "Hello," he said in a thick Nordic accent. "Can I help you?"

"Yes…" I hesitated, glancing around the shop, seeing boxes and crates and canvas rolls lining the shelves, along with gleaming brass musical instruments dangling from the ceiling. "I was told that you deal in tradesmen's tools?"

"Yes, I do. What do you have for me?"

"This is only temporary, you understand. Just for two weeks, maybe three."

"Of course. It always is." His voice was deep, his tones rough, "What do you have?"

I placed my own box on the counter and spun it to face him. "My work," I said, tapping the metal insets. At his nod, I opened it, revealing the racks and trays of implements. Lifting them out, I

71

arranged them on the counter, then pulled the silver ingot from its hidden compartment. I placed this with the rest, and watched as Issacson surveyed my offering, scratching his chin with a massive hand, and muttering to himself in his native tongue.

"I give you…fifty. You buy back before three weeks with seventy-five. Do you agree?" He held out his hand, gold rings glinting amid white fur and black pads. His thick dark claws were ominous.

Now it was my turn to calculate. Fifty marks would keep us for three weeks, especially as frugally as we had been living of late. The box—though priceless to me—was probably worth two hundred and fifty, maybe three hundred marks. Fifty marks was an insult, but we would barely be able to afford the seventy-five to buy it back. I had no choice. I shook his hand and watched as he filled out the ticket. I would have three weeks. If I couldn't buy it back by then, I would never be able to.

Going home, I wanted so much to surprise Hubert with a fancy meal, or even a few chocolates. I resisted the temptation, and only bought what meager food we would need in the coming week: a loaf of bread (day-old at half the price), a sausage, two cabbages, and three pounds of raw oats. I couldn't help but buy a single rose with the few pfennigs I had in my apron pocket.

I would make a stew as my grandmother had done in lean times. A quarter of a cabbage, added each day, as thin a slice of sausage as you could manage, and water and oats enough to keep it going. A low fire under the pot, and any scraps you could find to add in, and you had a meal that would keep a family alive. Just barely alive.

So, once home, I started the stew to simmering, tidied up our rooms, and placed the rose and remaining marks on the table. Hubert would be home soon.

He was flabbergasted, especially when I told him how I had gotten it.

The next few weeks went well enough, so much so that we still had almost ten marks left when Hubert began to get his extra wages, so I was able to buy back my box from Issacson with several days to spare. The extra money that Hubert was bringing home did help—indeed, if we hadn't been saving up to buy back my box, we would have been back to much the same level of income we had had when I had been employed.

I hated it. Hubert was either working or sleeping, which left me alone all day, brooding and waiting for him to come home and collapse. Sex had been out of the question for days now: Hubert was bone-weary, and i was in no state for courting of any sort.

A deep melancholy had begun to creep over me since that first day when I woke up and realized that I did not need to don my apron and trot the few streets to the foundry. Not even the successful return of my box from the claws of Issacson could cheer my gloom.

I did quite a lot of sitting, those first few weeks. Sitting at home, staring at the wall; sitting in the straße, envying the people bustling about on their own business; sitting on the front steps of my old smithy, which had lain vacant since that fateful day. A sore rump and sour stomach were the only fruits of my vigils—with one exception.

On a Sonntag after all but the most zealous churches had let their flocks out upon the world, I was sitting on a park bench, head in hands.

"Mama, why is that man crying?" asked a soft voice on the path before me. I half-considered raising my head to protest, but couldn't muster the strength even for that. So I sat, slumped over as they discussed me.

"These are hard times, little Maj. We're lucky your father invested so well."

"Is that why we thank God in church for the manny-"

"*Manufakturen,*" the child's mother corrected. "Yes, and that is why we are going to the dressmaker's now. You're growing so big."

"Mama," she said after a moment's thought, "I'm gonna give him my toffee-money. Would God like that?"

I realized then that my cap had fallen off, and was lying upside-down in the dust between my hooves, like a busker's bowl. Even as I watched, a tiny white-gloved hand appeared, and dropped three pfennings into it.

"I think he just might," the mother was saying. "You're such a good calf, Maj. What would you say if—after the dressmaker's—*I* bought you some toffee, as a reward for being so generous?"

"Oh, Mama!"

I looked up, watching the fat-bustled cow and her well-fed, well-bred offspring as they walked down the path. I wanted to leap up, to shout and fling their charity in their faces. The ache in my hands made me glance down: I had been gripping the boards of the bench so heavily that my nails had splintered the wood.

I was not normally a violent man, and not one to show so obviously the strength of my breed and profession. It terrified me, seeing those depressions in the wood.

No one seemed to be watching, so I bent, picked up my cap (ignoring the clink of the coins), and strolled out of the park as nonchalantly as I could. The coins jingled like Judas' purse.

Eventually the ache in my hocks brought me back to myself. A yellow fog had begun to settle over the streets, colored by the gas lamps still used in the seedier parts of the city.

My face felt cold and I realized, on examining my reflection in a storefront window, that I was weeping. Judging by the silvery tracks drawn through the hair on my cheeks, I had been for some time.

With a heavy sigh, I slumped against the window, dragging a sleeve across my face and making the coins in my cap jingle.

A chill ran through me, though from the fog or the thoughts that plagued me then, I knew not. Seeing the sign hanging above me, I made a decision: I deserved something. Something—I justified to myself—to warm my bones.

I stepped into the liquor shop, glancing up at the arranged bottles of spirits. In addition to the "toffee-money," I also had a few hellers in my pocket—money from a lunch I hadn't had the stomach to buy.

I had just enough to get a bottle of the cheapest schnapps, its harsh taste masked somewhat by peppermint oil. The otter behind the counter had huffed through his bushy whiskers as I placed the bottle and money before him. Clearly he made the same assumption about me that the calf in the park had. I didn't care. Not one whit.

So I took my alcohol and left the store, swilling a good long draft as soon as I was back on the street. The schnapps stung my mouth, and burned its cold fire all the way down my throat. I coughed and spluttered, thankful that the thick fog would mask me from the few other people on the street: I felt like a colt, taking his first drink from his father's stein.

The second sip went down easier. I was no great drinker ordinarily, but already I felt better, like how I had felt after a long shift at the forge, when I was finally able to set down my hammer for the day.

As I walked and drank, I suddenly felt so good that I could hardly keep from prancing down the street, singing as I went:

For I'm called Little Buttercup—dear Little Buttercup,
Though I could never tell why,
But still I'm called Buttercup—poor Little Buttercup,
Sweet Little Buttercup I!
I've treacle and toffee, I've tea and I've coffee,
Soft tommy and succulent chops;
I've chickens and ponies, and pretty polonies,
and *excellent* peppermint schnapps!

* * *

I woke with a start, to see the wood of our table swaying in front of my muzzle. I managed to swallow down the bile that suddenly crowded the back of my throat, and looked up into Hubert's eyes. I couldn't place his expression, so I opened my mouth to ask, and belched right in his face.

"Oh God," I whispered, clutching my muzzle in both hands, feeling suddenly very green.

Hubert, meanwhile, was spluttering, waving his cap at the air in front of him. "What is *wrong* with you, Tobias?"

I stared at him, feeling the whickering laugh bubbling up from somewhere in my belly. I slapped the table and guffawed, despite my still-queasy stomach: "Y-your face! Th' look on your face..." I devolved into helpless, breathless laughter then, slumping back onto the table. My cheek slid into a pool of my own drool, which only drove me further into hilarity.

"Stop it!" Hubert was shouting at me, his voice unusually brittle. "Tobias...Tobias, you're drunk. Please stop it."

I managed to reign myself in, digging my nails into my palm to help shake off the wool clouding my head. "Huber'...wha' time's it?" I slurred, my tongue feeling thick.

"It's nearly five. In the morning." He yawned, despite his frustration. "I just finished my second shift, and had hoped to find you in bed still...and here you are, drunk, muddy, and drooling. Tobias, what happened to the horse I fell in love with?"

I slouched back in my chair at that. Arrayed before me was the proof of his accusation: the smeared puddle of slobber, the empty bottle of schnapps, and two other bottles. I realized with horror that I had also drunk the medicinal alcohol we kept for emergencies, and drained the ornate vial of elderflower liqueur that Hubert had been saving. Small wonder that my stomach felt inside-out.

"Oh, Hubert," I sniffed, feeling my eyes sting. "I-I'm sorry. I…I-"

He slumped into the chair across from me, eyes hidden by the paw massaging the bridge of his narrow, aristocratic snout. "You what?" He sounded as tired as he looked. "What have you been doing all day? Our neighbors, downstairs, said that you had been dancing through the streets, singing some stupid barroom song. That's not like you; not like you at all."

I could remember the singing, the silly, frivolous lyrics; the lilting tunes; could feel my hooves tapping out threes and fours, even then. It wouldn't do to tell him why…to burden him with the pain I felt. So I tried to change the subject. "It was from *HMS Pinafore*," I protested quietly. "You remember, when they had translated it into German, and we went to see it at the National Theatre…"

"That was five years ago."

I sat up straight, feeling the disappointment pouring from his down-cast face, and tried to ignore the headache and the tears tickling my chin. "It won't happen again."

"You haven't answered my question. I thought you were going to look for a new position. I thought you said you were one of the best silver smiths in the city, that it would be a matter of *days*…Look, I'm exhausted. I've been on patrol for the past 16 hours. I need to sleep."

I was only too glad to follow him to the bedroom, to help him peel off his uniform, to massage some of the knots from his shoulders. But once we were in bed, he rolled over, presenting his lean backside. His tail was tucked tight over his rump, closing me off as readily as a locked door or a trundle board. I was not forgiven.

* * *

I woke the next day to a cold and empty bed.

Ever-punctual, ever-disciplined, he had arisen, washed, dressed, and left. And I had slumbered through it all, sleeping off my hangover like some ancient hedonist. Judging by the angle of the light streaming through our small bedroom's little windows, it must be almost supper time: I had wasted the whole day!

Knowing that I only had an hour, maybe two, before the shops and businesses started closing up for the day—the respectable ones, anyways—I threw myself out of bed. The currying brush ripped at the snarls in my hide, but it couldn't be helped; no one would hire me if I looked like I had slept on a doorstep.

So I brushed out the tangles and dried mud, donned my unused apron, and carried my box downstairs. For a moment, I was overwhelmed by déjà vu and had to forcibly remind myself that I was not going back to Issacson's pawn shop.

I will admit, the thought was tempting: I could sell my box—for scrap metal if necessary—and get a job as a drayman. Then I could work hard, just like Hubert, come home every day sore, exhausted. Maybe then he would forgive me. There would always be work for draymen, pulling carts, carriages, trolleys... And then I stepped out onto the street.

There were beggars now, even here in our respectable neighborhood. They were cleaner, I noticed, than those you'd find in other parts of the city, and for now lacked the signs of long-held desperation. Most of them were horses too, thick-muscled men with the tree-trunk legs and barrel chests (and cannonball rumps straining their breeches) that came from a lifetime of pulling other people through the streets. Any one of them was easily twice my size, despite my own arduous occupation.

As I watched, the draymen turned as one to watch something appearing up the street. At the same time a rattling, hissing, rumble became audible. Soon an automaton-driven omnibus drove down the street, its posted fare now half the price it would have been just a month ago. Even I could afford to use it.

No. My masochistic fantasy was just that—a fantasy. If the manly specimens of horseflesh loitering across the street from our flat couldn't obtain work in their own professions, there was no way I could even hope to. Besides, I would not have been happy as a drayman. Already my hands itched for a hammer, a chisel, a tricky bit of engraving to work out.

With a start, I realized the answer: the newspapers! I hadn't bought one in years, but I knew that *someone* had to do all that engraving. It would be a hard, detail-oriented job, but I wouldn't shirk from a little work. How could I, when I had been without it for more than a month?

Even as I ran down the street, that thought threatened to bring me to a halt. It really had been only two months. The fact that already I had grown used to sleeping a few hours extra every morning—and puttering around the house naked—did not bear thinking about further. I had once been better than this. If I ever wanted to return to a normal, productive life, I would need to be.

I had by now reached the offices of *das Signalhorn*, the city's main newspaper. Even from the *straße* I could hear the rumble of their great presses churning out the day's last edition. The building itself was uninspired; the only ornament on the dull gray-green walls was a series of plaster swags under the roof line, making the edifice look like a spoiled, half-frosted wedding cake. Still, I needed a job—and my old forge's structure had been no great thing of beauty either—so I stepped up to the door.

The entry hall was as drab as the exterior, with a staircase spiraling up out of the middle of the space, under which huddled the receptionist's desk. Doors and uncomfortable-looking chairs were situated about the perimeter.

"Tradesman's entrance is around the back," came a bored voice from the stairwell.

"Excuse me?" I looked up and saw a pretty but sour-faced young lady—a deer—descending the stairs. She was clutching a sheaf of papers to her starched shirtwaist as she repeated herself, speaking slowly.

"The tradesman's entrance is in the rear, sir."

"Oh." I had nearly forgotten what I was wearing: at first glance I *would* look like an average laborer and not the craftsman I prided myself on being. "No, Ma'am-"

"Miss," she corrected, not looking up from her papers.

"My apologies. I only meant, Miss, that I was here to obtain a position as engraver," I added, lifting my box for emphasis.

The doe looked at me thoughtfully, then swiveled in her chair to face a bank of disks mounted under the staircase's sweeping spiral.

She selected one and pulled it out from amongst its brethren. She flipped the end open and put it to her lips, speaking into the tube briefly.

Replacing the tube, she turned to me. "I doubt we have any positions, but our publisher, Herr Drucker, said he would see you—if he has time. Sit there." She gestured with a dainty hand at the chairs ringing the entry hall.

And so I waited, trying not to fidget. Though she made a fine front of ignoring my presence, I could tell that she was still watching me. Twice while I waited our eyes met. Both times, I was the one who looked away first.

As I sat, I could feel a snarl in the hide on my left hip, catching on the waistband of my trousers. It was all I could do to keep from scratching, to try and untangle it. The nagging tug of it nearly drove me to distraction: in that silent room, empty of any noise apart from the doe's papers and frosty glances, it was all I had to focus on.

After an interminable wait—which, given the lateness of the hour, was probably only fifteen minutes or so—a soft whistling broke the silence. The receptionist swiveled in her chair again, and withdrew the same speaking tube, uncovering the end and causing the whistling to cease. She lifted the tube to her ear.

Nodding, she replaced the tube, put the whistle-generating cover back in place, and turned to me. "Herr Drucker will see you now. You will have five minutes. Do not waste his time."

I leapt to my hooves, sighing with relief, but came to a halt at the foot of the stairs. "Excuse me, Miss, but which room am I to go to?"

She looked at me as though genuinely surprised at my question. "It's the door at the top, with his name on it."

I mounted the stairs, and sure enough there was a door right at the top, imposing and dark, with gilt letters spelling out the publisher's name. I knocked and a cheerful voice bellowed out: "Come in!"

Sitting behind an equally impressive desk—with chased silver corner caps, I noticed—was a burly brown bear, thicker by far than the rangy Issacson. His red velvet waistcoat strained as he leaned forward and extended his arm. His sleeves were pushed all the way up, above his biceps. As I shook his paw, I could feel my back starting to lather up in the heat of his windowless office; it was also, I realized, well-insulated from the bedlam of the presses.

"Well, lad, what can I do for you? Genevieve says you want a job, graven-ing our images, eh?" He chuckled at his own pun.

"Yes sir," I laughed along with him.

"We would need good craftsmanship, and fast results. Do you have any references, examples of your work?"

In answer, I smiled proudly and lifted my box up onto the green baize atop his desk. It felt good to see the eyes widen behind his pince-nez spectacles.

"That's very fine, lad, and all with photogravure?" He asked as he examined it.

I hadn't heard the word before, but didn't like the sound of it. Trying to keep my ears from canting back, I replied: "No, sir. Those were all sketched and etched by hand, by me," I added, just in case.

"Ah." That one syllable told me I would have no luck there that night. "And you've no experience with photogravure?"

"No, sir. I don't even know what it is."

"I barely do myself," he admitted, laughing bitterly, trying to lighten my growing dread. "The engraver uses photography and acid to etch an image on a printing plate. No chisels, no shavings, just science. We even have a little automaton that does most of the work for us.

"I'm sorry lad, but you've come a decade too late. I can't think of a single printer in town who still engraves by hand."

He stood, my box looking so small between his massive paws. "Thank you for your time, Herr Drucker. I'm sorry…"

"I'm sorry too, son. These are hard times, for all of us. Good luck with your hunt—I hope you find employment soon."

The sincerity in his gruff voice nearly made me lose my fragile composure. "Thank you, sir." I managed to croak as I slipped out of his office. I descended the stairs and was through the door without even a glance at *Miss* Genevieve, lest I see the smug smirk I was expecting.

* * *

I didn't notice until I got home: the publisher's claws had left grooves and scratches in the plates on either side of the box. I wanted to weep. I knew I could fix it, but only partly, and at risk of damaging the surrounding linework. No, it was better to leave it…or start over.

I crumpled to the floor, knowing that it was hopeless. I had no job in metalworking. Without a job, I had no access to a forge; without a forge, I couldn't re-make the plates on my box. And without re-making the plates, I couldn't get a job. The claw marks would have to remain.

It was late by then—I hadn't exactly been running back home— too late to try anywhere else that night. There was nothing for it but to sleep and try again in the morning, but not on the floor. I stood, stiffly: my body ached as it hadn't since father had last beaten me for "being a willful colt."

A deep sigh racked my body then. He *had* been a good father, and I missed him greatly. As I lumbered into the bedroom, I couldn't help but wonder if I would have even been in this predicament, were he still alive. Then wishful imagining was quashed by cold rationality. His small family-run smithy would have been forced to close, surely as any other foundry unable to afford the latest automata.

I would probably be even worse off then: I wouldn't have met Hubert.

As I stripped down, my fingers brushed against my sheath, the smooth grey velvet of its skin warm in the chill air of our flat. I had lost track of how long it had been since I last touched myself, let alone enjoyed any carnality. It couldn't have been since the night I came home from my job for the last time.

When I realized that the hair on my hip was still tangled, the frustration and self-pity finally overwhelmed me. Laying in bed, I began to weep.

* * *

I had a very strange dream that night, strange too in that I can still remember most of it. I was lying on a bed, naked, waiting for something. A door opened that I hadn't seen, and Hubert walked in. I knew it was him, even though he was a vague shape, built more like my father. As I watched, the Hubert-horse approached me, stroking his member.

He stepped into the light, and I could see that he held neither a fox's cock nor a horse's, but rather a sharp burin. The hands that held it, stroked it—making it flop as though it were flesh and blood— were also cold and hard, the grasping metal fingers I had seen in Heinrich Kley's drawings of the *Manufakturen*. The creature before me was no man, but a living automaton. And yet I opened myself to it, welcoming it into my body, sliding that chisel up under my tail.

I woke to find Hubert—the real Hubert—nestled behind me, like spoons. His member was tucked up between my buttocks. In that moment I loved him more than I ever had before. Grinding my hips backwards against his elicited a happy groan and a stiffening of his cock. I would, I realized with a new sense of determination, be better: a better man, a better boyfriend.

I must have dozed off again, because the next time my eyes opened, the ceiling and far wall were bright with the morning light coming in from behind me, warming the sheets where Hubert had been. As I shifted, I could feel that my rump was sticky, starting to crust over: the smell of fox, always noticeable in our flat, was now quite potent.

I sighed wistfully, wishing I could have been awake to help him, or at least to watch him. I loved watching his tail twitch and toes curl. I'd always envied his toes, and loved the way they would playfully grip my fingers when I rubbed his paws after a long day's patrol. I hadn't done that in what seemed like years.

I wrapped my arms around his pillow, holding it as tightly as I wished I could hold him. Our lives had changed drastically, and neither of us had noticed it. The degradation had begun, I realized then, long before my smithy had closed.

Perhaps that was why neither of us had seen it: it was too slow, gradual, insidious. As we struggled to compete against the burgeoning *Manufakturen*, my brother smiths and I had had to turn out more pieces, in the same time and for the same pay—that is, until the orders had stopped coming in.

Hubert, I realized, must have had it harder. His shifts and patrols had grown longer, as had the paperwork he rarely complained about. He rarely complained about anything, and I had for the most part ignored the strain he tried to leave at the police station. Metal— especially silver—behaves the way you expect it to. No matter how bad things may have been outside, in one's own smithy a burin of *this* shape, hammered in *this* direction with *so much* force will always make *that* cut. Not so with people.

Every day, on my short walk to and from my forge, I had noticed—and ignored—the changing mien of the city around me. He was forced to confront it, every day. Vagrants and farmers, seeking work in famous Gartenau, now without hope or scruples. Workingmen, like me, laid off, angry and idle, causing trouble out of sheer mischievousness. And then there were those who had fallen so far, who were so desperate to survive, that they had sold all they had, including themselves.

Hubert had to interact with them all, now moreso than ever. Thinking of his daily sacrifice, I clutched the pillow harder, feeling my eyes sting. Then I heard one of the seams pop. I gasped, and released my grip: the pillow was caved in at the middle, leaking a few broken feathers onto my thigh. At that moment, I didn't know whether I wanted to laugh at the dumb absurdity of it or to cry in frustration at another failure.

Instead I rose, fetched my small sewing box, and repaired the pillow. I may not have been much of a *hausfrau*, but my mother had taught me enough to be a little self-sufficient.

Today will be different, I thought. *Today, I will go and get a job.* I didn't know that I was wrong: I wouldn't get any work that day, nor for the two days after.

That first night of my new determination, as I massaged my sore hocks, I thought back over the day's results. I had started by going to the finest silversmiths in town—more than half of which had already closed. Most of the rest were letting their workers go. But those few I had been able to secure an interview with had all seemed to be saying the same thing: while my box was an "impressive catalogue" of the techniques I had at my disposal, they wanted something more… tangible. They wanted to see what my work looked like on an actual object, something that could be sold to a customer.

This had discouraged me, and—even as I shook hands and thanked them for their time—I was wondering where I could possibly find one of my pieces. Back in those days, all the work we did was commissioned, so every spoon and plaque and flask I had made was owned by someone, or had since been melted back down into ingots. I tried not to think of *that*.

And then I realized: not *every* item was lost to the whims of commerce. Three years before, I had hammered, formed, and engraved a flask. I had then given it to my fox.

Once home, I collected pen, ink, and a scrap of paper. Writing in the elaborate script that was now my normal handwriting—the result of a lifetime of decorating honorary plaques and commemorative chalices—I penned a brief note, asking him if I could borrow the flask. I made no mention of the brandy it contained, now the only alcohol we possessed, in the hope that he wouldn't think to object.

I placed the note on his bedside table, where he was sure to see it. Every night (or morning now, thanks to his double shift) before climbing into bed, he would wind his father's watch and place it there. I couldn't help but smile, as I climbed into bed myself, thinking of how dependable he always was.

* * *

The next morning, the note was gone. In its place, gleaming in the light of dawn, was the flask. It was, I noticed as I slipped it into my apron pocket, still full.

The flask did not help, however. Though I cast my search farther and farther afield, I found that few of the city's old smithies had remained in business. Gone it seemed were the days when Gartenau was famous for its silver—just as was Wessexshire for its wool, or Neuchâtel its timepieces. One such venerable foundry had survived by giving itself over to producing piecework for the *Manufakturen*. It was mind-numbing labor, churning out the same parts for hours on end, for long days and low pay. Still, I stood in line for the better part of a day in a desultory drizzle, trying to get even *that* job.

As I waited, I looked at the men around me: my competitors, I realized. They tended towards burliness; even working in silver requires a certain degree of strength. While I recognized a few, some even from my old job, most were strangers. We were silent, the rain and the knowledge that we could not all be hired keeping every man in a stoical silence.

Behind me was a massive bull. By his build and the rusty stains on his apron, I could tell that he had been an iron-worker. He had wished me luck good-naturedly—a sentiment I returned in kind—as he took his place behind me. The accent of his resonant contrabass voice was not of the city. I wanted to ask him why he had left the farmlands; they surely must still have had need of blacksmiths, of horseshoes?

As I thought that, I glanced down, tapping my hoof in a puddle. I had heard rumors that they were developing farming automatons too. I snorted derisively: it would never happen. Why, the image of a farmer in harness, plowing his own fields, was practically a national icon.

My snort startled the man in front of me, who turned around. Hardly a man: the colt likely had yet to reach his second decade, and had probably been an apprentice. Seeing the scared eyes and flared nostrils I couldn't help but pity the lad. Apprenticeship was supposed to be a time of security in a tradesman's life, where he could focus solely on learning his craft, when his only worry should have been pleasing his master. But when not even your master has work…

Before I could say anything, though, there was a ripple in the line of applicants, and a reedy voice rose above the patter of the rain: "Attention please, gentlemen."

Peering to one side, I could see that a fox in a cravat and an olive-green suit had stepped through the smithy's door. He held up both paws, a slash of white shirt cuff revealed below each dark-furred wrist.

"Gentlemen, I'm sorry. All available positions have been filled. We appreciate your time."

Not waiting to hear anything more, the colt whipped around in front of me. As he started to run down the street, I thought I saw tears glinting in his sunken eyes. It was probably just the rain.

The rest of the men disappeared almost as quickly: there was no sense standing in line and probably catching consumption for a job that didn't exist. And a bad job at that. I freely admit, a part of me was relieved that I was not one of the "lucky few." It seemed a soul-killing place, and I knew I could do better. Or could have done, a few years ago. Now everything was uncertain.

That was the closest I came to employment for a while. I even tried going back to some of the first smithies I had tried, but they refused to give me a second chance. One even had me "escorted" off the premises by a pot-bellied Alsatian guard.

After that, I nearly gave up on finding employment in my trade. It seemed that all of winter had swept in that week, blowing dead leaves into sodden piles that glistened with frost each morning. It was hard to resist taking a draft from the flask, just to bring a little warmth back to my bones. But with each step, as I felt it jostle and slosh in my apron pocket, I reminded myself of the look that had contorted Hubert's face that night. I could not disappoint him again.

So it was with some hesitation that I approached a pawn shop— not Issacson's—one sleety morning. I snuck in the shop door, the bell too cold to do more than clatter disconsolately, and tried not to drip on the displays. Despite my attempts to control it, my body spasmed as a clump of frozen rain slipped from the brim of my father's old wool hat and past my up-turned collar.

Through it all, the matronly nanny goat behind the counter stared at me. I didn't meet her eerie yellow eyes as I stepped closer. I had never felt comfortable around caprans, probably because of their race's pungent smell, and the inscrutable way their horizontal pupils seemed to stare right through you. I squared my shoulders, however, and tried for my best smile. "Good morning, madam."

"Good morning," she replied with that chilly false warmth I had been experiencing from shopkeepers and merchants for a while: the tension between scorn at my increasingly-desperate appearance and the need for customers of any sort. These were, it seemed, hard times for all of us. I pawned the flask, getting barely a fifth of its worth. Imagine my anxiety as she turned it around, inspecting its every surface, with the click of her hooves and the slosh of the brandy the only sounds above the background hiss of the sleeting rain.

It was a desperate move, I knew, but I hadn't eaten since the day before, and it would be another three days before Hubert got paid. We both needed food—and he never would need to know that I had pawned the flask. I don't know which would have disappointed him more: finding out that I had pawned it, or finding out that I had drunk it dry instead.

* * *

With food in my belly and enough coin in my pocket for several days' provisions, things didn't feel quite so bleak. Even the weather had lightened to a gentle, snow-like mist—cold, but not so insidious. The temperature had the added benefit of keeping down any offensive odors. My search for employment had by that point led me beyond the well-off areas of town, through the respectable trade districts, and even up to the grubby half-slums that had sprung up beside the massive fortresses of the *Manufakturen*. There was no work to be had there, either, not for someone without the small size and nimble fingers of a cub. I had reached the docks by then, where strong backs were welcomed.

It was also where the effluvium of the city emptied—like the rest of Gartenau's products—into the Salzach River, to be carried eventually out to sea. As I swallowed the last bite of my *wurstemmel* I stopped and watched the river swirling against the wooden bridge's pier below me. A glint of light had caught my eye: the gleaming scales of a fish head. It had gotten caught with a half-burned doll—a fox in a once-blue skirt—in the same slow eddy. I watched, tasting the dry roll and oily sausage I had just eaten, as they danced a slow minuet.

Before I knew it, I had grabbed the wood of the railing with booth hands and was bellowing into the fog-shrouded night air. It had been a primal, bestial, wordless yell. I knew my eyes must have been wild and my nostrils flared. Returning to myself, I glanced hurriedly about: I was alone on the bridge, and nothing moved on the banks on either side of the ice-clogged stream, one of the Salzach's tributaries. My ears flicked beneath my hat. I could still hear faint echoes of my shout bouncing back from the unseen walls around me.

I took a breath, feeling my heart thumping in my quivering chest. I had to lean forward against the rail, catching my breath, the eddy below me now mercifully empty.

But, once I could think again, I wondered at my lack of control. It hadn't been the fish head, nor the doll, nor the frozen yellowish foam floating between them. There was nothing in that swirling morass to have touched off such a powder keg within me.

I moved to push myself off of the railing where I had been leaning, suddenly grinning at a random thought: my grandmother would have said that my outburst had been caused by too much yellow bile. I certainly felt choleric, with the stress of my current jobless position. And then I heard the pop.

At first, I thought that it was a gunshot, off in the night, and my mind flashed with the vision of Hubert besieged by ruffians with pistols. But when another pop—this time the definite sound of wood splintering—rang out, directly below me, I knew what was really happening. Weakened by age, and wear, and weather, and now by my own weight, the wooden bridge's railing was giving out.

My stomach lurched and I again tasted my cheap dinner. As I fell, I caught a glimpse of the dim lamplight glinting off the corner of my box—I'd set it down to look over the railing, I realized with a sense of relief. Then I hit the water, almost flat on my back. I couldn't tell you which was worse: the hard smack that drove the air from my lungs, or the cold water that kept me from drawing breath anew.

It almost felt like I was outside myself, watching as my body floated, for an instant, and then sank. My cap stayed on the surface, and my apron fluttering up as I drifted under. Even from such a great distance, I could feel the water tightening cold bands around my body's chest.

And then my eyes flew open: above me floated bubbles barely discernible in the underwater darkness, faint glimmers sparking off their edges. No longer was I a detached viewer of my body's demise. I had to fight.

Hooves are no good for swimming. My father had once taken the family to Lake Wolfgang for a summer holiday, one rare prosperous year. He had shown me then how to fill my belly with air—his chest and gut swelling out as he demonstrated, taking long deep breaths—to keep afloat, while he flailed his arms and legs around, providing more splash than motion. My father was only graceful when there was hot metal before him. We stayed in the shallows, pushing off the bottom, gliding around slowly. A practice that is utterly useless when one is drowning.

Then something brushed against my shoe. I could feel the clink of metal on stone through water and bone: I had touched the tributary's bottom. I could sense it dragging across both hooves now, the current pulling me out to the river itself. If I didn't surface before then, I'd be done for, if not sooner. Already my lungs burned and I had to fight to keep my lips sealed against the icy water pressing in.

I let the current push me down, squatting with both hooves hovering above the rocky bottom, and then leapt. Or tried to: with all of my clothes dragging in the water and my strength flagging, the best I could manage was a weak push upwards. It was enough, though, and soon I felt the cold air on my fingers.

I slammed my hands down on the surface, managing to pull my head out of the water. The air crackled in my lungs, stinging and biting and welcome. I sucked down big gulps, feeling myself growing buoyant, despite my sodden clothes. Frosty wind slipped under my plastered-down mane, making my scalp prickle with the chill. And my father's cap was gone.

So too was the bridge. I had been carried further towards the Salzach, and was even then floating closer to the tributary's mouth. I struck out, flapping my arms, trying to swim towards the nearer bank. As I approached, I could see a staircase notched into the stone wall holding back the embankment. I managed to snag the bottom step with the tip of my fingers—for a second I thought I'd slip on the iced algae coating the granite, but I managed to heft myself up onto the slick surface. I huddled there, one leg still dragging in the water. The fear of death was fading, and I realized just how cold it actually was.

By the time I had made my way back to the bridge, I was shivering uncontrollably. My clothes were stiff with frost, and my ears were beginning to go numb at the tips. My box was still sitting where I had left it. As I brushed the splinters of railing off the top of it, I said a prayer of thanks, as best as I could through my chattering teeth. The walk from the river steps back to the bridge had been a frozen hell of gnawing worry—not only the fear that I wouldn't be able to find the bridge at all, but also that I would find the bridge empty.

Soaked, shivering, and weakened with relief and the knowledge that I had almost drowned, I hefted my box and started to work my way back to our flat. I rounded a corner and was pushed back by a sudden gust of wind, squinting to keep gritty snowflakes from blinding me.

Barely thinking by that point, I saw the glow of a red lantern a few buildings ahead of me. Sanctuary. It seemed like a blizzard was swirling around me, forcing me to lean forward to make any headway.

After what seemed an eternity of struggling, I had finally reached the ruby-lit doorway. Slumping against the leeward doorpost, I knocked frantically on the enameled wood as snow began to pile up around my hooves.

* * *

Smooth muslin sheets were tangled around my legs when next I opened my eyes. I was staring up at a white-washed ceiling with thick beams spanning its length, and was completely nude under the sheets and counterpane.

I tried to sit up, but a strong paw held me back. "You almost died on my doorstep," said a throaty baritone that emanated from a massive dirndl-covered bosom, which hove into view above me. "I have no wish for a frozen tradesman to scare off customers."

I rankled at that slight, and opened my mouth to speak, when the same paw descended to clamp—gently, but inflexible—around my muzzle.

"Hush."

Once I stopped trying to speak, the paw withdrew, allowing me to turn and view my benefactor. Sitting beside me was a St. Bernhardshund, easily ten or twenty centimeters taller than I, had we both been standing. Her thick winter dirndl of rich red wool emphasized her ample figure, with gold embroidery catching the firelight. Her apron, I noticed, was knotted on her right side, indicating that she was married, but no band adorned her finger—metallurgists pay attention to such things.

I did not see anyone else in my limited field of vision, but around me were the sounds of a crackling fireplace, the storm beating on the shuttered casement, and the rustle of a large household hushed by the weather. "Who are you?" I asked.

A hearty laugh was her response. "No, I imagine you wouldn't know me," she glanced over at where my apron and clothes were dripping by the fire. "There is no way you could have afforded our... wares."

That pause set my mane on edge. I had a growing suspicion, especially when she leaned forward and a gold pendant of St. Nicholas swung out from between her breasts.

"My name is Frau Hübsch, and you are now a guest of the Gallant Endeavour."

I had to stifle a gasp. The bed in which I had slept (after God knows how many other men and women) belonged to one of the most infamous houses of ill repute in all of Austria. I stuttered, trying to cover my sudden disgust. "T-thank you for saving my life, Ma'am."

"It's what any good Christian would have done," she said unironically as she fingered her pendant, with its engraved image of the patron saint of prostitutes. Changing the subject, she mentioned that I now owed her the going rate for one night's use of a room—less any "companionship fee," naturally. A year ago, it would have amounted to a day's wages: a steep price, but manageable, and certainly more than I would have elected to spend, given the choice.

Now, however, the amount would be ruinous. Perhaps, if I pooled our remaining funds, and if we could do without food for a few days, perhaps then I would have enough. Or I could try and barter her down to an amount I could actually afford, unlikely as that might be. "I can't pay that much, Ma'am. I don't wish to seem ungrateful, but perhaps we could come to some kind of agreement?" It is hard to bargain effectively while one is lying naked in a bed that is not one's own.

"I'm sure you can find the funds—you wouldn't want it to be put about town that you had an outstanding debt here, of all places. You must have a relative you could borrow such a small sum from discreetly, or perhaps an advance on your wages…"

I wanted to pull the bedclothes over my head, hiding like a child would. Instead, I turned to face her. "I have no wages. I was out looking for work when I…fell in the river, and then got caught by the storm. I have no way to pay you back—not in the amount you require, anyway."

She sat back, a paw to her white-furred chin. I watched as her gaze drifted from me, to my clothes, and finally to my box, sitting in a corner, just within my own sight. "I'd imagine I could take that and sell it for scrap. I don't know why you were lugging it around like

91

that. You know, I had to pry it out of your fingers when we brought you in-"

I could stand no more of it. I flung back the bedclothes and sat up, full of indignant admonishments. But the sudden rise left me light-headed, and I swooned back onto the pillows. "Please, don't," I managed weakly. "If I lose my box, I'll have lost any chance at being hired. It's the only proof of my work that I have left."

"Oh, you did that?" I could see her eyes gleaming with new interest, as her tongue flicked daintily out to dampen her nose. "You must be fairly well-read to have known those emblems and quotations—I even had to look a few of them up myself. Pity I've no use for a pewtersmith…" I resisted the urge to correct her. "Still, I'm afraid our prices are inflexible. We have college deans and high-ranking members of the clergy among our clientele, and *they* get no special treatment…when it comes to their bill, at least. I run a respectable business."

I almost laughed aloud at that despite my predicament; respectable, indeed. "Please, Frau Hübsch, I beg you to reconsider— would you beggar me after having saved my life? I *am* grateful, but I need to consider my own livelihood. I'm willing to do whatever is necessary; perhaps we can come to an agreement? Every month, I could pay you…" I checked my headlong rush when I realized that I might as well have been speaking to myself. The St. Bernard procuress was sitting, chin in hand, looking up and down my exposed body. I felt like nothing so much as a carcass in a butcher's shop. Thinking back on it, I'm certain that some part of me knew what was to come.

"Are you familiar with mythology—Anglo-Saxon, not that Greek stuff—Wodanaz and Wurdiz, the dwergaz and albaz? It's all very much in vogue nowadays. I noticed that you had a Mjollnir on that box of yours."

There was, of course, no such thing as a mythical hammer engraved on my box. I suspected she had mistook an anchor (intended to represent strength and constancy) for Thor's hammer. I did not have any opportunity to correct her, intent as she was on her own line of reasoning.

"It could work," she was saying. Suddenly, she focused full on me. "You said you would do anything to pay your debt, so long as you did not endanger your…career. Is that right?" I nodded. "Excellent. Now, rest up, we can start tomorrow with your training; it won't take long."

Flustered, I finally caught up (if only partially) with the torrent of her words. "But I can't stay here, Hubert must surely be worried."

"Who is Hubert?"

"He's my beau," I said softly, uncertain how she would react. I had of course heard stories of the Gallant Endeavour's "wares," but Frau Hübsch seemed a woman of strong opinions.

"You prefer the company of other men, do you? No interest in a pretty filly, or an experienced mare, eh?" I shook my head, not a little surprised by her forwardness. "Well, that's not so bad as all that. And, in bed, with your Hubert, are you the husband or the wife?"

I stared at her hungrily leering visage, which had the odd effect of transforming her matronly figure and traditional dress into something downright lewd. In that moment, she reminded me of the lusty barmaid I had seen once, smirking out of a book of racy woodcuts. I was so taken aback, in fact, that I answered candidly. "He usually mounts me, because I am too big for his liking."

"So I can imagine," She said, eyes fastened on my very limp sheath as she licked her chops. "Good. Men pay more for rarities. And we will make you quite rare indeed." She bade me rest, then.

* * *

I slept but fitfully, my troubled mind not eased by the storm's continued bluster. I had at first tried persuading Frau Hübsch to let me write Hubert a letter, so he would not worry to find our home empty. Pulling aside the thick brocade curtains, she had gestured out at the storm: no one would be out in weather like that; even the police would have hunkered down in some safe warm place. He had slept at the station on nights like this before.

And still I worried.

I woke when Frau Hübsch once more threw open the curtains, this time flooding the room with the bright white light one only finds on a morning after the city has been draped with an unsullied blanket of snow. It hurt my eyes.

"Ah, good," she exclaimed. "I see you are up already." Following her gaze, I glanced down, and immediately blanched. My rebellious member—despite the worries that had kept me tossing for most of the night—had latched onto some thread of a dream to hoist itself up to a moderate stiffness, presenting my benefactress with the view of a miniature mountain of bedclothes. She approached the bed, a gleam in her dark brown eyes making her look for all the world like a mountaineer preparing for the climb. I tried to back away, but fetched up against the sturdy headboard. Kneeling on the bed beside me, she flung the covers aside.

"Madam, please-" I tried to protest, but her soft paw on my flesh stalled all thought. This was not the firm clinical grip of my doctor, nor the half-afraid, half-worshipful caress of Hubert. These were the hands of an expert, knowing just where to touch, pull, or stroke to elicit the desired response. I was in the hands of a master of flesh, just as I was a master of sliver. I swelled to my full length: a respectable thirty centimeters of velvet grey, with just the odd pink splotch on shaft and head to add variety.

As the whole length unfurled, she proceeded to inspect every part, hefting my testes, examining my sheath. I found myself unable to resist her ministrations, not even when she lifted one of my legs (as though it weighed no more than a feather bolster) to prod beneath my tail. I will admit freely that it felt, on the whole, good.

And then the paws withdrew and my leg was allowed to fall back onto the bed. "Well," she commented, straightening her rumpled dirndl, "you seem healthy and responsive. Yes, you should do well."

Of course, I was still rather flabbergasted by my sudden arousal, and the just-as-sudden halt—especially so soon upon waking—so it took me a minute to retain control of my faculties. I could see that she had brought in a shaggy bundle, which lay on the stool she had been sitting on the night before. "I still don't understand what you expect of me."

"I'm offering to hire you; you were practically begging me for a job last night. Of course, we may need you to do the odd bit of heavy lifting—we tend to rearrange the furniture often, and you are stronger than any of the other boys."

"But what," I interrupted, "will I be doing?" I knew, well enough, what was going on; but still I could not let myself think the thought. "Am I to be some kind of porter?"

"No," she explained with exaggerated patience. "I am hiring you to be a paid companion, a consort, a prostitute. Honestly, I thought you were intelligent."

"But, madam, I…I have no experience! You can't force me to sell myself—"

Her anger was as frightening as it was swift. In a flash, her teeth were bared and her claws were digging into my shoulders as she pulled me to face her. "Look here, *boy*, it seems your body *is* the only thing you're willing to sell, and I am doing you a favor, hiring you like this. If I'd wanted a strong brute, I could have had my pick from hundreds of draymen. But I don't want an idiot in my employ. So you had best wise up, boy, and take what you're given." She released her grip, and I fell back onto the bed.

Her composure regained, she smiled, revealing far too many teeth. "So, Tobias, have I made myself clear?" I nodded, shaking worse than I had after my dunking in the river. "Good. Now that we've come to an understanding, we can proceed."

There followed a brief interlude in which she expertly quizzed me on my knowledge and experience of all things carnal. "Oils and clean washcloths are kept in the bed-side cupboards," she finished, "but you should always check before admitting a client."

She chuckled at a sudden remembrance. "He was only my second 'guest'—I was about half your age—and an archbishop too, if a bit elderly. We were less well-staffed in those days, and the previous client to use that room, an aristocratic donkey who had been feeling his oats from what I heard, had required the use of every single towel and most of the bedclothes to clean up his mess. It seems he was a bit tipsy too, and smeared things around somewhat.

"So when it came time to tidy up after my archbishop had had his way with me, there was nothing left in the room but my own costume. Though, of course, the smell of it when I returned to the foyer was so alluring that the next three gentlemen insisted on sharing my company at the same time." She smiled, almost abashedly, I thought. "Of course, I was in heat at the time. A pity, though. My archbishop died soon after: collapsed in a fit of apoplexy, right in the middle of his *Aves*."

She seemed lost in the midst of her reverie, and after the way she had lambasted me, I was loathe to interrupt her thoughts. But I had to ask. So, gesturing at the bundle she had brought, I inquired, "And that? Is that one of the towels?" If it was, it certainly looked well-used indeed: worn, scruffy, but at least it seemed clean.

"No, Tobias. That is to be your costume." She stood and unfurled the fabric. "I had told you my rooms were all themed. So, too, are my employees! You will be a fine Siegfried."

She had not told me about this arrangement—or if she had, it had been in the midst of one of her long-winded soliloquies. Nor had she needed to: I had heard rumors of what treats awaited those clients with bottomless purses and jaded palates. A room like a castle, where a guest could be heroic knight or rampaging dragon just as easily; a Roman banquet hall, filled with rare foods and rarer "slaves;" even a mock factory where courtesans masqueraded as the very automatons that had cost so many hard-working men their jobs.

I was to find out later that those tales were all—at one time or another—true, but that Frau Hübsch kept her rooms in an almost-constant state of flux. Her customers required and compensated her for this flexibility. I believe she also hungered after novelty herself. Perhaps that was partly why I had been hired.

She bade me dress, then, donning what turned out to be a tunic of shaggy wool, draped across one shoulder (and hemmed several inches too short in my opinion), and a pair of hempen buskins. I felt decidedly uncomfortable.

The costume was well-made, clean, and of good material, despite its intentionally ragged appearance. And I will freely admit that the straps wrapped around my hocks felt nice. It was not the clothes themselves that unsettled me, but what they meant. That, and the occasional frosty draft between my thighs. I was in this, as surely as if I had signed a contract.

Which was the next thing she had me do. The wages were surprisingly good; Frau Hübsch, it seemed, had no cause to cheat her employees. I signed an agreement promising that I would hold secret any goings-on that I witnessed. At first I wondered what court would ever have taken the testimony of a prostitute, but soon realized my error: it was not Justice we would be called on to protect, but our clients, from scandal-mongering journalists, avaricious competitors, and inquisitive family members. Most of our guests, I was to find out, operated under pseudonyms anyways.

We would work in shifts, like any other modern business—unless we were requested by special arrangement. And as I had my own flat already, I would not need to pay for room and board, a significant savings to one as desperate as I was. A part of me was actually starting to feel good about my new occupation.

She showed me what was to be my room, as well. It had been originally intended as a sort of wilderness room, with birch trunk pilasters and plaster boulders, for clients, she explained, who wanted to play at savages, or indulge in a Rousseauian ideal. A cleft anvil and wooden sword were all it took (barring a few runes painted on the rocks) to turn it into a fit setting for the Germanic mythological I was to play. Then she escorted me to the main lobby.

It was a large room in the style of a Roman temple, all white marble and gilt decoration, thanks to a judicious application of paint. Lounging about were the "boys and girls" of the afternoon shift, which I would be joining. They were a diverse assortment, their ages hard to determine—easily anywhere from fifteen to thirty-five—they were uniform in their leanness and languidity, if nothing else. Their races and costumes, however, were as wildly varied an assembly as I could have imagined.

Some only glanced up from their books and card games, but most at least graced me with wan greetings. The one vixen in the room eyed me hungrily, but it was a lithe zebra who leapt up to welcome me properly. He was dressed in a centurion's outfit, the leathern straps of his kilt falling even shorter on his thighs than did my own tunic. I gripped his outstretched hand, surprised at the tender lightness of his grip.

"Taj, help Tobias get ready," said Frau Hübsch. "The Professor will be here in an hour," and with that, she bustled through a door hidden behind a frescoed wall.

The zebra was still holding my hand, "Already have a date with the Professor, eh? She certainly isn't wasting time with you. I'm glad, too. I helped bring you in, and helped undress you. I think she's been waiting for someone to be a Siegfried: none of us could play the part."

Around the room, the other employees had returned to their diversions, with the exception of the vixen, who was fingering her purple kimono while she stared at me. Taj saw my gaze and pulled me back in the direction of what I had already begun to consider as *my* room. "Don't mind Elsinore. She's sick of playing 'la Japonaise'—even though she's requested more often than any of the rest of us. I think she was hoping Mother wouldn't have found a man like you and would have let her be an Amazon or Indian or somesuch."

"Who is this professor?" I asked as he pulled me through the door and into the little faux forest.

"Oh, he's a toothless old lion. I think he and Mother—Frau Hübsch, we all call her that—once had romantic entanglements. So now he gets a discounted use of the 'facilities' in exchange for his criticism of our more literary acts: like you. I heard he actually was a professor of Latin or Greek. He's very smart."

Together, we explored my room. The walls were painted with a mural of Black Forest trees, dark and foreboding, with the upper span of walls and ceiling painted the dark blue of a summer evening, lightening in color towards a sun bursting through bands of clouds. I caught my breath, wondering if perhaps this was a sign, if seeing my family's iconic symbol above the bed where I would be…working… if that could hold any significance beyond mere happenstance. The largest boulder in the room turned out to be merely a façade for the bed—which was firm and sturdy—and one of the false tree trunks opened to reveal shelves of towels, bottles, and a few male implements of various sizes and races.

Holding up an equine shaft, Taj declared, "I have one just like this, mounted onto a sword hilt. You'd be surprised how many of our clients like to be 'impaled.'"

I stared at the cylinder of polished wood he held, so familiar and yet so foreign. "And I'm supposed to use *that* on the Professor?"

"Only if he wants you to, or if he wants to use it on you. Sometimes they just want to watch us…" he popped the end of it into his mouth, licking the carved details of the flared head with obvious relish. I glanced down, and sure enough, his Roman kilt was starting to rise with the enthusiasm of his attentions to the false shaft he held. His eyes were closed and his nostrils flared. Soon, though, he pulled the tool from his eager lips and wiped off the clinging drool. "Sorry," he said with a sheepish grin, placing it back on its shelf.

* * *

The Professor was punctual. I was sitting on the bed-boulder, toying with my prop sword when he entered. Potbelly and thinning mane aside, he cut a dashing figure. Switching his tail out of the way, he shut the door behind him, the lock giving a decisive click.

I stood, striking what I assumed was an heroic pose. "Hark, who goes there?" I queried, feeling not a little silly. "Be you Brunhilde or Fafnir? Come forth, that I may know if my hole-maker, my sword, shall taste blood today—" by this point the Professor had his hand to his mouth, stifling his laughter without much success.

"I'm sorry, lad. You're just so serious. Yes, the role does require a certain *gravitas*, but you're acting as though your life depended on it."

My pose had slumped by then. "It does."

"Oh?" He stepped closer, removing his waistcoat.

"If I don't impress you…" I proceeded to explain my dilemma in a fit of candidness. He was, by then, sitting on the rock-bed beside me. He placed a paw on my knee. I hadn't noticed when I sat down, but the tunic had hiked up, leaving my thighs bare and my genitals exposed. His touch was gentle—if not fatherly, then at least avuncular—and helped me to relax somewhat.

"I see," he said, slipping his other arm around my waist. His finger pads were soft (truly the hands of a scholar) and warm against the slight chill pressing in from the storm outside. "And my earlier statement still holds. Get into the role, yes, but remember that you are meant to be an entertainer. People won't pay to be lectured at… believe me, I know. And talk to Frau Hübsch beforehand: she'll know what each client prefers. Use that to your advantage." His arms had pulled me closer, my head now resting in the crook of his neck while his paw worked its slow way up my thigh. "Work in a little sword play, a little word play; show off your assets—" A hand grabbed my arm, squeezing the biceps built up by my decades of metalworking. I flexed it, and had to smile at his involuntary gasp, the way the blunted claws dug gently into my hide, tracing the muscle. I didn't notice at first that his other hand had reached its goal and had begun caressing my sheath.

When I did feel it, my first instinct was to shy away, but his paw on my arm—claws no longer quite so gentle—kept me planted there, beside a lion who had started to moan. Of course, it could just as easily have been a growl, low and feral. I was afraid, then. One

99

hears tales of prostitutes found eviscerated and mangled, washed up on the riverbanks; and his rough tongue on my neck did not help assuage my misgivings.

I wanted desperately to protest, to push him aside and run for the door. But I knew that if I did (assuming I could even break free of his embrace) I would be done for. Probably not by the Professor himself, but just as certainly as if he ripped my throat out, then and there.

So I bit my lip and focused on the sensation of soft paw pads teasing the skin of my penis, drawing it further out. "That's what I like to see," the Professor rumbled, his voice husky. His hand gripped the base of my shaft, squeezing hard, trapping the blood there and making the skin gleam tight and dark. He held it an instant longer—and tighter—than I would have liked, then released it. "Well? I'm still dressed…" he chided.

It took me a moment to gather my wits, by which point he was starting to look impatient. So I leapt from the rock-bed and dropped to my knees before him, shuddering as my tunic's hem caught on my rigid shaft. With unsteady hands I traced along the folds of cloth at his knees, feeling the warmth of the legs beneath. As I worked my fingers up his trousers, I glanced up: the Professor's eyes were closed, and his mouth hung slack. When I reached his crotch—and the throbbing bulge thereat—his paw dropped onto my head.

"Get to it, boy. You know what to do."

I didn't, not really. But I had a fair idea of what he wanted, and I acted on that hunch. His belt flopped open to either side and a long moment of awkward fumbling resulted in his pants following suit. He wore, I was surprised to see, no drawers: laid bare was his stubby pink cock, gleaming against his creamy fur.

Tempted as I was to rush through and get things over with, I knew that my goal was to please the lion, no matter what. So I leaned in close, breathing deeply, watching his skin twitch and flutter as I exhaled, seeing the pulse in his member. The hand on my head began pushing down, so I opened my mouth and stuck out my tongue. His shaft was salty, but not quite as boldly-flavored as Hubert's. As the lion's sheath met my lips, I couldn't help but think of my fox. When was the last time I had done this for him, helped him relax after a long and draining shift? Waves of guilt and regret washed over me as I bobbed on the lion's shaft.

I missed him.

Having had enough of this, he grabbed my ears and—steering me like a velocipede—pulled me off his cock, then directed my snout under his balls. Thankfully, he was clean. This was something I had never done before, but my lips and tongue seemed to know what they were about as I licked his hole, guided by the occasional murmur of "deeper" or "slower," and rewarded by the breathy "like that."

Of this attention too, he soon tired. He rolled to one side and stood, stepping out of his pants, but leaving his stockings and boots on, as well as his shirt. I had gotten up as well, uncertain as to what he wanted next.

My ears flicked back at his feral grin: "You liked that, didn't you, horse?" He dipped his chin to indicate my still-turgid member, pulsing under its drapery of tunic. I nodded meekly, uncertain if it were the act, or the taste, or the knowledge that I had so debased myself before (and beneath) a total stranger in a way that I never would have for Hubert. But before I could wonder any more, he leapt on me. Pulling me down to meet his face, he kissed me, with an adolescent's desperate enthusiasm. Licking the slobber from my snout, he shuddered, probably with the knowledge that he was licking his own tailhole, by proxy.

We stood there—me half-couched, him on tiptoe—for some seconds, until he gave me a push that left me sprawled on the bed, my cock swaying and exposed like a ship's mast. With nimble feet and lashing tail, he stepped to the tree-trunk-cabinet—obviously well familiar with the topology of the room. He returned to the bed, his fingers already glistening with lubricant. Taking a deep breath, I prepared mentally, as I did whenever Hubert had had that same gleam in his eyes: I lifted my legs and loosed my hole, and tried to look alluring.

Imagine my surprise when the slick petrolatum-covered paw headed for my shaft instead. I couldn't contain the low moan, nor keep my hips from jerking up to meet his fist. This must have pleased him, for he bent round to kiss me again, nipping at my lips with his sharp teeth. I could taste a hint of blood when he withdrew again, but his paw upon my cock kept me from reacting as I normally might.

I licked my lips and watched as he clambered on top of me. He must have already applied the lubricant to himself, because when he straddled me and eased himself lower, my head popped right in. Unused as I was to it, the sensation of having my shaft so completely enveloped nearly made me come off then and there.

But he slapped his paw on my chest as he gritted his teeth and sank down further, and the cloying feel of petrolatum sticking to my hide brought me back to reality—for a time, at least. As in-control then as he ever was that night, the Professor began to ride me like a cub on a hobby horse, leaving me to dig my fingers into the bedclothes and try not to buck him off. Soon he settled into a rhythm, pulling up so that the flared edges of my head tugged at the inside of his tailhole, then sinking down until our hips met. A sweet torment. I watched him this way for a few minutes, his screwed-shut eyes and lolling tongue, his mane and shirt all askew. It was almost pitiable, the way his paunch bounced and heaved with his panting breath, above his dripping, bobbing member.

Instead of allowing my own heat to be dampened by less than passionate thoughts, I let my mind wander. The lion atop me faded into the background somewhat as I pictured—as I usually did on my approach to climax—the men I had seen recently. The bulk of Issacson hove into view, as I imagined what he would look like unclothed; then the familiar forms of the draymen materialized, like copies of my own body, writ large. I kept myself from envisioning Hubert, however, perhaps because I didn't want to taint even the thought of him with the knowledge of how low I had sunk, or perhaps it was because I was afraid that the disapproval of his image would cause me to lose my resolve.

Instead, it was Taj whose form finally resolved before my inner eye. My cock stiffened within the lion as I remembered the zebra's lean and striped form. He was built along the same lines of Hubert, but was younger and more energetic, where my fox was sedate. Frau Hübsch had not forbidden us from "practicing" with one another, as far as I knew. I suspected (and as it turned out, rightly so) that the little zebra would have much to teach me.

I pictured him as he had been earlier that day, a lean little centurion, likely only a hair over eighteen years old. As my eyes drifted closed, the Professor's tailhole became Taj's muzzle: licking, gripping, sucking, drawing me closer to my inevitable end.

From his perch atop me, the Professor growled, his body shuddering. He was close too, I could tell, and my own body reacted. Hips lifted to meet his. But in my mind, it was black and white hide, not tawny fur, that crouched at my groin. I recalled how eagerly (and easily) his lips had wrapped around the ersatz masculinity—how much more would he for a real man's member, and a fellow equine's as well?

And then, in my mind, those black eyes looked up at me, framed by the low hill of my belly and the silver visor of his helm. My untrained and ill-practiced body could not resist that last detail: snorting and moaning, I thrust up into the Professor, making him roar and dig his claws into my chest.

He shot his seed along my body, with a fair portion of it landing in my open mouth. I swallowed without tasting.

* * *

The Professor gave me what he jokingly called a passing grade, adding that "what he lacks in experience, he makes up for with his willingness to please." He added further that I would benefit from having other members of the staff instruct me in their particular specialities. And so my position at the Gallant Endeavour was made secure and official.

Given the relative lateness (a full two hours after the other members of the afternoon shift had departed), I was allowed to leave immediately after cleaning up. I donned my by-then quite dry clothes and collected my box. Seeing the ashes in the grate, however, gave me pause.

Ever since I had woken up in Frau Hübsch's bed I had been wondering what I could possibly tell Hubert. Being a policeman, there was no way he would approve of the Gallant Endeavour, let alone allow his own true love to work there. I liked it little more than he, but it had been the only position I could secure in all those months. I could not lose this job. I could not tell Hubert.

So I grabbed a hasty handful of soot and dusted it lightly on my shirt and sleeves and face before carrying my box out into the snowy white city.

As I walked, I allowed my story to crystallize in my head: I *had* found employ, but as a roustabout at the docks. Trapped as I had been by the storm, they had set me to shoveling coal. He would surely accept that, especially with the soot adorning my head and hands. I prayed that he wouldn't smell the sex, the scent of two men's sweat and seed. I had cleaned up as best I could, but his nose had always been more adept than mine.

I stumbled on a muddy, snow-covered cobble then, and nearly dropped my box. There was quite a racket as the tools jostled about inside. I clutched it to my chest and panted, waiting for my nerves to steady. It was then that I smelled the chocolatiers' shop: I was nearly home.

Leaping up the steps to our flat, I found the door locked and the rooms empty and cold. I had time. Hubert wouldn't be home from his shift for a few hours yet, and I suddenly realized just how hungry I was. As I secreted my box under our bed, I resolved to fix as good a dinner as I could for the both of us.

And maybe he wouldn't see that I was lying to him.

Lighting a small fire, I prepared for his arrival. Soon, cabbage and sausage soup was cooking, the table was dusted and set, and the bed made. I couldn't keep myself from giving my balls a tug or two as I adjusted the sheet, my trial with the Professor still fresh in my mind. Before I knew it, I was naked, my sooty clothes in a heap on the floorboards while I lounged atop the bed, hands running over my body. I hadn't appreciated my strength before; it had merely been part of me, like my voice or my hide's chestnut hue. As I stroked my chest, I could feel Taj's fingers prodding my pectoral muscle, as though to confirm to himself that it was real.

Letting out a moan, I realized—even as my cock began to push out—that I felt more relief in that moment than I had in a very long time. Not only was there a glimmer of hope, but I was actually looking forward to going in for my shift the next day.

Digging my head into the pillow and allowing my eyes to drift shut, I gripped my shaft with both hands. Like steam in a boiler, it swelled to fill my palms, hot and heavy and sensitive. My nostrils flared as I caressed the dusk-grey skin: I could detect no trace of the scent of lion, just soap. Sighing with relief I settled back into our old mattress.

My pleasure prevented me from hearing the door unlock, but Hubert's claws ticking on the floorboards managed to pierce through the warm fuzz of my self-enjoyment. I resisted the initial urge to leap up and hide my lurid display, and instead rolled onto one hip, facing the open door.

A few rays of afternoon light slanted through the half-shuttered window to spark upon his uniform's brass buttons. I smiled at my fox as I ran a finger along the thigh-draping length that had yet to reach full hardness. He opened his mouth, face blank aside from his constant weariness, so I spoke before he could.

"Welcome home, Hubert. I've," I flexed my groin, making my cock leap for emphasis, "missed you."

He grimaced, or tried to smile—I couldn't tell—and let out a deep breath. "Tobias, I'm tired—"

"So let's get you out of that uniform," I countered, propping myself up on one elbow. "Dinner is cooking, the rooms are clean. You've worked so hard for us, Hubert, and you deserve a reward."

I rolled off the bed and approached him. Placing a hand on his shoulders, I gazed into his amber eyes. When we had been courting, those eyes had always held a softness, a twinkle, and a depth. The drooping lids and downcast gaze that refused to meet my own made me want to weep. "My handsome fox, you are so brave. So strong." I stroked his cheek with the back of my hand.

We stood motionless for a time.

"I…got a job," I muttered, breaking the silence. Now it was my turn to look away. I had wanted to keep it a surprise until I had gotten my first wages—ignoring the fact that I could never tell him *where* I was employed—but that would have been cruel and unfair. My gaze returned to his face, where I could see doubt writ large. He had given up, as—to be perfectly honest—had I. "Yes, a job, a real job!"

"Where?" he asked, as though my announcement were just a dream on his part, or a cruel joke on mine.

I opened my mouth, and realized with quick terror that I had forgotten the story I had planned to tell him. If I tried to make something up, he might realize I was lying. So instead I said just "by the docks," and then I kissed him, full on the mouth.

His resistance slowly faded and his eyes closed as my tongue slipped between his lips. His mouth tasted awful, like stale tea and bile, but I didn't care: if I were to mention it, to balk at all, the tenuous spell would be shattered. I fumbled blindly with his uniform, finally managing to unbutton it.

The fabric rustled to the floor, followed with a clunk by his unbelted trousers. Breaking the kiss, I unbuttoned his underclothes, the white cotton union suit stiff and stained from too much wear and not enough wash. I let it fall to the floor as well, revealing his too-lean frame.

I ran my fingers lightly down the prominences of his ribs and, placing my hands in a girdle about his hips, drew him close to me, our loins pressing together. I kissed him again, and pulled him back onto the bed with me.

"I was thinking about you," I murmured, stretching the truth only a little.

"You're all I think about," he replied. His body was so light atop mine, his voice an embarrassed whisper. I felt dampness on my collarbone: he was crying, silent and still.

I pressed my face to his, cheek to cheek, muzzle to muzzle. "I'm here, Hubert—there's nothing to think about…I want you."

He sniffed and pulled away, looking down at me, trapped beneath the pylons of his outstretched arms. He seemed about to speak, so I flexed and made my cock leap up—still turgid—to nudge against his sheath. Any words he might have said melted into a low moan.

Feeling adventurous, I lifted my knees, rolling my hips back until my sac flopped up against my shaft's base. Taking hold of my legs, I pulled them further, spreading myself for my fox. I watched as his eyes flicked down, his muzzle opened and his tongue began to loll. I watched as realization dawned. "Come and take me, Hubert, I need you," I whispered; anything to coax him on, to fill the silence and keep him from thought.

Sliding a hand up between our bodies, I gave his sheath a squeeze, feeling it jump and stiffen. I smiled and pulled his it down to expose the pointed pink tip, so different from my own. Taj's form floated before my vision as I suddenly wondered what another equine's cock would feel like, in my mouth, under my tail, or pressed up against my shaft.

I hadn't noticed Hubert moving away until he returned with an engorged member and a petrolatum-slick finger, so rapt was I in the cognizance that my job would consist of servicing males of all types and shapes. Hubert's slender finger found easy access to my hole. I moaned encouragingly, pulling my knees further up my chest. My fox's eyes were hooded, sleepy, his narrow face expressionless as he guided himself into me.

It was no great feat to take his modest length in one long slow plunge: my body fairly welcomed him in. When his hips touched mine, it was his turn to moan, jaw slack, tongue lolling. I clenched gently—once, twice, thrice—and got a surge of heat in response, his claws pressing into my folded-up legs.

He did not last for too much longer. Fatigue, involuntary abstinence, stress, and my willingness combined to loose his self-control. I got the impression as he thrust slowly in and out, clearly savoring the sensation of flesh gliding within flesh, that he was as much interested in finishing quickly and going to bed as he was in bedding me. I did not take offense: the day had been long, and relief threatened to wash over me—relief and hope. Though it was only the gloaming hour, I could gladly stretch out alongside my fox to sleep on the bed we were currently rumpling. My own erection flagging, almost forgotten, draped along my belly, bouncing with each slow crash of pelvis against pelvis.

"Tobias," he grunted, barely audible, a pleading edge to his voice. I was confused for a moment, and then I remembered. How could I not have noticed the knot swelling, pressing against my entrance, already almost too big—if it slipped in we would be tied, joined for long minutes, unable to separate or even merely assume more comfortable positions without acrobatics either of us had the energy for. He had shown me a trick, in the long-ago days when our love was blooming, and I used it to good effect on that snowy evening.

Shoving a hand between our bodies, I encircled the base of his shaft below the bulb-shaped heat of his growing knot. Holding tight, I used the meat of my palm to create a barrier, a stop-gap keeping him from plunging all the way in.

"Oh, Tobias," he groaned as my fingers tightened and my innards began to milk his shaft. His eyes screwed shut, his face contorted as he fought with himself. Fangs bared in a snarl as bestial passion overcame exhaustion and discipline alike. Despite my hand, his wild thrusts brought the knot up against my skin, its heat making me moan despite myself; I nearly released my hold of him, but instead squeezed all the tighter.

He barked, quick, high-pitched yips that must have been audible on the street outside, despite the thick blankets of snow. Spent, he slumped against me, cock still twitching within my encircling fingers. Gently, I released him, allowing him to roll onto the bed beside me.

I wiped us off with a rag, feeling oddly parental. I was struck by the knowledge that this man loved me, that he was working himself to the bone to keep us alive, and that—despite it all—he had not entirely given up. And now I was helping, adding once more my wages to the household, or would be soon. I tried not to think about *what* I would be doing to earn those wages.

Instead, I set to tucking in my softly-snoring fox and further tidying up the flat. The stew I set by the frosty kitchen window in the hopes that it would furnish us both with a hearty—if cold—breakfast when we woke. Lingering, I gave myself a currying, aligning sex-mussed hair so I could sleep easier. Finally, I felt weary enough to slip between the sheets with Hubert.

Tired though I was, my mind would not let me rest. Even as the last rays flicked through the shutters, chased soon after by the dancing fugitive glow of the street's gas lamps, my eyes refused to stay closed; the rising heat at my groin would not be ignored.

I rolled away from his side of the bed, lest my swelling prod his backside and disturb him. An eternity later, I could stand it no more. Slipping from the enveloping warmth, I trod as lightly as I could to the foyer, the furthest point in our few small rooms from the bed.

I sat down on the bare floorboards, cold quickly seeping into my equally bare rump. My nipples hardened, my shaft pulsing, my fingers nimble despite the chill. I pleasured myself there, one hand on my cock and two fingers shoved into my still fox-slick hole. I worked at my own body with the intensity of a machine, desperate for release, for exhaustion and sleep and quietude. And I thought of Taj, of his stripes and the velvet grey skin tucked between his pert buttocks, his eagerness and his exotic allure. His scent and touch suddenly fresh in my mind. And still relief was a long time in coming.

I awoke late the next morning to find a cold bed and half-empty stew pot, and a heart-shaped piece of foil-wrapped chocolate, placed square in the center of the table. An hour later I arrived at Frau Hübsch's brothel, donned my costume, and checked that the fake tree had a sufficient stock of clean towels.

INITIATION

Initiation

by Kyell Gold

In 1886, a wide concourse opened between Picadilly Circus and New Oxford Road. Thousands of people walked the newly named Shaftesbury Avenue each day, and of course the list of merchants who had petitioned the Queen to locate their establishments there was far longer than the list of available spaces, so only the best lined the thoroughfare.

About a third of the way down from the Circus, a side street led from Shaftesbury Avenue into a small cul-de-sac. No street sign named it; a select few knew it as Shaftesbury Court, and though there was no particular secret about it, they liked the fact that this information was not widely known.

Shaftesbury Court consisted of exactly seven buildings, only one of which need concern us here: a discreet brick edifice with marble cornices and an elegant and restrained wooden door, which gave the impression of wealth only to those who knew how to discern crystal from glass, or ebony from treated mahogany. The door bore only the number 9 and a small knocker which appeared to be brass, in the shape of a fluffy tail, elegantly curved outward from the door.

Behind the ebony door with its crystal panes stood a smartly dressed dhole, his reddish pelt set off by his immaculate dark blue velvet suit. Hollingsworth attended the door faithfully every evening from five until eleven, and it was no good pretending to be on a mythical guest list, because Hollingsworth knew all the members of the club. If you lifted the knocker and let it fall without identifying yourself, you would hear his rich, accented voice say, "This is a private club, sir." There would be no more than that.

On the evening of March 25th, 1891, a chilly wind blew through the narrow court. A portly otter drew his fine woolen coat more tightly about him as he approached the door of number nine. Behind him, a slender fox, younger but with a similarly fine coat, lagged a few steps behind, stepping delicately over the cobblestones to keep his paws dry and trying to keep his tail off the ground.

The otter, whose paws were already wet, turned and gestured impatiently. "Come along, Elliston. There's a fine line between proper and dainty, you know."

"Begging your pardon, Mister Smythe," the fox replied, navigating a particularly large puddle and arriving at the otter's side, "but on the whole, I would rather you suffer the inconvenience of a few moments' wait than risk catching pneumonia or the ague."

"One catches the ague from being in the tropics, not from splashing through puddles," the otter grumbled. "Little water never hurt anyone."

"My aunt Belinda died from a grippe she caught as a direct result of slipping from a poorly seated stone and landing in a puddle," Reginald Elliston said, "and I have a second cousin who caught pneumonia from standing outside in a beastly wind like this one, so if you'd be so kind?"

"Deuced frail family you have," the otter said. "No Smythe ever died on account of weather. Hello, Hollingsworth," he called, lifting the knocker and dropping it to make a loud clack. "Smythe and guest."

The ebony door swung silently back to reveal the imperturbable dhole. "Good evening, Mister Smythe. And this would be young Master Elliston?"

"Yes," the otter said as the fox's ears flicked back. He looked at the dhole, but got no flicker of emotion in the return look.

"Pleasure to make your acquaintance, sir," Hollingsworth said, bowing slightly. "Best of luck in your application tonight."

"Thank you," the fox said as he followed Smythe into the anteroom.

"You see," Smythe rumbled as they wiped their paws on the thick carpet, "no need to worry about tracking water into the club."

Reginald handed his topcoat to Hollingsworth, who waited patiently for Smythe's. The otter unfastened it, but left it on as he pointed out various features of the room to the fox. "New electric lights throughout the building," he said. "No stink of gas. Fixtures are all Venetian glass, of course. Just installed last fall. Ah, I see you've noticed the original sketch by Constable. Look at the linework."

Reginald examined the picture. "I don't suppose most people comment on the linework first," he murmured. "He appears to have exaggerated the man's... finer qualities somewhat."

Smythe chuckled, shedding his coat and handing it to Hollingsworth. "Get used to it, m'boy."

The dhole took the coats and vanished through a door just behind his station. Reginald caught only a glimpse of a row of neatly hung identical blue topcoats before the door swung shut again. He nodded to himself, following the portly otter out of the small antechamber. Certainly everyone in the club appeared to keep up with the same fashions.

"The Tempest was built back in '53 as an actors' studio," Smythe said, waving a paw around the large circular room they emerged into. "It changed paws several times before the Society purchased it in '73."

Reginald looked around and stroked his chin. Five wooden columns, each carved to resemble a whirlwind, defined a crescent through the room, from where he stood to another door across the way. To his right, on the narrow side of the crescent, hanging electric lamps dotted the ceiling, though the dark patches above them showed that the lights had recently been candles.

On the other side, the ceiling rose up to the second story at least. A soft murmur of speech arose from the couches and stuffed armchairs below the open space, arrayed with their backs to the columns to face a small wooden dais in the center of the area. Behind the dais, against the wall, a short dhole tended bar, serving a clear drink to a tall badger.

"Stage is original," Smythe said. "From the Old Vic, they say, a prop from some drama or another." He sniffed dismissively. "That's Chambers, behind the bar. Makes a capital martini. I recommend it. Let's see, that's Beddington sitting down with his gin and tonic. The two on the couch are Quince and Wilson. They're always like that."

The fox managed a slight smile at the two raccoons leaning against each other on the couch, one with his paw on the other's knee. The otter shrugged. "Second Circle is a harbor of sorts from the bonds of society," he said. "Besides, they're from the New World, you know." They walked along the columns, looking back at the chairs that had come into view. "Oh, good, Worthingsley-Hill is here. You know him, of course. From the Stratford Worthingsley-Hills."

"Of course," Reginald said. He inclined his head to the short red fox, who looked up from his conversation with a plump stoat to return the slight nod.

"And he's talking to the newest member, Lyman Sellers. He joined last month. Quite tip-top." He looked at Reginald with a raised eyebrow. "I wager you'll do just fine."

Reginald kept his ears up, despite the churning in his stomach. "Thank you, Smythe," he said.

"The president will be up on the balcony, probably with the vice president." Smythe waved up to the crescent-shaped section of ceiling, and Reginald saw stairs leading up to it. "But you'll meet them all in due time. And that other door back there, that's the necessary, and the private rooms." He gave a broad wink.

Reginald smiled nervously. "Jolly good," he said. "So, ah, when do the proceedings commence?"

"Oh, posh," Smythe said. "There's no proceedings. You get up when you're ready, tell your story, and we've enough members here to approve you. You will be approved, no fear. Just tell that story the way you told it the other night."

"Thank you," Reginald said. "Join me for a quick one before I start?"

Smythe chuckled deeply. "My boy, no Second Circle member would dream of embarking upon a presentation without the proper lubricant. Martini?"

"Thank you," Reginald said again, smiling around at the other club members, who were just beginning to notice him now that he and Smythe were walking towards the bar. "How long does the story have to be?"

"As long as it is," Smythe said, and clapped the fox on the back. "You've no need to fret, boy. Chambers!" he called as they approached the bar. "Two martinis."

The dhole smiled. "Of course, Mister Smythe. Welcome, Master Elliston."

116

Reginald kept his ears fixed, but his whiskers twitched in surprise that the bartender knew his name too. He noticed that Smythe was watching him with a grin. Of course the staff would all have been told that he was applying for membership tonight. Certainly this was a change from the gentleman's clubs he was used to, where the staff remained aloof.

Then again, those clubs were not, he admitted to himself, the more desirable clubs to belong to. But they were the best a young gentleman could afford, and most of his fellow clerks belonged to the same ones. Part of the allure of Second Circle was not only the particular affinities of its members and the startlingly low dues, but the class of member. Raccoons from the New World, for example—where else would he be able to meet them in such a casual setting?

Chambers set two martinis on the bar. Smythe picked up both and handed one to Reginald. He raised his glass. "Cheers."

"Your health, sir," Reginald said, lifting his glass to match. He noticed that except for the two raccoons, most of the people in the room were at least glancing in his direction. Beddington, the tall badger, was openly watching him. He could see some indistinct muzzles in the shadowy balcony and the shine of a pair of eyes. By the scent, there were half a dozen people up there looking down on him.

They drank at the same time. Reginald raised his eyebrows as he lowered the glass, the sharp and sour taste of the martini lingering on his tongue. "Superb," he said.

"Indeed." Smythe turned back to the dhole. "You use the same ingredients as the chaps down at the Cap and Kitty, Chambers?"

The dhole showed teeth in a smile. "To my knowledge, sir."

"I don't know how you do it. First rate."

"Thank you, sir." The dhole bowed slightly.

"Come along, Elliston," Smythe said, leading him to a pair of unoccupied chairs. "Let's sit down a bit until you're ready, shall we?"

"Actually," Reginald said, taking another sip, "I'm ready now."

"Capital." Smythe cleared his throat, getting the attention of the raccoons and the overt attention of the other. "Fellow Second Circlers, Please allow me to present a young gentleman whom I'm certain will capture your…imagination. Master Reginald Elliston."

Polite applause filled the room. Smythe nodded toward the dais, and Reginald took a deep breath, and then stepped up, glass held as casually as he could currently manage.

"Good evening, gentlemen," the fox said, and raised his glass to the balcony. "I would drink to your very good health."

Some of the people raised their glasses, others simply smiled. Reginald took another drink and let the liquor fill his muzzle before continuing. "I have recently returned from an expedition, scouting territories for my father in the depths of Africa, and I would regale you with a rather surprising experience I had while there."

"It was the heat of summer, and to one accustomed to our pleasant English summers, the brutal heat of Africa was nearly unbearable. In the town of Mgongo, the natives are a curious race of dark-furred pygmy foxes with great spreading ears and tan underbellies. Despite their dark coat, they trot about cheerfully in the midday sun as though it were no more than a springtime morning, whereas I found myself quite unable to move between the hours of eleven and one-thirty, as my chronograph measured the day."

"Now, in Mgongo, the natives go about barely covered at all, and after several days in the summer heat, my purser and secretary, as well as our two British servants, all fell out of the habit of wearing their shirts. Of course, I carried on as any gentleman would, doffing my clothes only to put on my dressing gown, so as I sat in the hut they had set aside for me and ate my lunch in the shade, I was treated to a lovely display of young native men parading past my window with their sleek muscles on display. From that distance, it was barely obvious that they rarely bathed."

He paused to touch his nose as though recalling the odor, and to his delight, the room filled with a soft chuckle. Emboldened, he went on. "I had been endeavoring to negotiate with the chief of the village to allow my father's company exclusive access to the river, and the concept of exclusive access was proving rather difficult to convey. The river that ran past Mgongo was shared by many tribes, although the Mgongo foxes did use their bend exclusively, as far as I could tell in my month there. My job was to convince them to make war on any foreign boat that didn't sport our particular insignia. A simple matter, you might think, but it was devilishly hard. Their chief kept asking why they would go to war with other tribes they didn't know,

118

that just because they wanted to sail down the river there was no reason for the Mgongo to stop them, it wasn't as though they were attacking, and so on."

"Truthfully, there were two other tribes I could have talked to, but the Mgongo foxes were also located at the base of a convenient trail into the mountains, which might well prove useful in the future. Also, the other tribes were both monkeys, and I felt it would be best to forge an alliance with other foxes, as strange as they might seem."

"And," he said with a grin, "I found it hard to leave all those attractive youngsters."

The crowd murmured again, and he saw smiles on the faces of those nearest him. His stomach was settling now that he was into the story. "About two weeks into my stay, I noted that all the young men in the village left one afternoon. I couldn't help noticing, as my lunchtime display was exceptionally dull that day."

"The younger cubs were fascinated by me and often came over to see what I was doing. I had several sweets which I gladly shared with them, and fortunately I'd kept some in reserve. When the first one showed his curious little snout, I tempted him with a Callard and Bowser toffee, and he found it irresistible. I asked where all the young men had gone, and he said they'd gone to the river, but that he wouldn't be allowed to go 'til he was older. It was some kind of togetherness ritual that the tribe practiced once a month."

He heard a snort and saw Beddington grinning widely at him. For a moment, he faltered, and then went on. "It turned out to be an initiation of sorts. None of the Mgongo foxes knew the exact date of their birth, but when a boy was considered of age, he joined the men of the tribe on the next monthly ceremony. If there were no new members, it appeared they would perform the ceremony anyway."

"I began to pursue a new tack with the chief. Could I join the tribe, I asked. As an honorary member, you know. If so, would they attack these other ships? Well, they had some difficulty with the 'honorary' part, but they were quite willing to take me into their tribe, and they eventually said that if I furnished them with descriptions of my enemies, they would fight them for me if need be."

"I was obliged to bestow all the gifts I'd brought on the chief and his family, but after a fortnight of sweltering heat broken only by fierce rainstorms, I succeeded in procuring an invitation to the next initiation ceremony. Traditionally, the father presented the son to the tribe, but they were not unfamiliar with the case in which a father was not present. The chief himself would present me."

"In the course of my negotiations, I'd seen rather a lot of the chief's son, a fox by the name of Anari. His father was old and dignified; he was young and dashed handsome, for all his three feet of height. When it became clear that his father would present me at the ceremony, Anari took to passing by my hut during the mid-day heat. My translator, being used to the tropical climes, went about his business while I rested, so I had no way to speak to Anari, but we made ourselves understood well enough."

Reginald paused for another drink and lifted his eyes as though looking away into that far-off jungle. He tried to picture the young pygmy fox in front of him, wearing nothing but a barely modest cloth around his waist, and described him for his listeners, as it was about time for the story to arouse a little interest. "The Mgongo had little understanding of modesty; the crude loincloths they wore served primarily to guard their privates from damage as they made their way through the brush. In the village, the cloths frequently slipped low, providing enticing glimpses of just the tips of the delicate valuables they were protecting."

"But of course, I was the perfect gentleman and never so much as glanced in their direction. For more than a second, anyway." A small ripple of laughter went through the room. "We communicated with pictures drawn on paper and in dirt, with gestures and sounds, and we both talked even though we couldn't understand the words each other said. I gathered that he was looking forward to having me along on hunts, and perhaps participating in some other activities as well."

"Although they had no concept of modesty in regards to exposing themselves, they did keep certain activities private. But once, when I turned quickly, I caught Anari with his paw beneath his loincloth. He removed it quickly, leaving a noticeable protrusion beneath, but when he saw my smile, he returned a generous one himself."

"So it was no surprise that on the day of the ceremony, when I handed command of the expedition over to my second, Anari was at my side as the chief led me and the others down to the river. They had demanded that I dress myself after their fashion, but I refused to do so in sight of my men. Running around like a savage…" He chuckled to show how unthinkable that would be.

"Once we had left the village behind us, however, I realized that for the good of my father's trading practice, I would have to sacrifice the dignity of the British gentleman. Fortunately, I may not have mentioned that the cloths the Mgongo wore covered them only in front. After walking behind a large number of uncovered shapely derrieres, in the warmth of the tropical jungle, the aversion to removing my garments was somewhat less than it might normally have been, especially as I was provided a small clearing for the purpose."

"I waited for someone to provide a cloth to cover myself, but none was forthcoming. Eventually, through my Mgongo translator, the chief made it clear that I would not be given a cloth until after the ceremony, so I was obliged to walk down the path completely a poil. The considerate Mgongo surrounded me on all sides so I would not risk damage from plant or predator, but it became obvious that their motives were not completely altruistic, as several of them appeared to take inspiration from my explorer's mien and mounted expeditions of their own to uncharted areas under my tail and below my tum. Not that these expeditions were unwelcome, but I had no bally clue how to respond to them. They appeared not to expect any response, so I endured their touches with a smile and tried to remember which were the bolder ones, for later reference."

"We were walking away from the river, and presently the path wound upwards at a rather steep angle. The Mgongo hung back, letting the chief go first, followed by myself and Anari. Courteous of them, I thought, until a breeze caught the underside of my tail and I realized what view they were getting. I won't say I found the thought particularly unpleasant."

"At the top of the ridge, I had to stop and catch my breath. The chief had stopped anyway, and pointed down the other side. There was a beautiful waterfall a hundred feet below us, churning up the water of an otherwise sparkling pool. That, it appeared, was our destination."

"Had I not been worried about the beastly insects, I would have appreciated the view much more. Our ears seemed to be moving of their own accord at the sounds and brushing of the little flying devils, and soon enough we began descending into the ravine. The noise of the waterfall grew louder and louder, my fur getting damp from the mist as we drew closer, but at least the flies seemed to dislike the moisture."

"We reached the pool quickly and circled around the edge. I soon saw our destination: a wide rocky space clear of vegetation, large enough for the whole tribe to assemble. They did so, taking up seats on rocks with some small bickering over what I assumed were the choicest spots. Anari sat near the front, while his father drew me to the side of the pond and turned with me to face the tribe."

"I was still entirely unclothed, of course, and if I'd been mildly titillated at the thought of the tribe watching my tail, I now had to face the lot of them, staring without any pretense at my other... assets. I was somewhat nervous, truth be told, but I can't say I didn't enjoy the attention, and presently there was a bit more for them to stare at."

"One of the younger foxes trotted about the clearing picking some leaves, which he distributed to the group. The Mgongo chewed them with great enthusiasm, so I followed suit and found them to have a slightly bitter taste masking a sweet under taste. Anari caught my attention and swallowed with great exaggeration, so I did the same."

"When everyone had gotten enough leaves to start chewing, the chief introduced me with a great fanfare in Mgongo, which I could not understand, as my translator was not permitted to speak to me during the ceremony. I'd been prepped with my responses, of which there were three, and I could still recite them for you now, though I see no Mgongo here to understand them."

The crowd chuckled, and Reginald saw that most of them were quite intent on him. All the ears he could see were cupped forward, all eyes fixed on him. It was not difficult, in those circumstances, to imagine himself being studied by a tribe of pygmy foxes. "When I'd properly given all three responses, the chief indicated I should jump into the water. It looked a bit chill, but an Elliston has never backed down from a challenge, so in I went." He saw Smythe cover his muzzle, no doubt remembering Reginald's distaste at getting wet earlier in the evening.

"The water was in fact surprisingly warm. I surfaced to the sound of paws on rocks, and within moments, splashes surrounded me as the Mgongo joined me in the pool. From this point, I didn't know what to expect, though I had an idea, and I looked to Anari for guidance. Even though my translator remained nearby, the roar of the waterfall seemed much louder than it had twenty feet above on the rocky ground, so he would not be much use to me."

"Anari beckoned me over, and I saw that about thirty feet further from the waterfall, some of the Mgongo were climbing up onto a rock ledge that extended about a foot below the water. I could see the water dripping off of their fur as they shook their lithe bodies and full, bushy tails. They'd removed their loincloths, and so this was my first chance to get a good look at how they stacked up to the fine British fox in certain areas, and I regret to say that the Mgongo compared not only favorably, but impressively, considering the size of the rest of their body. Indeed, a few of the chaps seemed to be specifically intent on displaying the extent of their, ah, endowment for me, without any shame, and upon viewing this show, my own pride was stirred…among other things…so that I, in return, showed them just what a good British fox was made of when I climbed onto the rock shelf to join them."

"Anari led me to his father, the chief, and pulled me down on all fours in front of him. Well, there was little doubt by this point what was intended, and my blood was quite warm with the idea of it. The warmth of the sun and water, the roar of the waterfall, the rich, moist scent of the jungle and the foxes, all this created a powerful surge that I felt unable to resist. I daresay those leaves had something to do with it, too."

"The chief settled himself behind me, placing his paws in quite inappropriate places for a gentleman of such short acquaintance, but I was past caring. I believe I made some entirely unseemly noises that were covered by the waterfall."

"Anari, meanwhile, had walked about to stand in front of me, and from the placement of his hips near my muzzle, it was quite clear what was expected of me next. I obliged happily, the feeling not unlike tasting some exotic tropical fruit. His father, in the meantime, was now resting both paws just above my tail, and something else just beneath. He pushed a little further, and I gained a new appreciation for the Mgongo physique."

"It wasn't terribly uncomfortable; actually, it became quite pleasant when combined with the activity my muzzle was engaged in, and presently it became even more than that. When I tried to move my paws to accommodate myself, Anari gently moved them back to the water. The way I was kneeling, as I rocked back and forth, the surface of the water was lapping where my paw could not, which simply enhanced the feeling."

"There was little question when the chief had finished. He clutched my hips and rested his head against my tail and then barked something I heard even over the roar of the waterfall. I would later find out that it translated to 'Welcome.'"

"Anari had definitely been waiting until his father finished, because it was only a few moments later that I heard his guttural barks and was presented with incontrovertible evidence that he, too, was finished."

"I licked the taste from my lips and had to shiver as the chief stepped back. The warm breeze on my tail didn't last long, as someone else stepped up to take the chief's place. I looked back in surprise and saw one of the other elders, and then I felt him—larger than the chief, even. He didn't acknowledge me, intent on his activity. When I looked back, Anari had moved to my side to make way for another young warrior, who smiled at me and presented himself for the same treatment."

"Anari let his paw caress my ribcage as I lowered my muzzle again. Beneath my tail, the other elder was grunting as he joined himself to me, and I fell into the rhythm again quickly, actually enjoying the press from behind and the taste in front."

"As soon as one finished, another stepped up to take his place. After the first few, however, I believe none of them actually finished with me. They made a few token moves to let me know them, then retreated and allowed another to take their place. I confess I lost count after a space, and as I looked around in between licks, I noticed that the ones who'd had their turn with me were now happily occupied with each other, while the ones I hadn't serviced in some way were patiently, or not so patiently, waiting their turn."

"I was quite worn by the end of it, and ready for my own turn, which was provided, finally, by Anari. He knelt below me and worked back to allow me access to him. I tried to be gentle, but I fear I'd built up rather a lot of tension. Fortunately for him, that also meant that it didn't last very long, and in no time I was having to make sure I didn't force his head beneath the water as I bore down on him."

"That seemed to signal my entry into the tribe. I played with a number of other Mgongo then, in a happy daze that I suspect was partly the result of the leaf I'd chewed. Its properties seemed to increase one's stamina as well, for the ceremony went on well into the late hours of the day."

"When we'd worn ourselves out, the foxes showed me how to catch the fish of the pool, by this time attracted by all the motion and unusual, ahem, additions to the water. We scooped them out, most more successfully than I, and clambered out onto the rocks to dry our fur in the late afternoon sun.

"Anari stayed close to me the whole time, and we talked in our language of gestures and expressions, though we did not touch once we left the water. He was happy I had joined the tribe, and he hoped I would stay, but he knew I would not. I told him in return that I would like to stay, but that I also owed allegiance to my father's tribe, and the concept of belonging to two tribes at once he understood, somewhat to my surprise."

"As the sun dropped in the sky, the Mgongo began to get up and fasten their cloths around their waist. Anari made me to understand that it was important that the women never see a gentleman's privates, because they would try to steal the man's essence and become a man themselves. I assured him that things were much the same in my homeland." The room was filled with chuckles once again.

"I did, however, feel rather left out, as I had no covering for my own well-used privates. Upon expressing this to Anari, he gazed quite openly at my midsection and grinned as he extended in his paw a cloth of the same sort he was wearing. Some thoughtful Mgongo had provided a much longer strap than usual, and the cloth fit snugly around me, revealing nothing from the front." He put down his now-empty glass, reached a paw inside his jacket, and drew out a folded piece of rough cloth. "I brought that back with me," he said as he unfolded it and held it out to the group.

There was an appreciative murmur, which lasted until he folded the cloth back up and replaced it in his pocket. "I walked back proudly clad only in this, a member of the Mgongo tribe."

"Model it for us, then," called Smythe, who'd clearly been waiting for this moment, and who got a laugh for his pains.

Reginald grinned at the otter and looked down at him, ears and muzzle held in mock hauteur. "Private shows only, old chap," he said. "Needless to say, I changed back to my proper clothing before rejoining my crew."

"Much as I would have liked to have remained for another month, duty and my other family called. I did assist the tribe in a hunt, but," he looked around the room and smiled, "that's a story for another time. I thank you all, gentlemen, for your kind attention to my words."

Smythe laughed and clapped his paws together. "Good show, Elliston," he said, and the others joined in his applause.

Reginald bowed and stepped off the dais. From above, he heard a smooth voice say, "Thank you, Elliston, for that charming tale. Please repair to the foyer while we consider your membership." After a pause, the voice continued, "I assure you that our entrance ceremony is not nearly as energetic as you may be accustomed to."

He laughed himself then, bowed again, and walked past Smythe's grinning whiskers back to the foyer.

Hollingsworth greeted him there with a slight bow of his own. "I quite enjoyed your story, Master Elliston," he said. "I have heard many tales in this club, and I confess I am quite unfamiliar with the habits of the Mgongo tribe."

Reginald grinned. "They have escaped notice for centuries," he said, feeling free to continue the fabrication. "Pure luck we happened upon them, really. Secretive little blighters."

"Indeed, sir," Hollingsworth said, and Reginald thought he could detect just the faintest hint of a smile. For a few moments, he pictured Anari again, the savage's sweet smile and supple body, but even his imagination couldn't keep his tail from twitching nervously. "How long do they usually take, Hollingsworth?"

"After a story of that caliber, sir, no more than five or ten minutes. Ah, see, here comes Mister Smythe now."

The otter was striding up to Reginald with a large smile on his muzzle. He shook the fox's paw warmly. "Congratulations, my boy," he said, "you're in the Second Circle. May the Lord have mercy on your soul." He said the last part with a formal air and followed it with a wink.

Reginald grinned widely and clasped the otter's paw. "Thanks awfully, Smythe," he said. "Jolly decent of you."

"Think nothing of it," the otter said. "I merely got you past Hollingsworth. You earned your place."

"Righto," Reginald said happily, and raised a paw. "Good evening, Hollingsworth."

"Good evening, sir," the dhole said, and gave Reginald a mysterious smile before turning attentively to the door again, settling against the wall and looking for all the world like one of the souvenirs some member had brought back from a faraway land.

Smythe grinned at the fox. "Come on now," he said, tugging Reginald's paw. "Let's go hear another story."

I have chosen to dedicate this story to the "fucked up girls" and "lost boys" of history who have fallen through the cracks.

Moral Folly

by Miriam Curzon

"Power operated as a mechanism of attraction; it drew out those peculiarities over which it kept watch. Pleasure spread to the power that harried it; power anchored the pleasure it uncovered.
Pleasure and power do not cancel or turn back against one another; they seek out, overlap, and reinforce one another. They are linked together by complex mechanisms and devices of excitation and incitement."

—Michel Foucault
The History of Sexuality Volume 1: An Introduction

* * *

"Your paper is fanciful and unprofessional," my advisor, an elderly stag, scowled at me from across his desk, "This is amateur work without proper research or logical connections. You presented an objective conclusion from a subjective observation. What you claim as a shared cause of madness—regret—is unjustifiable in contemporary scholarship."

I bit my lip. Father always told me our kind belonged on the scaffolds, scaling over the peaks of buildings with our paws caked in mortar. We were the elite masons and bricklayers like our forefathers. If we were intended to be elite thinkers, God would not have created our bodies that are so adept at climbing. After all, no other creature can out climb a squirrel in London.

"I am concerned, Mr. Morris, you are close to your final exams and thesis, but so far you have only displayed a merely adequate level of work. You have practically squandered your benefactors' contributions to this institution."

My heart dropped in my chest with each passing word like I was drowning in a pond. Honestly, how is madness not fueled by regret, I was full of regret and despairingly close to hysterics. Quite a lot in common with the sedentary, soldiers, the senescent, the dispossessed I studied, maybe that was my path. I had thought that University College with their embracing of secularism, of foreigners, of females, of the coming new century would be a welcoming environment. Even here, at the end of a century of industrialization and scientific revolution, power remained with the elite pedigrees and not the red-furred bricklayers.

"You should think about what is best for you and your kin, I doubt you can afford to continue here should you fail to earn satisfactory marks from this department."

I nodded, my ears folded and my eyes downcast. Father would be furious, already mad that I opted for a course in Philosophy somewhere other than a proper Church of England university; after all, what would Queen Victoria say?

"Are you listening, Mr. Morris? You better shape up because right now you are not graduate material."

I was used to anger, but not this dispassionate disappointment. Facing bitter anger daily at home, I could handle, but this detached response to my failure had my stomach irate. I barely managed to contain tears, which flowed following the meeting. On a bench in Russell Square I cried in the shade of an oak tree as paws pattered past.

A shadow approached me and through my tears the glint of a polished silver case caught my attention. The case made a soft click and popped open to reveal a row of finely wrapped tobacco. "Have a cigarette," a thickly accented voice said.

I plucked one from the edge of the case and wiped my eyes on my jacket sleeve. He looked to be slightly elderly, a dormouse, more common on the Continent than here, with bits of white mixed in to his predominantly gray muzzle. The case closed and he tapped the end of his cigarette against it. "May I sit?" he gestured to the space beside me on the bench covered by my tail.

With a quick flutter and shuffle my tail draped over the edge of the bench into the patchy grass. I rolled the cigarette between my claws. The dormouse sat beside me, sliding the cigarette case into the inner pocket of his velvet jacket and withdrew a matchbox. His dress was of moderate means, better than mine, and professional. The match flashed into life and he cupped the stick and gestured to me. I leaned over and the cigarette flared to life, filling my lungs with the burning smoke. Cigarettes were a luxury I could not afford, but I had my fair share from other generous individuals and some friendlier acquaintances. He lit his own and extinguished the small torch with a flick of his wrist. "My name is Dr. Ernst Schreiber. I am new to London."

Between his name and accent, he must be from one of the central empires in Europe. He offered his paw and we shook, his whiskers twitched as he let out a puff of smoke. "Christopher Morris," I answered.

"I know you, Kristof, I have read your last paper."

He continued after a pause for a drag on his cigarette, "Very interesting. Clearly thought out, albeit completely wrong. Although it is not wrong to engage in experimental abstract thought, these British universities are hardly the place for such things."

Schreiber's words continued, accompanied by the sharp intake of smoke and the drawn out exhalation of tainted clouds. "You claim that regret is an underlying symptom of the troubled mind, but that is wrong or perhaps the wrong word."

With another long pause he leaned back against the bench resting his right arm along the back of the bench behind me and rested his left leg on his knee. He took another deep draw and exhale of tobacco. "I believe the term sexuality is better suited. Sexuality of both mind and body."

Ash fell from my cigarette, forgotten between my right index and middle fingers. With one last drag, Schreiber stood. "Come to the seminar. Tomorrow at 7:30. I think you will find it interesting."

His cigarette crumpled beneath his rubber sole. "It was pleasant talking with you Kristof," he offered his paw again and we shook, "Until tomorrow, then, 7:30."

I watched the thin furry tail disappear into the flow of bodies cutting through the garden. Sex. The cigarette fell to the ground and I stomped it out. How could that be possible? Sex is sex: an act of acceptable procreative means. Orimpure acts based in lust. Or monetary transactions. Of course I heard that institutes of philosophy and psychology in the Continent were examining a connection between deviancy and madness, but not here in London. Such matters were of a legal nature, not a psychic or philosophical debate. Throughout the three-mile walk to home in East London I continued puzzling over Dr. Schreiber's assertion. My puzzlement continued until I found myself on a stool in the lecture hall at 7 in the evening the next day.

The lecture was brilliant. Halfway through the seminar, my already perked ears jumped. "A young scholar of this university suggested the underlying symptom of madness, as he referred to mental distress, is an extreme case of regret. While his theory is wrong, he was on the right path. Mental illness has an underlying cause relating to an individual's psychosexual development. For many of the poor, sex is a commodity for personal survival, a traumatic break from the survival of the species. The rich hysterics suffer from the repression of sexual instincts, demands placed upon them by their parental authorities. The soldiers are troubled by an imbalance between their exclusive male camaraderie and healthy marital relations. The aged suffer from the loss of sex and either repress memories of their sexual history or over indulge in memory and fantasy."

The flaws of my thinking and conclusions glowed bright and certain. Every stipulation I had made, I re-examined. My walk home was a flash of theorems. At the end of the walk the only reasonable conclusion I could make was Schreiber's clear genius. His theories were so clear and understandable, but most certainly unpopular.

The next day, I sat on the stairs to the college while finishing half a cigarette from my acquaintance Charles, who just finished imparting on me the aim of Kantian ethics and economics. We shared little in common, but we both were among the few from East London. He had to rush off to meet his fiancée, a concept I had yet to consider. Each hasty tobacco flavored breath came as the door of the college opened and closed. There was little else to do but wait and see if

Professor Schreiber walked past. He had no office I could find and even if I knew his address I surely could not show up unbidden. My cigarette down and I then had no method of calming my nerves or keeping busy.

Without the tobacco, my tail jolted whenever the doors opened or someone would walk up the stairs. I did not know if I would find him coming or going from the building. My ears swiveled with each Continental accent. Some time long after the death of the cigarette he appeared from the front door. Similar in attire to the day we met, he started down the stairs, papers under his arms and his gaze pointed at the ground. "Professor?"

Schreiber did not even look in my direction. I walked over to his side and matched pace with him. "Professor?" I repeated.

He glanced at me, his whiskers bristling. "Sorry?" His eyes opened wider when he saw me. "Oh right, you. Doctor, please. I am a doctor first."

"Certainly, Doctor Schreiber."

He shuffled the folder of papers around and grabbed me with his free arm. "Come Herr Morris, join me for a pint."

Before I could utter any mark of protest or disinterest. Schreiber guided me by arm through the crowds down passed Woburn and Russell Square. Along Montague Street past the British Museum, and a few blocks more to High Holborn. Holborn I was familiar with, but I rarely ventured south of Holborn. My tail buzzed with psychic terror when Schreiber guided me further south down Chancery Lane. I looked around, ears twitching, when we reached the intersection and headed east along Fleet Street. Horror stories, fact and fiction always unnerved me. I could not ignore the stories, but I could avoid the places. Places like Whitechapel, Covent Garden, and, of course, Fleet Street. We stopped in front of the dark paneled windows of a tavern called the Old Bell.

The dark and dimly lit tavern was hazy with smoke and the smell of sweat. With the promptness of a regular, Schreiber crammed me into a corner of the bar with an ale before both of us. Between the loud murmurs and laughter my ears had trouble locking onto the sound of the doctor's voice. He clapped a paw on my back as he took a swig of the dark ale. "What did you think of the lecture, Kristof?" His silver cigarette case hit the bar with a delicate clink.

"I was quite fascinated, sir." In an instant I held a lit cigarette in paw.

"That is what I am paid for, son."

I saw him glance at my untouched glass and back at me. "What grabbed your interest the most?"

There was another glance to my untouched glass, which I picked up in my free paw and took a deep gulp of the malty bitter ale. The ale was strong with a slight burn in my unaccustomed throat. "I was quite drawn to your explanation of psychosexual trauma as the basis of sexual deviancy."

His ears perked along with his hunched shoulders. My ears picked up a long, but hesitant sigh. "It is not so simple, dear boy," he said with a shake of his head. "Psychosexual trauma and deviancy are certainly linked, but they do not share a definitive causal relationship. There are plenty of deviants without a history of trauma, there are plenty of traumatic histories without expressions of deviant behavior."

Schreiber turned toward me, and I felt my tail press between my back and the wall. He wagged his cigarette at my chest. "You see... out there, in the world-" he paused, punctuating his thought with exaggerated gestures,"-in society, in politics and religion, deviancy describes acts deemed-unnatural. But in our field of research, we cannot take deviancy as an unnatural act without scientific evidence that these acts are, indeed, unnatural."

He paused and blew a cloud of smoke. His head turned and stared at his glass for a period before taking a drink. "Take for example the subject of sexual inversion, or homosexuality as it is oft referred to in Vienna. Current research in Austria suggests that there is a natural element to the desire for the same sex. No trauma or psychic link can be made between all of the test subjects to suggest otherwise. Here, right now, there is-without a doubt-at least one invert. There are also, without a doubt, a pawful of males who have experienced a temporary state of inversion."

Before he could continue, I took a deep drink of ale and a hearty intake of my cigarette. "Doctor Schreiber, please be my advisor," I blurted out, throat still charred from the shock of smoke and alcohol.

After a period of silence, cigarette puffs, and a drink of ale, Schreiber put a paw on his papers and a paw on my shoulder. "If you have another pint, and help me with my research, I will."

Euphoria resounded through my chest. "Unpaid, of course," he added.

I clamped on his paw and shook vigorously. This would save my degree. In a few years I could have a paid position and be well on my way to a doctorate. I ended up having two more pints with the doctor. We parted a few hours later near Aldgate. For my first ride on the underground I was drunk on ale and unparalleled excitement. Somehow, I managed my way off the train at Old Street. In the gutter outside of the station I had to steady myself against the brick facade as I vomited, an unsuspected turn of my stomach. My stomach soured, my throat dry and irritated, the taste of bile and old ale in my mouth, I walked the remaining block home, happy.

* * *

Three Years Later

I completed my degree as I had originally intended to, much to the faculty's surprise. My thesis on comparative philosophies of deviants was well received by many and with guarded suspicions from others. In honor of my work, and my desire to remain working in the field, the college rewarded me a salary to continue my work with Dr. Schreiber. As I proved a constant with the doctor's work, I became more personally involved with his life. He introduced me to his wife, Ana, a stout dormouse who, despite her motherly appearance, did not dote on me as others of her sex, age, and demeanor. On the contrary, they treated me with respect, as one would treat a fellow colleague. They were the ones I shared my academic accomplishments with as my own parents never had much to say. In my mind there could be nothing better than being treated as an equal by Dr. Schreiber who I held in deep love and admiration. More so at the crest of a new field of inquiry just as the 20th century was upon us. Excitement replaced my nervousness, which opened plenty of analytical talks of Jack and Todd at the pub on Fleet Street. During one of these talks that Dr. Schreiber invited me to assist him in his more clinical work with patients. A week later, I sat on a stool behind Schreiber, facing the patient, in a long rectangular room.

For the first hour or so, I simply observed the patient while copying down verbal exchange and the male badger's facial expressions. This was the first time I had to transcribe Dr. Schreiber's spoken words and his accent led me to several words spelt with his heavy Bavarian accent. Otherwise, I was invisible. Aside from the occasional glance from the extremely gray badger, I felt I did not exist, as I expected. Then Dr. Schreiber's words caused my heart to skip and I missed what he said. He repeated, "Herr Morris, would you be so kind as to remove your clothing."

"Doctor?"

I felt the veil lifted, both Schreiber and the patient turned to me. "Go on, my boy."

I searched the dormouse's face for mirth and play, but all I saw was the straight muzzle and eyes, not even his whiskers showed sign of gaiety or want. My limbs were heavy as I placed the stenographer pad on my stool. I hung my jacket on the rack by the door and unbuttoned my vest. "Dr. Schreiber, I am not sure I feel comfortable undressing," I said, turning around.

Schreiber had turned back to the badger, the badger still stared at me. "Keep going," Schreiber replied, without glancing toward me, "This is important for both research and diagnosis."

The badger shifted, still sitting on his paws, his dark beady eyes still watching. I shrugged off my vest, and without further question I disrobed until I stood nude, facing away from both the doctor and patient. "Sir?"

"Now go back to taking notes, Kristof."

Schreiber did not remove his eyes from the patient. I took notes as before, but now I could not be more visible. The badger's eyes stayed on me until the questions had finished and I had redressed. Not once had Schreiber turned to me. When the orderly came to collect the patient, he left the room visibly aroused. I handed my notes to Dr. Schreiber when I was dressed again. "Thank you, Kristof, you were most helpful. I hope I can rely on you again."

I opened my muzzle to speak, but all I managed was a nervous gurgle. After I cleared my throat, I asked, "What are you researching?"

For the first time since I had undressed, Schreiber turned to me. "Let's discuss this over a drink at my house."

I followed the mouse silently out of the hospital and to the train to Aldgate. The flat he shared with his wife was above a grocer's shoppe. His study was small and filled with the stench of tobacco and near rotten fruit from the window beside his oak desk. I sank into the smaller of two chairs and Schreiber stood by the window. He picked up a matchbook from the brass ashtray beside his desk. For a moment he just looked out the window and shuffled the matchbook in his paws. "I apologize if I made you feel uncomfortable, Kristof," he began, turning to face me, "but this was an experiment that could only happen once. The patient was committed for displaying homosexual tendencies, but also shows a high interest in mixoscopophilia. He has admitted to experiencing sexual pleasure in the viewing of young nude male bodies."

He paused to retrieve a cigarette from his case, leaving the it open on his desk. "I am trying to determine whether his desire to watch naked males is symptomatic of repressed desires or an independent act of sexual deviancy."

"So, one conclusion is his psychosis is rooted in repressing his natural desire, assumably of inversion or pederasty. The other conclusion would be-"

"Exactly! A deviant act unrelated to his natural desire."

I rubbed my temples and stood up.

"I hope I have not offended you."

"No, sir," I replied, "I find chairs uncomfortable."

"Not enough room for that bush of yours," Schreiber grinned.

I nestled up to the window and plucked a cigarette from the case. "Isn't this a bit extreme? This is a new area of research. The Continent may lead in advances in psychology, the concept of sexual inversion as natural may be correct, but the Crown still recognizes inversion as a deviant act against nature. How can you hope to prove your theory when we don't yet recognize any deviant act as natural?"

"The Crown, the government, these are all symbols due to be replaced. Science and philosophy will advance. The field is new, yes, but growing by the day. You and I, our colleagues across Europe, we are the ones that get to draw this line and we can not be fickle or squeamish, we have to be thorough to produce cognizant arguments backed by scientific evidence."

Schreiber beckoned me and I leant forward as he struck the match to light my cigarette. As he proceeded to light his own I perched myself in the open window, allowing my tail to hang out to be buffeted by the wind. He looked at me with those eyes I had come to know as sincere and serious. "I asked of you what I have because I trust you. I hope my trust was not misplaced." He kept his gaze even with mine, our cigarettes smoldering in our fingers.

I did not think this was an issue I could or was even worth challenging. His eyes searched me and for the sake of the last few years I answered, "no."

Schreiber's face lit up, his whiskers and tail wiggled, and he pulled me from the window into an embrace. I felt warmth and respect from my elder and I hugged back with my admiration. "You can trust me, Kristof, as I do you."

The next several ninety-minute sessions with the badger, Schreiber experimented using me. Sometimes I would be naked prior to the patient's arrival, sometimes I would partly undress, and sometimes I would not undress at all. I continued to take notes, both for the doctor and myself, and settled into this method. Soon enough, I realized I no longer cared that I was naked, or that I assumed the symbolic position of the badger's desired object. Honestly, I came to enjoy myself, which seemed to encourage the badger even more, so much so I could smell it clearly. Rather than sitting on the stool with my knees together, my normal position, regardless of my dress, I would sit with knees ajar.

After a month, it became clear that the patient's mixoscopophilia was likely a symptom of repressed homosexual desire. The days I remained dressed, he would enter aroused, but would shuffle uncomfortably in his chair, eyes darting between the doctor and I. When he left he walked with a dejected shuffle, his gaze fixed at the floor, any sign of arousal gone. Schreiber's concluding experiment caught me by surprise, the badger's wide eyes showed a similar response. "Would you masturbate for the patient?" he asked with the same tone and decorum as his initial request for me to undress.

I sat on the stool, my knees locked together. The request frightened me and the notepad fell to the ground and the pen rolled across the tile floor. My shoulders hunched over and I buried my paws in my naked lap. Blood pulsed in my cheeks as I hid my nakedness from the badger. The request thrilled me, which is another reason I covered my lap. The patient was the deviant, not me. My promise of trust weighed heavy in my mind. I opened my legs again, revealing my paws clutching my swollen sheath and emerging arousal. With a brief glance at the back of Schreiber's head, I locked eyes with the patient and withdrew my paws from my sheath. I gave the badger an unobstructed look at everything. His eyes widen as more of my shaft surfaced. The air filled with a mix of masculine odors. Throughout the act, the patient's eyes locked with mine. The gray irises shifted only when the badger rocked hard enough the chair moved, unable to provide any relief to the tent in his trousers. Like I had done occasionally for the last decade at home in the darkness of my shared room, beneath my blankets, just as my elder brothers had. Like I had more frequently in the past month, I masturbated.

Through the hot beating of blood in my ears I heard Schreiber's accented questions. "You are agitated. Do you find my colleague's actions arousing?"

"Yes."

"Do you wish you could touch yourself?"

"Yes."

"Do you wish you were masturbating my colleague?"

"Yes!"

"Have you ever masturbated another male?"

"No."

"Have you fantasized about masturbating another male?"

"Yes."

"Did these fantasies start during puberty?"

"No."

"From before?"

"Yes."

"Thank you, I think we have reached a good stopping point. Most enlightening. Herr Morris, you may get dressed."

Stop. The words echoed in the pounding blood. The patient's eyes remained on mine, but felt different, almost pleading with me not to stop. I closed my eyes, took a deep breath, and bit my lip. I stopped. Before the orderly arrived to take charge of the badger, I was fully dressed. My heart pounded. I drew my jacket tight around my stomach, pushing the rushing blood and arousal deep inside. Some slow minutes later, Dr. Schreiber patted me on the shoulder and left. Alone, I walked around the room to the chair where the badger sat, damp with sweat and thick with musk. I turned and walk to the chair where Dr. Schreiber always sat. He had sat there and calmly requested me to perform a sexual act in front of the patient. Not once in all these weeks did he turn in my direction. I steadied myself against the oak chair and took a deep breath. My body still ached and I wanted to finish right there on the spot. I tasted the faint fruity tobacco laced scent that followed Schreiber. There was something off, something spiced and malty, like the bitter ales we would share at the tavern. My stomach convulsed and my tail went erect. I rushed out of the room, embracing the stench of the hospital corridor.

That night the memory and the ache remained. The room was empty, my brothers off with Father at a worksite on the southern coast. Despite the freedom of a seldom-empty bedroom, I could not shake the lack. The memory of the badger's eyes staring into me would not leave me. Those eyes, burning with desire, kept my stomach in knots and my sheath aching for a touch I could not fulfill. With quiet steps on old floorboards given to creaks, I crept passed my parents' bedroom and left my home. I weaved through the quiet streets with only my father's old wool coat covering my bedclothes. A voice nagged in the back of my mind. This is wrong. I should return to my bed, but I persisted through the blocks to the park. This late at night, there was only the occasional vagabond fighting the cold of the coming winter. I knew I should be frightened. That was the feeling I knew, walking out in the dark of East London with streets still lit by the somber amber gas lamps. Instead I felt only a tantalizing excitement of eyes in the shadows.

I pressed my back into rigid bark of a barren oak. With the dirt path just on the other side of the tree, I grasped my aching sheath and closed my eyes. I sought the memories of the last month, of this afternoon. The badger's eyes and scent, the feeling of being watched and Schreiber, always turned from my naked body. In the chilly air, my erection burned in my paw. My lip tasted of the blood pounding in my ears and heart. The wind would rustle the leafless branches, which sounded like someone could be close by, watching. With my eyes closed, anyone could approach and watch as I committed this heinous act. What if it was the patient? What if it was Schreiber? Nonsense, of course, but in my mind reason was replaced by a rampaging desire. I imagined Schreiber sitting in front of me, his back to me like always. His head began to turn, and my back slid down the tree until I crouched above the roots and dirt. Then his eyes met mine, just as the patient had. There was something wrong with me, I knew. When I came, it was different from all the times previously. I clung tightly around my coat and ran. There was a line and I had crossed it.

The next day I did not go to the hospital, I spent a few days salary on cigarettes and matches. On the steps of the university, I smoked through the chimes of Big Ben. My stomach felt wrong, my fur was a mess, my eyes drooped. I counted the clock chimes with each discarded cigarette. By the time I was out of cigarettes, my throat burned, and the four o'clock bell rang. Lungs protested the walk to the hospital and the flights of stairs to his office. The door was open and I could smell his presence in the room. My legs seized in the hallway just before the doorway. They burned, my muscles trying to force me to turn around. The same feeling I had just before my last meeting with my former advisor in university.

"Mr. Morris, don't just stand out there. Come and tell me why you were not here for today's session."

My tail whipped behind me, frazzled by Schreiber's interruption. I skulked in, the weight of shame holding my head and tail down.

"What seems to be the problem?"

I slid on to the stool I should have been on for the last several hours. "I'm not sure I am comfortable with what you have me do anymore," I muttered.

"We will try some other methods, then. Our approach worked for Robert, but we certainly cannot expect the same result from the same exact methods. What brought on this change?"

"Worked for whom?"

"Robert, the badger we have been treating."

"He's cured?"

"I would not say he is cured, but we pinpointed the source of his madness and I prescribed a course of action to occur outside of the facility. Now, would you explain this change in your position regarding treatment?"

Frustration burned in my throat like the last half-dozen cigarettes. "I am not comfortable with, well, masturbating in front of patients. It is wrong."

"There is nothing wrong with what you have done. These are experiments, this is science, and it worked. Therefore, there is absolutely nothing wrong with sexually stimulating a patient to produce results."

"It's wrong!" my lungs burned and I coughed heavily, my voice stressed from a cigarette too many.

Schreiber straightened up in his chair. "Something is wrong," he paused, "but not our method of treatment or your feelings about the treatment. Please explain how you arrived at your conclusion."

"It's wrong," I protested quieter.

"What is? Masturbation? Sexually stimulating a deviant patient?"

"I enjoyed it! I was embarrassed, at first, but then I enjoyed it. I wanted him to watch me. I masturbated in the park, last night! I enjoyed it! It's wrong!"

I gripped the edge of the stool between my knees as Schreiber relaxed back into his chair. He pulled out a watch and looked at it for a moment. "It is getting late, I must insist we continue this conversation at my home."

My heart pounded in my chest. My limbs and muscles would not move. My jaw ached. My mouth was dry. My legs moved only when I felt the warmth of Schreiber's paw on my shoulder.

The trip to his flat was a blur. Not the fast kind like on the underground train, but the kind that is slow and unfocused, viewed through a droplet of water on a windowpane. He sat me in his study with a cold bottle of ale. "How many brothers do you have?"

"Three."

"You are the youngest, correct?"

"Yes."

"Did you share a bedroom?"

"Yes."

"For how long did you share a room?"

"I still do, only my eldest brother moved out."

"When did you have your first orgasm?"

"I guess, thirteen?"

"Where do you normally engage in onanism?"

"Our bedroom."

"So you regularly masturbated in bed in front of your brothers?"

"We all did, sometimes, in the dark." I sipped from the bottle.

"Then would you not say that mixoscopophilia was a fact of your sexual development?"

"I suppose it was, in a way."

"Now was there any precipitating event to last night?"

I took a deep breath. "I could not sleep. I kept thinking about everything that happened and I was so aroused, but just the fantasy was not enough."

"Were you alone in your room?"

"My brothers are all out for a job."

"Well, the reason you went out to the park to masturbate last night was because, real or imaginary, your brothers were not there to watch you. A simple case of mixoscopophilia, which will likely diminish when you get married."

"I thought about you!" I shouted.

"Shh. Calm yourself."

"I thought about you, watching me, while I masturbated, in a park!"

Silence followed my declaration. I turned away from Schreiber and felt my eyes start to water. That was when I felt warm breath and bristly whiskers against my forehead. He took the half empty bottle from my grasp and placed a handkerchief. "That is simply a natural progression of our relationship and your sexual desire. How is your relationship with your father."

Schreiber was back in his chair watching me. I wiped my damp face. "My father? I really don't see or talk to him much."

"Yet, you live in the same house."

"He is busy running the business."

"A family business, I assume?"

"Yeah."

"A family business that you are not a part of."

"No, I wanted to go to university, Father did not like it, especially a secular school, but Mother convinced him."

"I am fairly certain that you must have subconsciously constructed me as a replacement father figure, after all, I have no sons, and have come to regard you as a father may regard a son."

"But my behavior, my... desires," I complained, "They are unhealthy!"

"What makes you say that?" Schreiber asked, propping his head up with his paw.

"The badger."

"He was committed for his behavior."

"Well, shouldn't I be committed?"

"I do not see why. You are not a danger and I can provide any counseling you may need. I honestly can say that I doubt you would benefit, in anyway, from a sanitarium."

There was a knock on the door. "Just a moment, Ana," Schreiber said.

"Yes, dear, dinner is ready."

The doctor stood up and walked over. He pulled his handkerchief out of my grasp and looked at me. "Stay the night, son. I would like to show you something. Come by my room after bed."

He placed a paw on my shoulder and squeezed.

After dinner, Ana provided me with some of Schreiber's sleepwear and bid me goodnight in a small white bedroom. The bed was lumpy and stiff, the sheets threadbare and weathered. I pulled off my shirt and sat on the bed corner. The only light in the room was the small gas lamp on the bedside table. Schreiber's shorts were big on my slim waist and his nightgown only just reached my waist. I folded my clothes and placed them in a pile on a small wooden chair. Outside the tiny porthole window all I could see were faint outlines of buildings in the darkness. There were tiny lights, a mix of old gas and new electric lamps, toward Tower Bridge. My ears perked up, I could hear a faint sound similar to the creaking of wood.

I turned from the window and walked to the doorway. There were soft noises coming from the dim hallway. At the end of the hallway, a door was slightly ajar accompanied by a faint amber glow of a gas lamp.

I figured it must be Schreiber and walked down the hallway. As I approached the slightly open door, my nose wrinkled at a strange, unfamiliar scent. When I glanced into the gap, I came whisker to whisker with Schreiber. "Be quiet and watch, just there," he whispered.

I nodded and he walked away from the small opening in the doorway. He approached the bed and I saw Ana sitting on the bed, her back against the headboard. Her thighs parted as Schreiber slipped between them. They shared a kiss, nothing more than a simple peck, but full of tenderness. He caressed her cheek. I steadied myself against the doorframe. Schreiber slipped his shorts off and I pressed my free paw tight against my stirring groin. I caught a flash of pink and a tawny sheath below his belly. His paw slipped over the pink flesh, giving it a few strokes. My own member had slipped out and down one of the legs of my shorts. I gripped my erection with my free paw and watched Ana's back arch. Schreiber glanced to his right, and then buried his muzzle in his wife's neck. His hips began a slow thrusting motion that soon sped up. I doubled over, pressing down on my erection and abdomen. My eyes did not move from Schreiber's pistoning hips. Ana's hind paws entwined with the doctor's, his tail waving in the air with each thrust. On occasion, Schreiber's head would turn to the right before returning to Ana's neck or chest.

After several minutes, I had to bite my fist, the pleasure mounting deep in my abdomen. I slid down to the floor, my paw covered in hot semen. I took a tentative lick, not wanting to wipe the remains of my orgasm on my fur or the doctor's clothes. As I finished licking the distasteful solution on my paw, I looked up. My eyes locked on his, the taste of my shame still on my tongue. Schreiber returned to his lovemaking and I sat on the floor, dumbfounded and aching from arousal until they finished. They put out the lamp and I fumbled my way back to the room. Throughout that night I repeated the act, theirs with my mind, mine with my fist, and licked clean my spilt seed time after time.

Sometime well into the next morning I was awoken by a timid knocking at my door. I tucked myself back into the shorts and pulled the gown down as far as I could. The room smelled as I would expect: male squirrel semen.

"Christopher?"

"Just a moment," I answered.

I could feel the blood in my cheeks and I knew the stench permeated the room. For a brief moment I paused with my paw on the doorknob, trying to moisten my dry mouth. The door opened and Ana greeted me, her own spot of redness in her cheeks. "Ernst wanted me to give you this," she said, handing me a folded piece of paper, "I am about to head to the market, would you like something? Tea? Coffee? Something to eat?"

"No, marm, I should get home before Mother worries."

Ana nodded and walked away. I sighed and changed behind the closed door. The folded sheet of paper just had a date, time, and location in Schreiber's ill written hand.

"My office, tomorrow, 16:00."

I slipped out of the house in my own clothes before Ana left. The short ride to Old Street I spent mostly asleep. My loose tucked shirt and unbuttoned waistcoat reminded me of the drunk and rakish few I would see in the morning on my way to university. Unaccustomed to partying or staying out late I never quite understood the meaning to their appearance. Now, in their place, as clear as day, the disheveled look is an apparition of shame. After all, what is the point of putting yourself together after a night of deviance. I felt dirty, and, perhaps if someone else saw my signals and recognized them, I would feel lighter.

Mother was out when I got home. Evidence enough that I was not too missed. Father and my brothers were still out in Brighton. I slumped through the house and curled up around my tail. Muzzle nestled against my thick bush, a common pose of younger years, I slept straight through to the next day. Two nights without much sleep were more than I could survive.

The next day, in Schreiber's office, I was greeted by a smile. "Feeling better?"

I shrugged as he guided me to my stool. My stool was moved. Today it sat in front of Schreiber in the position of the observed not the observer. "Have a seat, we should continue our discussion."

I climbed on to the stool and hooked my hind paws around the stool legs. Schreiber just looked at me. Under his continuous gaze, I began rocking on the seat. His head cocked to the side and the chair started to rock with me, only flicks of my tail stopping me from tipping too far.

146

"I see there is some pleasure in mixoscopophilia."

I stopped rocking and the stool came to a sudden stop, my body swinging dangerously forward. "But, I cannot say how much enjoyment was the act of mixoscopophilia, itself, or a subconscious response to engaging in a deviant act."

"Can't they be the same?" I asked, "Maybe mixoscopophilia is only enjoyable because it is taboo."

Schreiber sat further back in his chair, resting his leg on his knee. "So the act of deviancy is empowered simply because it is deviant? I think that just might be a good hypothesis. Although, it does little to solve our little puzzle."

"Did it feel any different? Watching, rather than watched?"

"I don't know," I confessed, "I liked watchi…"

I blushed and fell silent.

"You liked watching, but was your evident desire built on observation or fantasy of being?"

"What do you mean? Fantasy of being?"

"Imagining you were a part of what occurred rather than a witness."

I shook my head. "I don't know, sorry."

"Well then, what did you focus on?"

"You, sir."

"To be me in coitus, or with me?"

"With…" I paused, the realization of what I said immediately apparent, "With you."

Dr. Schreiber visibly twisted in his seat, switching his crossed legs around. "Well, I guess that pushes us closer to a conclusion, but muddies the water, so to speak."

I felt itchy. Itchy and hot. He just looked at me and stroked his whiskers, expressionless. "I didn't sleep much that night, it was like an opiate . I kept going after that first time looking through the crack in the door. Back in the room I masturbated several more times, I couldn't think of anything else."

I shifted in the stool this time, the cotton trousers trying to contain the memory of two nights ago. "Shouldn't the next be an experiment? See if my symptoms are a matter of simple mixoscopophilia or inversion? Whether you are a fixed or symbolic object?"

The dormouse sat bolt upright, but hesitated, his lips parted and silent. I was confused. Never in the years we have worked together has the doctor ever been so a loss for words. "Shouldn't we test to see where my delusion lies? Whether my desire is based in deviancy or inversion? If it is limited to you and who you are in my fantasy?"

"I suppose, I could contact Robert. I believe he is about the only subject we could have at this time."

"That would work, but, sir, you are already here, shouldn't you be a part of the test as well?"

Schreiber looked up at me, his leg falling from his knee to the floor. Blood pounded through my body. I slipped off the stool and stepped towards Schreiber. Each step followed the next in a slow march. My throat felt dry, my clothing insufferable, itchy and hot. When I slipped into his lap he shivered. Deep-throated whimpers followed as I settled my weight onto his thighs, my legs astride his belly. My tail shook from his heat. I leaned against his chest and wrapped my arms around his neck. The embrace felt queer. It did not feel like I imagined it should feel. There was no tenderness, the way I witnessed him and his wife embrace in their bed. Instead, it felt almost as I would imagine hugging my father in his lap.

I began to untangle myself from Schreiber when I felt a light touch on my lower back. Another one followed the first touch, light and quick. Schreiber's paws settled on my back, still just a light touch. I stopped moving, now perched on his lap with just my wrists on his shoulders. With brutal force he pulled me against him. He buried his whiskers in my neck just above my collar.

Teeth brushed my fur. Nostrils flared against my throat. Schreiber grabbed the back of my head and pulled back. His tongue traced up along the fur of my bare neck to my muzzle and kissed me. The back of my head burned in his grasp. My cotton pants stretched tight against my groin. Overcoming the shock of Schreiber's sudden passion, I squeezed my thighs around his waist. His paws slid to my front and pushed my coat off. Before the coat hit the floor he was undoing my waistcoat. Schreiber ran his paws back around to my back, underneath my waistcoat and pulled at my tucked in shirt. I pulled my arms back, flinging my waistcoat off. He licked around my muzzle, pulling my shirt up over my back. Our lips parted and

Schreiber tossed my shirt behind him. Schreiber buried his paws in the fur on my back, raking his claws against my spine.

It soon became all too apparent that my pants were in the way and difficult to remove. Schreiber managed to hook a claw in the waistband, but my thighs stopped them from moving too far down my hips. He manage to create enough space to stick a paw down my front. I gasped against his whiskers and his tongue darted in my parted muzzle. His paw slipped along the underside of my shaft and cupped my sack and sheath. With his free paw, he steadied my hips by grabbing the base of my tail and his claws followed the curve of my rump. I shivered in Schreiber's grasp, his paw squeezing my equipment and freeing my bits from my trousers. For the first time since he first touched my back, his muzzle left mine.

Schreiber pulled on my tail and I felt his claws press into the cleft of my rear. His other paw pulled up and I followed, my hips rising as he pulled. My heart jumped in my chest as I felt his whiskers tickle my sheath. I steadied myself on his shoulders. Schreiber bent further and drew his tongue along my sack and up my sheath to the flesh of my member. Then I lost my grip on his shoulders and my thighs went slack. The immense shock of pleasure at his tongue, followed by the warm wetness of his mouth overwhelmed me. I fell backward, slipped from his grasp, and hit my head on the floor. My vision blurred and blackened, I could no longer hear the pounding of our blood or our labored breathing.

When my sense returned, I was on the floor, a pile of clothing underneath the soreness burning in my head. My pants were gone, along with my underclothes. Schreiber knelt next to my head, peering down at me. While I lay naked, he remained fully clothed. I could see his protrusion in his pants, the dark brown cloth nearly black at the tip. His scent was spicier, maltier, a vague remembrance of three days ago in this very room. The dormouse dropped a paw to my chest and stroked along my breast and stomach. I reached up toward him and took a hold of his waistcoat. With my strength, and his help, I returned to his lap, the lump in his trousers pleasantly pressing against my perineum. This position allowed me to hook my thighs around him, my sheath, reawakening, pressed against the slight round of his belly.

I kissed him and his arms wrapped around my back. Schreiber's waistcoat was dispatched with urgency, followed by his shirt. His muscles flexed in my grasp and he stood up, grunting in to my muzzle. My thighs latched tighter and I slid my arms up under his arms. His hot breath tickled my whiskers. I heard ruffling cloth and the clang of his belt striking the floor. I wanted to feel his bit and bobs. My desire overwhelmed my logic and I let go of his shoulders. Schreiber was there to catch me as I almost slid from his hips. His equipment burned into my paw. The mouse's body quaked against me. We dropped back to the floor, Schreiber sliding between my thighs. I loosened my grip around his hips, allowing him freedom of movement.

His fur tickled my bare shaft as Schreiber shifted position. I was soon engulfed again in his muzzle, this time with no fear or possibility of falling. Sitting up, I stroked his head as his tongue lapped at my tip. My eyes pinched closed, and I bit back a moan. My orgasm hit with no warning and Schreiber drank my semen. We parted, both breathless, chests heaving from exertion. "Ernst." The name escaped my muzzle before I could stop it.

He wheezed softly, and coughed. "I saw you do it the other night. Never tried it myself."

"Ernst," I repeated and threw myself at the kneeling dormouse. I did not wait or tease, but slipped his member into my muzzle. Ernst collapsed forward on to my back, forcing more of the shaft in my muzzle and along my tongue. My hindquarters slid back and I ended up laying chest down along the floor, my head deep in his lap. I could feel his plump sack pressed between my chin and his upper thighs. The scent of his crotch filled in the flavor draining down my throat. Ernst whimpered against my spine. He caught a loose flap of skin between his teeth and nibbled. I gurgled and choked as the flow of seed welled up in my throat. "Stop," Ernst moaned, sending vibrations along my spine.

We decoupled, his member glistening with a mixture of saliva and semen. Ernst steadied himself on his knees, shoulders heaving. He glanced up at me with a smile, his cheeks flushed pink. Without a word, he crawled to me on his knees. I leaned back as he crawled on top of me, hips slipping between my thighs. The slippery shaft slid across and beneath my sack. Ernst buried his face in my clavicle and

150

then buried his member in my rump. I let out a hoarse cry. He had hilted inside of me. His hips began to move. I wrapped my arms and legs around his body, blinking tears from my eyes. Trying to forget the pain, I forced my mind to remember the sight of Ernst taking his wife. He was between her thighs thrusting, she was beneath him moaning and writhing in pleasure. I tried to picture myself in her place, as one feeling pleasure from penetration, but the pain overwhelmed the fantasy with each motion Ernst made inside of me.

Ernst knocked me back to reality when he pulled at my right leg. I unwrapped my legs from his waist, but held on to his back with a vice like grip. He pulled on my leg and grunted, "Roll over."

He maintained a grip on my hips as he helped me roll on to my stomach. The next time he pushed in my body convulsed. Sparks shot through my body and out through my sheath. My penis, which had retreated amidst the pain, emerged with each of Ernst's thrusts. On my hands and knees I began to moan each time I felt the dormouse's member buried inside my gut. Ernst wrapped his arms around me, hooking one around my chest and one around my hip. Each time my body jolted from a thrust, the tip of my member would just touch his one paw. I soon began thrusting my hips on my own, trying to get as much of the foreign touch on my hardness as I could. He shifted behind me and I felt his thighs pushing against mine. The thrust became deeper and shorter, but faster.

Without warning, he grunted into my neck and enveloped my hard stick from sheath to tip. I was pulled up and back against him by his other arm, which grabbed my left breast. He pressed his muzzle into my neck and under my jaw, licking or drooling, I could not tell which. Ernst hoisted me back until I felt the firm muscled thighs beneath me. Once again sitting in his lap, I bounced with each thrust. With each thrust my slick member slid in his paw. My hips moved independent from my brain, seeking out as much pleasure from Ernst's hardness. We devolved into a writhing heap. Pleasure and desire could be the only powers that kept our bodies in place. When Ernst flooded my rear with warmth, I erupted, spurting my seed over the floor, his paw, and my stomach. He slowed and I could feel the rapid rise and fall of his chest against my back. I eased myself off the quaking member, grabbing it as it left my body.

Ernst convulsed at my touch, a reaction I mirrored when I turned and settled in his lap, brushing my tender rod through his fur. After a few pumps of my fist his member retained its rigidness. Kneeling over the dormouse I kissed him and slid back on to his hardened stick. Mine made a mess of his stomach, leaving the fur damp and sticky. His moan echoed in my mouth and we began the dance again. This was something far different from what I witnessed in his home. We continued into the night, overwhelmed in the pleasure possible in our union, our descent into depravity and madness; a celebration of the power in pleasure.

* * *

"The pleasure that comes of exercising a power that questions… the pleasure that kindles at having to evade this power… the power that lets itself be invaded by the pleasure it is pursuing… power asserting itself in the pleasure of showing off, scandalizing, or resisting… these attractions, these evasions, these circular incitements have traced around bodies and sexes, not boundaries not to be crossed, but perpetual spirals of power and pleasure."

—Michel Foucault
The History of Sexuality Volume 1: An Introduction

To my own "Buttercup," who knows who he is.

Summoning

by Tym Greene

I stood, examining my handiwork: it would do. The full moon, and the seven candles arranged on the conservatory floor, illumined the chalk lines, the drops of blood and trails of silver dust placed in strategic locations. This might just be the night when…

But I couldn't bring myself to think on that, not so close, not after so long. Such a long, lonely road it had been.

I stood stroking my tail, occasionally plucking out an errant strand of hair before forcing my hands to release their grip. It would not do to go down that path, not again; I had picked myself bald in patches before, in the years since I had lost him. I did not want Rafael to see his lion looking like some mange-riddled tramp. Instead, I ran my hands down the front of my waistcoat and turned to my desk.

Gliding a hand across the marble top, I examined the books and charts spread atop it. Things were so close to fruition; it was almost as though I expected to find some mistake, some slight yet grievous error that would jeopardize the whole affair. Once more my hands brushed down my vest, and this time continued until they found the lewd bulge distorting my trousers.

I had read—in the writings of Nicholas Flamel, Nostradamus, and other similar authorities—that a libido denied had tremendous powers for focusing the occult energies. Small wonder that many of the most efficacious practitioners were also highly religious men. How many of my early attempts had failed because of that lack of focus, of dedication? Not this time, I thought, giving my engorged sheath a too-sharp pat. I winced at the pain, but that was the point, wasn't it?

Able for the moment to ignore my need, I went back to double-checking my preparations. I would not have been able to come even half so far had it not been for Father's death. He might not have approved of this, but he would have had to admit that I had finally "put my mind to something."

I switched off the desk's built-in electrical lamp, and then my hands once more found my tail; thinking of Father, claws again plucking hairs one by one. He had spent so much money on my youth, I now knew. I had never imagined that the abandoned violin lessons, forgotten French, and constant changes in my schooling would have amounted to much, but—once I inherited his balance books along with his fortune—it was all there in his neat hand. He had always been willing enough to pay, and had he not, I would not have known Rafael.

My beloved Rafael, soon I'll be with you again...but at what cost?

I stretched my back, sore from bending over my tomes. "Your lion's not as spry as he once was," I said aloud with an ironic smile, feeling aged beyond my thirty-three years. I sighed, leaning against the desk, the cold marble top reminding me of his soft cool fur, always so pristine and white. I could have given my father's entire fortune up just to watch Rafael grooming himself again, those piercing pink eyes flicking up at the mirror, catching me, and warming with his welcoming smile.

But that vision faded, along with the pristine fur and lively eyes. Now there was red staining cheek and chest, languor in body and mind, and the incessant deadly cough. I had held his hand, done what little I could. I had worn no mask, nor even a handkerchief tied around my snout, but I had not died. I often wished I had, cursing Father and his hardy family line.

It had taken a mine shaft to finally kill the old lion, or perhaps it was his drinking, or both. But he had never taken ill, nor had I, and so I had to kneel there in our little room while no-longer-beautiful Rafael coughed up his life's blood on the counterpane and on me. I still had that soiled shirt, the blood now brown stains along the linen threads.

It was the shirt I had worn that night and day, holding him. That first month of grieving, that first month of inconsolable solitude, it had still smelled like ferret. I had come, in the years after, to be grateful that I had kept it, along with a few other mementos—his brush, for example.

Both items were sitting, that moonlit night, on the conservatory's bare stone floor, each in its own loop of chalk, tying it to the main pentacle. Five years might not seem near enough time—especially for a dilettante such as I had always been—to learn enough of the darker arts to be able to perform a summoning, but Rafael's death had had the side effect of siphoning away all my distractions. Nothing else mattered.

I felt a hollowness in my belly and realized I could not remember when I had last eaten. Running a hand through my mane, I found it stiff, grimed with sweat. The conservatory was the largest room in Father's mansion, still devoid of plantings, and with its floor carved out of the living rock it had seemed perfect for my pursuits. It was indeed, but the summer sun had been merciless as I set things up over the past few days. My shirt was stained and rumpled, and my mouth tasted of ashes. But the moon was already nearly at zenith, and I had to hurry. There was no more time.

Staring out the sand-pocked glass I stood, looking down at the twinkling lights of Father's mining town, down below his lofty mesa, and tied my mane back with a ribbon. A single stray lock could spell disaster, I knew, undoing all of this work in a trice.

Father hadn't understood my disinterest in crinolines and rouges and tittering dalliances, nor in what lay beneath them. He had ascribed my grief after Rafael's death to my "fragile and tender" nature, and the fact that I had not seen death before. If I had not been at school in Canada, I might have been drafted to fight for the Union. Father would have liked that. Instead I was failing my courses and letting my ferret have his way with me. With a shock, I realized that I could no longer recall the exact details of his face, the sound of his voice, the way his body pressed against (and within) my own. I could ascribe words—flat, lifeless words—but I could not feel it again. How long had I been bereft of even these simple recollections?

My resolve steeled, my sense of urgency rekindled, I took my place at the diagram. All was in readiness.

Dropping to all fours, I leaned forward. My chin hovered barely an inch above the chalk outline. As proscribed, I exhaled

157

slowly, softly, as though whispering in someone's ear—Rafael's ear. I pictured the woodcut diagram for this step, my breath coming out like the printed wolf's, curling like an Indian pictograph. The silver dust seemed to sparkle a bit, and the chalked lines had taken on an otherworldly hardness, almost etched into the stone floor. I had to quell a surge of triumph: it was working, yes, but it was not done yet.

I reached out, and with one finger extended, began to tap at the stone within the easternmost arm of the pentacle. Tap-tap. "Evocatio," I murmured. Tap-tap. "Evocatio."

There was a sudden hitch in my breath: was that someone standing behind me? No, I could see myself, prone, lit by the flickering candles, reflected in the night-black panes of glass. I was still alone. The presence I felt could only mean that the ritual was still working. "Rafael Steele," I said with a shuddering voice, far softer than I intended. "Rafael Steele, I summon thee. By blood and fur I summon thee. Thrice by three, I summon thee."

I paused, doubt flooding my mind—had it been "thrice by three," or was that for some other spell? If only I'd had the patience to rehearse the incantation. That was when I saw the golden glow: a single strand of hair, laying across a chalk line, had begun to iridese. It was thick, brown, wiry. It had come from my own tail. One by one, the candles went out, and a basso rumbling shook the conservatory around me, threatening to shatter the windowpanes. I had failed. It will be at least another lunar cycle before I could—

And then I heard the breathing, saw the glow of embers above me, the moonlight glinting from ebony ram horns.

"Rafael Steele?" I asked, my voice all a-quaver. "Thrice by—"

"Hssk Naal!" The voice was low, gravelly, like the rumbling of boulders underlaid with the roar of a bonfire. It set my fur on end and made me bow my head in involuntary obeisance. "Who Naarghen? Who summons Boesom?"

I dared to look up again, and saw a ram-headed beast, smoking a cigar as thick as my wrist. A long slow pull made it flare momentarily-brighter even than the moon, its orange glow glinting off a thick hairless chest, shaggy arms, bird-talon feet, and the glossy black shaft, quiescent—for now—between his thighs. The beast's eyes, however, were the most unsettling: a deep featureless black, like Chinese lacquer or a pool of crude oil. I saw them shift, as though he were looking down and seeing me for the first time, still cowering on my knees before him.

He shifted, claws digging into stone as though it were sponge cake, and plucked his cigar out to blow a smoke ring. "Who summons," the creature said, in more conversational tones, "Boesom, Lord of Arroyos and Mesas?"

"Lord of…?" I looked around, confused, and then realized that Father's mansion had indeed been built upon a mesa, the flat top forming a perfect foundation indeed, the cellars under the main wing having been hewn from the living rock as well, and the excavated stone dressed and used in the rest of the structure. It had been left intact under the conservatory—a fact of which my knees were even then reminding me. I thought of the fortune that had been lavished on this, which was to have been Father's home as well as mine. Such a pity he died not even a week after the last board had been nailed in place, the last of the mail-order furniture delivered. There remained some rooms that still smelled of paint.

The demon stepped closer, his talon setting down right on top of the chalk line, where my errant hair still spluttered and fizzed. That had been the weak point, the knothole in my hull, and now the ocean was rushing in to meet me.

"Who," he said slowly, bending down to blow smoke in my face, "summons Boesom?" He had, I noticed, a bowler hat tucked between his horns. It was the only clothing he wore.

"Anselm Julian Henderson," I replied automatically. "But, I didn't summon you…O Great One." It wouldn't do to upset him, and nearly every demonological text was in agreement: demons were prideful things, and if not appeased—

"Then why am I here, hmm?" This time the gout of thick smoke engulfed my head, then settled around my neck, encircling me like a scarf, or a shackle. He stepped still closer, my chalk lines clearly no impediment to him.

Gasping at the smell of brimstone and sweat and rich tobacco, I tried to retain my composure. "I did not call upon you, O Boesom. I was trying to summon my…a friend." Even with his ebony shaft dangling a scant foot from my head, I was suddenly loathe to reveal the truth about my relationship to Rafael.

He looked around, seeming to notice his surroundings for the first time. "This…friend… is dead, yes?" I nodded. "This is set up correctly, given the time of year and the moon's phase." The demon seemed able to read my occult preparations as easily as I might grasp the meaning of a child's primer. I gestured at the offending strand of hair, and it was his turn to nod. "That would do it, yes. That also explains why you are now bound to me."

I just knelt there, staring up at him and his matter-of-fact demeanor. Of all the sciences, sorcery is notorious as the least-rational, the least "scientific." I had known this when I began my tuition, had known that the slightest irregularity—a difference of time, the conditions under which ingredients were prepared, the pronunciation of a single word—could cause the failure of an experiment, or worse. It seemed I was facing that worse. "Bound?"

"Until you fulfilled your contractual obligation—of which there of course isn't one—or I release you." He leered down at me, jetting smoke into my face again, his liquid black eyes catching the cigar's glow and keeping it.

At that moment, I felt as no lion ought: I felt fear. A small part of me wondered if this is what Father had experienced, as the rough mineshaft walls sped past. I blinked and the eyes were before me; I could no longer feel the floor beneath my knees.

Boesom had lifted me so that our heads were level, using his otherworldly power to levitate me. One massive hand cupped my chin, bringing my gaze into better alignment. "Yes, I like you," he rumbled. "A bit skinny, but that mind…that mind is just begging to be twisted in the right direction."

"Please, Great One, I did not summon you, nor have I entered into any contract. I merely wished-"

"To call up your old lover? I know. I read it in your soul. I cannot help you. he is…" and here he cocked his great head, as though listening to a voice in his ear. "Yes. He is up above, and therefore unable to return to Earth. I am surprised you didn't check that first."

And there it was: the result of my monomania. I had been so consumed by my need to see Rafael again that I had ignored even the possibility that he was unreachable. A simple Pershing Gold Test would have told me as much. Only spirits still focused on earthly affairs were able to be summoned. That is why even the master practitioners of my field could only speculate on heaven: no one had come back from there. Hell, on the other hand, was close—as near as the brothel down the street, the bottle in your hand, the hatred in your heart.

And this demon had seen right into my heart. A demon could not lie—oh, he could obfuscate, evade, omit, or even dissemble—but he could not actually lie. Whatever else, Rafael Steel was lost to me. In that moment I tried desperately to recall him, his gentle tenderness, his laugh, his scent, but I only could dredge up the words describing him, the mental image of the single photo I had of him, stiff and formal. I didn't even notice as the demon's telekinetic grip upon me shifted.

It wasn't until my high-collared linen shirt fell open, exposing my admittedly unimpressive chest, that I realized Boesom was undressing me, taking as much slow pleasure in his new bondslave as a child might with unwrapping a Christmas package. "Please, Great Boesom, Lord of Arroyos and Mesas, spare me at least a shred of decency," I objected, struggling to keep my pants up against his inexorable, invisible force.

He laughed, by way of response, and I caught a flicker of motion in the periphery of my vision. Glancing down, I saw that arm-thick, rather-equine black shaft pulse and engorge, lifting up until it was at right angles to his avian thighs. The head was pointing straight at me. It had been long, so long, since I had tended to my own needs, let alone been within touching-distance of someone else's maleness.

About a month after Rafael's death, I had sought out a former classmate.

Jeremiah—a rather pudgy black horse—by then had built up a modest trade in the smaller enchantments. He too was unattached, and had admitted to having fancied me somewhat; I hadn't even noticed him, beyond our shared coursework, too wrapped up in my darling ferret to even think of other men. Once Jeremiah and I had undressed, however, I knew that I'd made a mistake. He was almost the polar opposite of Rafael: ebony, stout, brash, and with a blunt member almost twice the size of my beloved's refined tapering shaft.

His tongue beneath my tail had been nice, and with eyes and nostrils closed I could almost imagine that it was Rafael's snout pressed up there…until the tongue was withdrawn and replaced with thick, hot, horsecock. It was all I could do to keep from shredding the bedclothes as he spread me wide. Thankfully, he liked tight holes and finished quickly. I snuck out with his seed soaking the seat of my trousers, leaving him snoring on a bed smelling of lion sweat.

I felt my balls drawing up as I looked upon the demon's—my new master's—shaft and recalled my sole failed fling. "Please, Great One, Please..." I whispered.

Thick fingers scratched down my bared spine and dug gently under my mane. "Poor kitty," he rubbed, blown smoke once more engulfing my head. I moaned despite my terror. "Come, I want to survey my new temple." He gestured and I found myself standing on my own feet, bare pads shuffling through the chalk lines and avoiding the melted clumps of silver dust as I followed him through the door and into the mansion proper.

He had a nice rump.

I had to pause at that thought, snorting to clear the cigar smoke from my nostrils. I had never—had I ever?—been attracted to hindquarters, and now it was what kept and held my attention on this demon before me. Two hemispheres of muscle covered in black feathers, with a snake's tail and diamond scales leading up his spine. Then we stepped into the hallway where every lamp was burning bright, and I saw that Boesom had not a snake's tail, but a whole snake! It bobbed and shifted with every step, palm-sized head staring right at me, smiling.

Those eyes were the same deep-oil black as Boesom's own. Then the tongue flicked out, and the snake head spoke. "I am pleasssed," it said with a tinny version of the voice coming from the demon's ram head; like listening to a Victrola recording. "Pleasssed that you are... sssuccumbing ssso willingly. I never asssked for a ssslave, but you ssseem to be quite willing."

Willing.

Had the demon been reading my mind? He must have, and yet why was I so willing?

My thoughts were interrupted by sounds I had never thought to hear in the grand house my father had had built: laughter. The clink of glasses. Music. Indeed, from the plink of a piano and the rhythmic tread of feet on a wooden floor, it sounded more like a saloon than a high-class party. As we approached the ballroom, I noticed furniture, paintings, fixtures placed in the hallways and open rooms we passed. Items that Father had purchased, ordered, and had shipped here, whose crates had never been unpacked. Now they were arranged comfortably, tastefully—even to my un-artistic eye— and yet with a certain purpose, as though the whole mansion was now part of some massive occult preparation. I was also aware of a presence as we walked…no, several presences, like passing through cold spots hovering in mid-air. I shivered, feeling my fur bristle. Then we reached the ballroom.

At a gesture from Boesom, the cigar in his hand making a sigil of smoke, the double doors flung themselves side, revealing an empty ballroom. But as soon as I registered that thought, reality shivered around me, and I suddenly saw with eyes unclouded. There were demons all about! Lesser than Boesom, I was somehow able to tell, subservient, but no less impressive in the variety of their forms. They milled about the ballroom—which had indeed been converted to the semblance of a saloon—drinking and chatting, and all as naked as Boesom himself (barring a scattered handful of choice accessories).

Meekly, I followed him through the crowd and up to the bar. There, leaning against a polished redwood plank that looked both sparklingly new and at the same time worn by decades of hands and glasses, was the bartender. He wore nothing more than a drayman's harness, which highlighted the bulky muscles of his canine body, but from the neck up he was a cactus. I stared as a split opened across the demon's neck, looking for all the world like a spiky green jack-o'-lantern. "What'll it be, boss? Brimstone whiskey? Or something more refined tonight?"

"Hellfire wine, Deelutau, for me and the lion." The cactus-headed horse grinned wide and seemed to wink at me, though he had no eyes at all. He placed two delicate glasses on the bar and proceeded to fill them with a thick blood-red wine. I couldn't help but notice that my father's monogram, which he'd had etched and gilt on every glass, had been transmuted into an elaborate pentacle.

I took the glass Deelutau was holding for me, and allowed Boesom to clink his against mine. The harmonics of the glasses had also been altered, it seemed. The tone resonated through me, making my tail bristle and my sheath plump up.

"Drink," Boesom commanded. I found myself unable to disobey, so in one long swallow I downed the entire glass. Fire poured down my throat. It was not the acid burn of the cheap wine Rafael and I had sometimes bought—indeed, the hellfire wine had only the barest thought of a taste—but rather the burn one felt when standing before the boiler of some great ship, as though the boiler were within one's on blood. My head ached and my claws extended of their own accord, digging into the polished parquet of the ballroom floor. I licked my lips, catching my tongue on a fang. My teeth seemed overlarge.

I winced, feeling wine-soaked saliva sting the cut on my tongue, tasting my own blood. A rush filled me: never before had that copper tang been so…erotic. It was all I could do to keep my free hand limp at my side. Deelutau refilled the glass in my other hand, and suddenly I didn't see any harm in giving my shaft some attention.

It needed little coaxing to come forth into the hot smoky air of the ballroom-bar, and Boesom, glancing down, began to rumble. I pressed against him, side-by-side, his vibration setting my fur on end. I quaffed my second glass, the inner heat seeming to bake my very bones. An odd protuberance met my fluttering fingers then: looking down, I saw not the tapered tongue-pink shaft I had known since puberty, but an angry red length with a swelling bulge on either side of its base.

"I have a dog's dick," I said, half-belch, half-giggle.

"So you do," replied Boesom, his ponderous hand resting on my head, fingers palpating my ear. I started to purr. Lions ordinarily cannot purr, of course, but at the time it felt as natural as the taste of blood in my overfull mouth, the weight of the ram demon's hand on my skull. "Deelutau, I think we'll finish this up in a more comfortable setting." Boesom's snake tail arched up and curled around the bottle, but not before giving the mouth of it a few licks.

Feeling a bit silly, I waggled my fingers at the bartender, the expression on his saguaro head impossible to read. Then I summoned the demon I had so inadvertently summoned through the crowd he had summoned. I was finding it hard to focus, as though my vision were a daguerreotype where everyone—everything—had moved slightly during the exposure…everything, that is, except Boesom. Still, I caught glimpses of the minor demons we passed, impressions of transition lines between scales and fur, stone and flesh, metal and feathers. The composite monsters pressing around me, brushing against me, reaching out to stroke my tail, grip my flank in passing… these lesser demons seemed to me more real, more welcoming than any of the real people I'd known since losing Rafael.

After an eternity, we reached the back wall, where curtained rooms lurked that had never been part of the architect's design. Red velvet and flickering candles marked these as boudoirs of the sort one might see in a Carson City whorehouse. But where lush beds would have been, each one had instead a low pillar of rock rising from the floor, the same stone as that upon which the mansion itself was built. Boesom led me past the others and to the middle room, larger and more lushly-decorated. The rock pillar bed was oddly shaped in this room as well—no mattress-shaped rectangle, but rather a rough-edged roundness. I blinked, and realized what it was: a scaled-down copy of the mesa on which we all stood, an altar to Boesom, Lord of Arroyos and Mesas. I stepped forward, polished wood turning to rough dry sand beneath my bare paws, the candles winking from within bleached skulls and tumbleweeds, and the cinnamon-sweat taste of the ballroom air becoming the tang of incense.

I turned to look up at Boesom, and felt my knees weaken. He towered over me in this altered room as he first had in the conservatory. Gone was the fatherly twinkle in his eyes, the playful attitude. I saw him, I realized through the haze of the unholy alcohol, as he truly was: a demon of high order, with a domain that covered far more than the government's Utah Territory. Boesom ruled the whole of this Wild West. I fell backwards onto the mesa-shaped altar, my changed shaft pointing straight up like an obscene gravestone. My glass shattered on the stone beside me, the fragments turning to dust and desert sand.

After taking a long drag on his cigar that seemed to pull the all light from the room into its glowing tip, he blew out a cloud of smoke that bound me in place, as though my mind no longer had any control over corporeal matters.

"Now it is time," he rumbled, stepping ponderously closer. "Already your form has begun to debase itself. It is time to relinquish to me your immortal soul." It sounded like part of a ritual, but the way he said the words made them seem tailored specifically for me. "But," he added thoughtfully, "you must beg for it."

I stared up at him, uncomprehending. It was only then that I noticed my nose pushing forward, stretching, fur dropping out to reveal something black, glossy, hard. This is all real. I hadn't imagined my fangs growing sharper, my cock changing shape, my face becoming avian, the ballroom bar and the other demons. "Pleath…" I said weakly, automatically, stumbling with my new be-fanged beak.

Boesom loomed higher, swelling visibly. "Say that again," he murmured, reminding me suddenly of Rafael, how he would ask me to repeat some trifling naughtiness that promised to send him over into climax. But that memory too had become flat, more like a book's illustration than something that had actually happened. My father was dead, and I had no interest in taking over his business. Even my studies in the occult sciences, my driving passion of the previous five years, held no promise for me now.

My gaze rose from my shaft to Boesom's equine rod, and from there up his body, watching the slick muscles work to pull desert-hot air into his lungs, and expel it even hotter. I looked into his eyes, those shifting pools of blacker-than-black.

"Please."

Like filling a canteen to the brim before a long journey into the desert, I poured myself into that one word: my pain, my loneliness, my shattered hope, the desperate physical need I had for so long ignored. Even as I said it, I could see Boesom's body shudder with energy, his horns growing to add another full curl to their length. Flat square teeth bit into his cigar as he grinned. "Yes," he hissed long and low, his voice doubled by the snake head at the end of his tail.

I felt the blunt scaled snout nose up between my thighs, pushing them wide to be caught in his strong brutish hands. Then the forked tongue entered me, dampening my hole with too-thick saliva, readying me for Boesom, Lord of Arroyos and Mesas.

He slid into me easily, putting the lie to my five years of self-imposed abstinence, filling me up. I moaned, looking down, half expecting to see a bulge in my belly. Instead I saw long smooth scales, like those on the underside of his tail. I could feel the demon's shaft tensing, hotter than any blacksmith's iron and just as dense; my own shaft was beginning to drool a glossy black fluid that smelled-

I had to catch my breath then, to keep from crying. The unnatural slick essence my member was producing smelled like Rafael had, the first time we had had sex: there was even a tinge of the sulfur from a textbook preparation that had exploded in our faces, prompting us to hurry back to my nearby flat and its bathtub. We had been so eager and clumsy that night, but there had been passion too. I fairly reeked of ferret for days after.

Boesom withdrew his shaft almost all the way, lodging his flaring head just inside my hole, seeming intent on stretching me out. One of his hands strayed to my chest, caressing the smooth scales that had replaced fur and nipples and bellybutton with a pale yellow armor. When he thrust in again, I noticed another smell emanating from my cock: the hot-house roses Rafael had surprised me with one winter night, for no reason at all. Another thrust brought another scent, and at this one I did cry, even as my body thrilled from the slow, masterful fucking.

The slick black fluid seeping from the tip of my shaft now had the unmistakable tang of blood and sweaty linen. The odor of the night he finally died.

The snake head had curled its way around Boesom's magnificent rump and now hovered inches above my drooling cock-tip, staring at me. And that was when the puzzle pieces all fell into place for me. I was bound to this demon already—he had told me so when he first appeared—but it was an ineffectual bond, a technicality. What he wanted (what he craved, if his thrusting was any indicator) was something deeper. His blunt fingers dug into my shoulders, spearing me further onto his cock. I could feel his balls, hot as coals, singeing the fur on the underside of my tail. It was time.

"Please," I whispered to the snake, the word soft and round in my beak, as though it were a lover's name. With rattlesnake speed, it dove onto my cock, jaw unhinging to encompass the knot, muscular throat milking me of every drop I could produce. Boesom hunched over me, chest-to-chest, sweat beginning to steam. I could feel part of myself boiling away, reduced to a thick black concentrate and pumped out.

He bleated, sounding suddenly very vulnerable, and I felt his balls draw up. Resting my head against his curl of horn, I murmured

167

into his ear with absolute certainty. "Please, my lord, claim me." The snake sent his fangs into my shaft, flooding my blood with venom.

In an instant, everything was changed. Gone was the tender hesitancy of the demon, replaced by the demeanor of a powerful beast in rut. I could have sworn that I was melting from the inside as he bred me—and in a sense, I was. My own member seemed to be in constant orgasm, spewing out my soul for the snake-tail to consume and replace with poison that set fire to my blood and twisted my mind into a blackened knot. And I loved it.

Somehow, I regained enough control over my contorted being to clench my hole around my lord Boesom's shaft. This was the final piece: I had to welcome it, seal my own fate, and I did so gladly. His fingers—on my thighs now, holding my legs skyward—gripped so tightly that blood began to drip down his wrists and onto my bellyscales. He came with a bellow that threatened to cleave the altar on which I had sacrificed myself, as well as the mesa from which it had been grown. I could have sworn that I could taste in the back of my throat the seed that filled my guts.

Then his tail withdrew from my shaft, licking the last drop of concentrated soul from my tip as it pulled away. A quick glance showed that the fang wounds had already healed. Releasing my aching legs, Boesom leaned forward and kissed me. His powerful tongue tasted of hellfire wine, cigar smoke, blood, and roses. Our eyes met, and it was all I could do to keep from crying again, or shouting, or kissing him back again. I knew my place now.

Instead, he helped me to my unsteady feet. With a wave, he reformed my wine glass and refilled it from the bottle he had brought from the bar. I followed him back out to the revelers in the ballroom.

I later learned from one of the other demons that the men and women in Father's little mining town below had looked up to see the light coming from the mansion that night. Lights, and music, and the sounds of a party, the likes of which none of them had seen, let alone expected from me. There were comments and snide remarks about how I had finally thrown off the yoke of his influence…how little they knew the truth of it.

The next morning, hoping perhaps to earn a bit of cash in carrying my supposed guests back to town, a drafter pulled his cart up to the porte-cochère. The mansion as he found it was empty, truly empty, as though everything of any worth had been removed long ago. Years-worth of dust had settled evenly on the floor, and there was a smell about the place... Some people say it was brimstone, others charcoal and spilt wine. They found, of course, no traces of me nor of the celebration they had seen the night before.

As for myself, I never looked back.

Tithes

by Chris "Sparf" Williams

"Now now, Sir Reginald, please control yourself!"

The boar's ham-sized fist left a gust of wind in its wake as it passed mere inches above the ears of the red fox, who scrambled backward to avoid the second blow which followed immediately. The boar, eyes ablaze with mindless fury, roared and stamped at the ground. Alexander leaped to the side just as the charging Sir Reginald Catesby reached him, rolling into the dust of the garden path and pushing himself back to his feet just in time to see the boar smack headfirst into the brick wall of the garden's perimeter.

"Alex," shouted an alarmed voice from the veranda. The fox looked up into the frantic, impossibly blue eyes of another boar. Before he could move or speak, a blustering rumble rose from the staggered Sir Reginald, leaning against the wall to steady himself.

"I told you to stay inside, boy. You've done enough damage to the family name already," rumbled the boar, still leaning heavily on the brick.

"Sir Reginald," said Alexander, dusting off his jacket and straightening his waistcoat, "If you'll permit me to explain-"

"There's nothing to explain, chicken thief. I know what you are." grumbled the boar as he rounded on Alexander.

The fox raised both paws in a placating gesture. "If you please, Sir Reginald, such language is hardly necessary. This has all been a great misunderstanding."

"Father, if you would just listen-"

"Shut it, Philip. This ain't the time for your limp-wristed chattering," The boar spat.

Philip looked stricken. He opened his mouth to speak again, but instead closed it and slunk off into the house, risking one last, worried glance back at Alexander, who stood squared off with the hulking mass of muscle that was his father. The fox stood like the branch of a willow before an oncoming hurricane. Philip gnawed on his lip momentarily before disappearing into the house.

"Sir, I-"

"Shut your cocksucking mouth, you filthy degenerate."

"*Really*. So that is how it is to be played. If you will just listen to me for a moment, Sir Reginald, I can explain the source of the rumors that have quite plainly come to your ears."

"I know where they come from. They come from Father Andrews, so there ain't no point in denyin'em."

Alexander began to laugh. "Sir, would it surprise you to know that on no fewer than three separate occasions I have had to rebuff the amorous advances of the good priest?"

"Liar," shouted Sir Reginald, but did not take a step forward, nor throw a punch. Alexander smiled inwardly. He had his attention now.

"Oh no, sir, I assure you, it is the truth. And because I spurned his attentions, he has contrived to cast aspersions on my character. I regret that it involved your son, but Philip is my dearest friend in all the world. It was the simplest matter to plant the seeds of doubt among his parishioners and then to come to you directly with his poisonous accusations."

"Andrews is a man of God. He ain't interested in the type of sin you're tryin' to lay on him."

A quavering, just slightly, in his voice. A momentary loss of confidence. Excellent. Just a little more...

"Sir Reginald, I must be blunt. A priest is in a position wherein he is thought to be above reproach. But it is from exactly that position that the greatest evils can be done, do you not agree? And think about it for a moment, both your son and I are active, physically fit, and dare I say, rugged? There isn't a hint of effeminacy about either of us, but yet how many times have you seen the rector behave in a way that, were he not a priest you'd think were the mannerisms of a rent boy on the street?"

"I...well... now that you mention it-"

"He's—and you will pardon my indiscretion here sir—a prancing, limp-wristed fairy if ever I saw one, and in my profession I have seen many, always trying to hide their twisted, unholy desires. Always, their mannerisms slip through. I trust that this conversation will not leave these walls, for a man of God is powerful indeed and I, but a lowly author and poet, already of questionable morals where society is concerned, could not hope to counter him in open court."

The boar folded his massive arms. The action stretched the already tight fabric of his vest and tailcoat. Simon quietly swallowed, his mouth beginning to dry up. His eye fell on the gold rings he wore around both of his tusks, symbols of both his wealth and his influence. His sheer size conveyed all that needed to be understood about his power. The boar towered over him, and could likely snap him like a twig. He had to resist the innate urge to tuck his tail between his legs. Instead, he forced a soft smile and a tail wag. The boar's green eyes pierced straight into him. He felt as if they were literally drilling holes through his skull. A deep rumble issued from the boar's chest.

"Hnn…"

"I know what I've said is a lot to take in, Sir Reginald. Please, take some time to think things over fully. In the meantime, given the rumors flying about, I think I should make no further visits to your home to visit with Philip, at least for the time being. That should help allay some of the ongoing rumor-mongering."

The silence between the two was interminable. Alexander dared not twitch a muscle lest he set off the boar's rage once more.

"You should leave, yes. By the back exit. I'll consider what you said, but I'm not makin' any promises that you and I are gonna be friends."

Alexander scooped his silk top hat from the patio table, adjusted it on his head, flicking his ears to adjust the specially designed holes for comfort, and with a wag and a bow excused himself through the servants' entrance at the rear of the house and made his way to a neighboring street via an alleyway.

Well, that could have gone better, old chap.

Alexander leaned wearily against a pillar-box near the curb, finally letting his breathing return to normal. He hadn't realized he'd been holding each breath while talking to Sir Reginald until

173

that moment. That was the closest he'd come to being beaten up over his romantic proclivities since he was a kit. He smiled, now, remembering his first kiss. Not from some sweet, coy female, who giggled and led him away under the cool shade of a mulberry bush, but another young kit, the son of his family's gardener. Patrick, his name had been. He'd showed Alexander so much about caring for the flora of the iconic English garden, and was so warm and open, that Alexander couldn't help falling in love with him.

Of course he knew it was wrong, even then. His father had been a barrister and he caught wind of the cases being rushed through the courts. The polite term was "gross indecency." But still, the first time the young male had timidly taken his paw had been magical, as if lightning had shot through Alexander. He tingled even now at the memory of that. Then, in the shadowed cloister of hedge maze, when he'd worked up the courage, and kissed him. He remembered the thundering of his heart and the return of the lightning in his veins at that moment.

Rumors of Alexander's indiscretions had contributed to the early death of his father, worn down by the private, unspoken scorn of public opinion and gossip. He could still feel his father's icy gaze from what turned out to be his deathbed. It was the societal scorn that dogged him. Alexander Stewart, the son of a decidedly middle-class imports merchant, with an equally pedestrian brain, had risen to some notoriety by being every inch the stereotype of the crafty fox. He had certainly surpassed his father's wildest dreams for him. But like Icarus, such a rise could easily precipitate a catastrophic fall.

"Alexander."

The fox suppressed his natural flinch at having been snuck up on, and did not turn to face the source of the voice. He did not need to.

"Don't you think tempting fate is a bit risky given what just happened, Philip? I don't relish the thought of spending years of my life smashing boulders in prison."

The boar huffed and stepped out of the shadows. Alexander caught the scent of salt.

"I'm sorry, Alexander, truly."

The boar sniffed. Alexander caught sight of his puffy eyes and realized what the salty scent had been. Philip had been crying.

174

The puffiness marred what were, while not traditionally-speaking 'handsome', at least unique and striking features. His bone structure with its pronounced cheekbones could stand up to any classical Roman wolf's statue in Alexander's opinion.

The fox slipped his handkerchief from his pocket and put his arms around Philip, holding him close in the relative seclusion and safety of the alley. He wiped the taller boar's eyes with the cloth.

"I'm sorry, Alexander. I didn't mean for this to happen," sobbed the boar, burying his face into the fox's shoulder. Alexander glanced around to make sure he wasn't being watched, then held Philip tightly against him, stroking his wiry mane.

"My darling, I'm sorry too. Unfortunately for the time being, I think it best that we separate. Our friend the priest, though in dire need of being taken down a peg, is more or less unassailable."

The boar wiped his tears on his sleeve and cleared his throat. "There's a way, Alexander. There is a group of people who work for my father who—"

"No, Philip. I think it's better that we don't try. We will only make things worse for ourselves." The fox sighed and pulled back so he could look into Philip's goldenrod eyes. "I hope that one day we can once again spend our nights in each other's company, Philip."

He stepped back, holding the boar's gaze.

"But not now."

* * *

Alexander's tail lashed furiously as he stalked his way to the lavishly appointed rooms he kept near Whitehall. His paw ached from the death grip with which he clutched the cold, heavy metal of the head of his cane.

Andrews.

"And thus do I clothe my naked villainy with old odd-ends stol'n out of holy writ, and seem a saint when most I play the devil," the fox muttered, recalling the sinister machinations of Shakespeare's hunchbacked king Richard III, though perhaps Cardinal Wolsey from Henry VIII would be a better comparison.

A hansom cab rolled by on the cobblestones of the street, splashing a puddle of standing water onto the pavement ahead. Alexander

175

stopped, staring. He swallowed, feeling the lump in his throat. The priest's intelligent eyes and smirking, arrogant face filled his mind. The mouse mocked him, laughed at him from the unassailable tower built on a foundation of false piety. The fox gripped the cane more tightly, feeling the slight stab of pain that brought focus.

Alexander could sue him for slander. There was, after all, no evidence of the carnal crimes that the rector intimated. The fox had been very, very careful of that. He frowned.

Wilde had proven the futility of fighting these people in court. Alexander did not want to fall so far as that. Firstly, he was not nearly so well known and respected in literary circles and among the general populace as Wilde had been. That alone made his chances for a positive outcome less salutary. Second, while he was quite well-to-do by any modern standard, a court battle could end that in an instant.

Sir Reginald Bolingbroke was the other variable. He was, though blustering and physically intimidating, one of the best businessmen in all of the Empire, and squeaky clean as far as his life was concerned. He was a member of several clubs, all of them completely aboveboard and boasting the highest ranking members of the peerage and in some cases members of the royal family itself. Given his working class upbringing, which still leaked out in the boar's rough speech and manners, his rise was seen by some as indicative of the Empire itself. He had a reputation for being God-fearing and pious, absurdly over-generous in dealings with his employees and exacting in his demand that the strictures of business be always observed. He had once shut down an entire factory floor because he had discovered that an appropriate contract was not in place regarding incoming raw materials. His assistants and partners had all assured him that it would be fine, that it was a minor mistake and not worth the cost of shutting down, but according to the story, Bolingbroke would not hear of another moment of work being done until the paperwork was properly signed and in his hands. He had even paid his workers the full day's wages when he sent them home.

The one thing that did not seem to come near him was embarrassment or scandal. No one had managed, though many had tried, to find something to discredit the magnate. It was as if he were coated with a fine oil, and nothing stuck or could grip onto him. His rivals tended to self-destruct, hoisted by their own petard when some scheme or another collapsed around their ears, and the downfall of these creatures only increased Sir Reginald's influence. Obviously if he were able to maintain the high road when his competitors were behaving in a dastardly or immoral way, then he was one with whom it paid to be friends. Unfortunately that meant that he would do anything necessary to protect that reputation, and if that meant kicking Alexander to the curb to keep scandal away from his son and by extension, himself, then so be it.

Alexander sighed and continued on his path, stepping lightly over the water spread in his path by the cab. It felt disgusting, somehow. Slimy. He didn't smell anything particularly disgusting in the water, but the feeling set his fur standing on end. So that was it? Andrews was invincible and his only hope of freeing himself from the threat of persecution and imprisonment brought on by him and his flock was to kneel to him and pay him homage as if he were, if not the Christian God, then the Greek god Dionysus.

The thought of it, of pleasuring the doughy, unpleasant, small-minded little mouse, made his gorge rise. He swallowed and took a deep breath to center himself. This would be resolved, one way or another, and dwelling on it, worrying at it like a feral dog with a chew toy, would not help matters. His ears twitched. It wasn't the worst proposition he could imagine, simply agreeing to the rector's demands and being done with it. After all, wouldn't that leave him free to…

To what? Secretly court Philip? *To what end?* asked that cynical part of his mind. *What is the purpose, after all, if you can never publicly proclaim your love?*

If it must be secret, then it must be secret. At least it will be a love that is my love and not forced or false or desperate, he answered himself.

And without meaning to, he turned on his heel and set off for Saint Matthew's, the parish led by that pious mouse of God, Galen Andrews.

* * *

The edifice of Saint Matthew's was of the new aesthetic, almost colonial in its simplicity. Its lines were clean, its stone façade as yet unstained by the poisonous London air. Alexander paced up and down, staring at the building each time he passed it and feeling his heart sink lower and lower into the pit of his stomach. Part of him, the part that saw the filth of the world and the motivations of sentient creatures for what they were, knew that submitting to this would not make the scandal disappear. This was the blind hope that led all victims of blackmail into their inescapable quagmire of shame and obedience. But on the other paw, what hope did he have that it could go away on its own?

There was none, and Alexander knew it. His whiskers and tail drooped as if the raincloud that had been hovering over him since he had left Philip's house had burst, soaking him ears to tail in regret and hopeless despair. He swallowed the lump in his throat and pushed open the door, stepping from the relative warmth of the sunlight into the cool vestibule. There were no worshippers in the plushly upholstered pews quietly berating themselves before an effigy of Christ. No line of them waiting their turn at the confessional. In fact, there was no effigy of Christ, or ornate stained glass windows depicting scenes from the Bible. The windows were colorful, yes, but abstract, displaying only the symbol of the cross. Even the cross above the altar was sanitized. Simple, plain, and unadorned. It always felt to Alexander that churches like this had taken all of the flavor out of religion lest someone start to experience a positive feeling.

"Alexander Stewart," squeaked an unpleasant high-pitched voice from off to the fox's left. The rector stood at the foot of a carpeted wooden staircase leading into the bell tower. The mouse was a few inches shorter than Alexander, lean, but with just a hint of pudge about the belly from a life lived mostly without difficult physical exertion. He was dressed simply, in black trousers and a grey shirt with its priest's collar intact. "I had been wondering when you would grace my sanctuary with your presence."

"You knew I'd come eventually."

"Quite, quite. Please, won't you step into my office? It is a fair bit more comfortable, and more private. I am sure you would not care for our conversation to be overheard."

Alexander gritted his teeth and followed the mouse as he led the way through a door to the side of the vestibule. The fox's paws sank into the lush carpeting that had been laid down the center of the corridor. No squeaks of old wood or building settling reached his sensitive ears. Everything looked as if it had just been built.

The office was furnished with fine mahogany, from the desk to the shelves and the decorative wood accents that stood out from the pale blue of the walls. The accents were plain and unadorned, but pretentiously so. It made a show of being simple and unadorned, rather than simply being so. rector Andrews slipped into the padded leather chair behind the desk. He looked like a child sitting in his father's study for the first time, but there was no childlike innocence in the diminutive rector. His unblinking grey eyes moved like little machines, analyzing the fox, taking in every slight movement, every twitch, every uncomfortable shift.

"I assume by now you've had a chance to *converse* with Reginald?" The mouse's short muzzle cracked into a nasty grin, revealing pearly white, perfect teeth. The sneer in his tone, despite the placid look on his face, made Alexander want to snap at him. Instead, he gritted his teeth, feeling the pressure that bordered on pain as his back teeth made contact and kept going. Were his teeth not the teeth of a predator he was certain he'd have cracked them.

"Converse would be a nice way of putting it."

The mouse rasped a laugh. "Oh yes, I'm sure. Reginald is known for his temper, after all. Quite the champion boxer in his day. But where are my manners? I haven't offered you tea or biscuits. I have a lovely selection available. One of my few indulgent vices, you know."

Andrews opened a wooden box, offering a selection of teabags to Alexander. He almost reached for one. God knew he could use the drink to steady his already frayed nerves. His tail twitched and lashed behind him through the rail of the chair and it was all he could do to remain still.

"No. You know why I'm here, and I'd rather not prolong it."

"Suit yourself," said the mouse warmly, closing the box and placing it back in the desk drawer from whence it had come.

"Now what is it you want me to do for you?"

The mouse's grey eyes twinkled. "Oh, many things, Alexander. I have so been hoping that you would change your mind."

"You didn't leave me a choice."

Andrews chuckled, shaking his head. "No, I suppose I didn't. But let's not dwell on the unpleasantness of such things. The Lord has delivered you to me so that I may purge you of your sins. By His grace you will be forgiven and purified."

"Purging me of sins?"

Alexander shook his head, disbelief dripping from his expression.

The mouse stood up and came around the desk, never dropping his warm, genuine smile. The longer his face maintained that expression the more the fox's fur stood on end.

"Through the shepherd shall the sheep know the abiding love of our Lord. Trust me, Alexander. We can know the Lord together."

Everything inside him screamed for him to run. Alexander's heart pounded, and he found himself forced to control his breathing to keep it steady. The priest placed a paw on his thigh. Alexander couldn't move, now.

"If- if we do this, will it be over? Will you let me live in peace?"

"The Lord brings us all peace, Alexander."

He still hadn't moved his paw. The fox felt a stirring in his sheath, the tightening of his trousers. His eyes stung at his body's betrayal.

Andrews abruptly moved away behind the fox. He heard the clicking of the door lock, and the creaking of the mouse's light footsteps as he returned to view.

"Just to make certain no one interrupts us. Can't imagine that they would, but you know, someone might get the wrong idea."

Alexander successfully fought the urge to bolt when he felt the tingling caress of the mouse's fingertips along the sides of his neck.

This is for Philip, he told himself, squeezing his eyes shut and forcing his shoulders to relax under the mouse's attentions.

"Mm, that's it, my fox. Just relax. Everything will be fine. The Lord is with us in His divine perfection."

Oh how Alexander wished the mouse would stop saying things like that.

"Now, stand up, my fox," said Andrews, again stepping before Alexander. This time, his paws found not the fox's thighs but his own paws, taking them and lifting them in a gesture of helping him to rise. He did so, his body mechanically obeying even as his mind tried to retreat. He had thought this would be so easy, coming here.

If he just submitted this once, he could be free. He repeated that to himself like a mantra as the mouse looked him up and down.

"Disrobe, Alexander."

Alexander snapped back to attention, startled by the directness of the command. "What? Here? But, there's no bed or-"

"The bed is sacred to marital relations. You are a sinner and you will kneel in the dust like a sinner. Thus does the Lord prepare our souls for redemption. Disrobe."

"I want your assurance first that when this is done, you will leave Philip and I in peace."

"Through the Lord, all men find peace. I represent the Lord."

When Alexander reached for his jacket's lapels, he hesitated again.

"Disrobe." The word was now a command, sharp as a thunderclap. The fox squeezed his eyes shut. Just this once. For Philip and for freedom. He could do this. He had to do this. The jacket fell away. Then the waistcoat joined it, crumpled and discarded.

God forgive me...

The fabric of his trousers brushed against his sheath through his undergarments, sending a spasm of unwanted pleasure through him. He felt the heat rising in his cheeks and ears. His tail clung to his leg. He felt his member begin to peek out. Inwardly he swore, he screamed, he begged his body not to do this, not to react. He had wanted to do this without the feeling of desire, to be a neutral plaything, a doll that the mouse could use and discard. He had not wanted to be himself, with desires and yearnings and the ache of a body demanding release.

"Your body is addicted to its sin, I see. Filthy fox. Do not hide your nakedness before the Lord! Remove those garments of shame!"

Alexander swallowed, focusing only on the physical task at hand and doing everything he could not to think about the grey eyes of the mouse wandering over him. He pulled the undershirt over his head and dropped it to the floor. The air in the office felt cool on his exposed fur. He gripped the band of the constrictive flannel underpants, hesitating only a moment before pushing them down to his ankles.

The musky scent of his arousal reached his nostrils and he felt the cool air on his exposed member. Finally opening his eyes again,

181

he looked at the Mouse, who stood rapt at the sight of the fox's naked form.

"Oh, my. The Lord built a glorious specimen in you, Alexander."

Alexander's ears and tail drooped under the mouse's unyielding gaze.

"Now," the rector said. "Kneel."

Alexander stooped, dropping to one knee, carefully keeping his expression neutral. Inside, his mind raged, swore, demanded that he not submit to this indignity. He could feel the lineage of his father's howling with rage, commanding him to spit, to bite, to claw, to fight his way to freedom, but that freedom was a cage and he knew it and so he quietly waited, his expression reflecting something akin to admiration of the pudgy rector, still fully clothed, standing above him.

The flash of pain across Alexander's muzzle drove everything else from his mind. He was laying on his side. When did that happen?

"You kneel on one knee to creatures of this world. You kneel on two knees to God, sinner."

The fox suppressed a growl and returned to a kneeling position, this time obediently on both knees.

"Now pray."

"What"

Smack! This time the blow struck him from the other side.

"Pray. Pray for your salvation from sin. Confess your loathsome desires to the Lord." Here, the mouse placed a stoneware crucifix on the edge of the desk. "Bow before God, on your hands and knees. Avert your filthy eyes."

Oh God this is really happening.

In his mind, Alexander was already retreating to his boyhood place of safety. He bent over onto his elbows, lowering his head to the floor, eyes squeezed shut. He chose to do this. He chose to allow this to happen because it was the only way to be with Philip in any measure of safety. But now that he was here, compromised, on the floor of the rector's office, being 'cleansed of his sins', the fox was regretting not being crafty enough to find another way. There was *always* another way for a fox.

He felt the cleft of his rump being slathered with something slippery and knew what was about to happen. He forced himself to relax, keeping his eyes shut and thinking of that country estate, the sunny summer days when he had been innocent and played games with the first love of his life, when that first kiss had happened—

"Mrrrrf!"

He felt the sting of the mouse's member pushing its way into him. He was not accustomed to being the receiving partner and even Andrews's mercifully diminutive size stabbed like a knife.

His own shaft throbbed and ached. The mouse was not large but was managing to hit something within the fox that made his traitorous body somehow even more aroused. He could feel the drops of fluid landing on the wooden floor beneath him. His eyes stung as he fought back tears. For Philip, this was worth it. For Philip and for freedom.

The mouse was muttering prayer after prayer, each one growing louder and more fervent than the last, begging for Alexander's salvation from his horrible sin. His thrusts grew wilder and more powerful with each moment that passed. Alexander felt himself gripped tightly by the hips and pulled against the mouse, who pounded into him ever harder, with the regularity and force of a steam engine.

"God forgive him his sins!"

He felt Andrews stiffen and send several spurts of hot seed deep within him. The pressure inside him lessened as the shaft was retracted, with the rector shooting more sticky fluid onto the fox's rump, tail, and lower back. Alexander heard a light thump as the rector fell backward off of him. He turned to look and saw him already pulling up his pants. Alexander lay on his side, feeling disgusted, broken, and violated. But it was done now. It was over.

Andrews stood up and walked to one of the side doors leading to the rector's private living quarters.

"Get out of here. I'll see you back here tomorrow," he said, not looking back.

"What," Alexander yelped, the tainted feeling growing inside him subsumed within the electric jolt of shock, fear, and anger.

"You didn't think it was going to be that simple, did you? No, no, my child. The Catholics have one tenet that I agree with. Some sins require penance. Yours is not nearly over. In the meantime, I would not suggest that you try to mingle very much in high society.

183

I think you'll find a good many doors closed to you," he said, cold disdain apparent in his tone. "Also, use that spare bathroom to clean yourself before leaving. Try to leave without doing so and I'll make sure you're put into prison for your depravity."

Alexander tried to stand, tried to force his body to work long enough to get his hands wrapped around the mouse's scrawny neck, but found that he couldn't bring himself to claw his way off the floor. His heart and insides felt like they'd been eaten by acid.

The mouse was gone, the door shutting with a resounding thud, followed by the faint sound of the lock mechanism.

Alexander curled around himself and sobbed.

* * *

The fox wandered aimlessly for hours, having managed somehow to clean and dress himself and stagger out of the church unhindered. He cringed under the cold glares he occasionally perceived from passing strangers. They all knew. They knew what he was, what he had done. He knew it.

He found himself in front of yet another church, staring up at its gothic edifice and the stone angels of various species staring down at him solemnly. He thought of turning away, but he did not know of anywhere he could go. He certainly couldn't go to Philip, not after what he'd done, and not still covered in the mouse's rank scent.

He'd done as ordered and cleaned himself, going so far as to brush what for a church mouse must have been a very expensive perfumed powder into his fur. Even so, every so often the mixture of the perfumed powder and the musk of the mouse's loins wafted into his nostrils, and he had to hold onto a nearby wall to keep himself from collapsing in tears in the middle of the street. He'd wind up in Bedlam for sure, at minimum, and if any canids were serving as doctors or orderlies, and smelled the musk of another male…well, once he was declared sane enough for trial, he'd be sent to prison, breaking rocks by day and likely being broken nightly, just as the mouse had broken him, before dying in disgrace, likely contracting the various diseases of the night.

The fox gnawed on his claws without realizing what he was doing. The pain as his sharp fangs dug into the flesh around the base of his claws jerked him back to awareness. All of the rage and humiliation flooded over him as the world came back into focus. He didn't need to confess his sins. He needed Philip. He wanted his boar to hold him and kiss his cheek and nuzzle his ears and tell him that everything was going to be okay, that everything was forgiven and that nobody really knew that they had been seeing each other.

The fox did not sleep a wink that night. Every time he tried, his mind conjured up images of Andrews atop him and inside of him, filling him with disgust and humiliation all over again. And his body betrayed him each time, his member stiffening and aching for contact and release. And each time he gave into the urge to take himself in his paws, the mental image would shift to a heartbroken, sobbing boar, his eyes searching Alexander's and conveying but one unspoken, silent question. *Why?*

When the harsh light of dawn finally broke through the grimy windows of his bedroom, he wasn't sure whether he had slept at all. He dragged himself out of his bed, then combed scented powder through his fur, brushing extra into the fur on and under his tail, hoping that the scent would have faded by now. Not that it mattered much, as unless he figured out a new plan, he would be covered by the mouse's musk again this afternoon. With that thought threatening to make him sick, he shook his head, hoping to clear it. He had to focus and puzzle out the logic. Andrews wouldn't have done more than make veiled comments about him and Philip, and only to certain key people. He couldn't be too obvious about anything or he'd tip his hand. At the least he'd lose what he'd set out to gain, Alexander's obedience and compliance. And his silence. Alexander clenched his fists. Not for the first time, the thought passed through his mind that there was no way out without removing the mouse permanently. If he did so, however, he would become an instant suspect in the case. No doubt the rector's rumor mongering would give him all of the ready testimonies that the state could desire when prosecuting him, and Alexander Stewart would find himself at the long end of a short rope.

He clenched his fists again, listening to the pleasing sound of his knuckles cracking, and stormed off towards the church, turning the problem over in his mind at every angle and finding no solution. So that was it then. Barring taking his own life, or killing the rector, there was no escape. He was the rector's whore, or he was an outcast from society, or he was in prison. Or he was in the gallows. What would Philip say?

The fox rubbed his eyes. They stung from the salt of hours of crying and from lack of sufficient rest. He'd already lost Philip. He had to assume that. If he didn't, he was a fool, simple and naïve, and unworthy of serious consideration. His ears burned with the heat of shame. *No.* He gritted his teeth. This was not him. This wasn't his doing. He saw his writing desk, strewn with papers and sections of a new draft of a novel. He glared, bleary-eyed at the papers, and slumped across the creaking wooden floor, scooping a stack of them up and flinging them away like a flock of startled pigeons. The bells of the great clock tower chimed the hour, and Alexander realized that he had to prepare to meet the unholy priest yet again. He slipped into the bathroom and began to make himself presentable.

This time was quicker. The mouse didn't have time to take him from behind like before. This time, the order was to kneel and pray, and to open wide. Alexander didn't like to brag, but that was something he *was* good at, and it showed. He had milked the rector dry in under ten minutes. It was a mercy that Andrews had something of a hair trigger and at least he could finish him off and be gone. If he had to continue servicing him for the foreseeable future, at least he could deny him the pleasure of a lengthy interlude.

The taste though, lingered, and served to remind him of his shame. He had scrubbed at his tongue with the wool of his coat, with his own fur, his claws, even a scrap stick he found along what passed for a garden path near the back of the church—the mouse had told him he was no longer to arrive or leave by the front doors of the church. Too much potential for scandal, after all—but he could still taste the musk.

Finally, having spent two hours in a tavern guzzling the cheapest gin he could stomach, the flavor of the mouse's seed no longer permeated his mouth. Well, it did, but with the world having gone a little unstable as he staggered his way out of the establishment, and his face having gone somewhat numb, he found that he no longer cared, either about the taste or his destination.

Getting drunk was stupid. So, so stupid. What was he doing? He shook his head and nearly fell flat onto the ground. He was a fox. If he was going to live up to one stereotype he needed to live up to another, and figure his way out of this mess. It wasn't divine punishment. What he had wasn't a sin. Love was not a sin! The rest of society might not agree, but to the devil with the rest of society! Alexander shook a silent fist at the carved crest on a municipal building as he passed it. Philip could help him. Philip would know what to do. He wasn't as clever as his fox paramour when it came to games of wit and wordplay, but he had been raised by the wiliest businessman in the Empire.

A flash of light ignited in his cloudy brain. Philip had said something about people who worked for his father. Maybe he already had an idea, and as usual Alexander was too busy wallowing in his own feelings to notice. The fox couldn't remember if there was more to the conversation, but he wobbled off to where he could find out.

* * *

The sun had long since set when the fox finally summoned enough courage to stagger out of the darkened alley across from Lord Bolingbroke's town home. Alexander watched as the hulking boar hauled himself into his carriage and drove away, probably for a night at one of the music halls. When the vehicle had rounded the corner and disappeared out of sight, he strolled casually—or as casually as one in his current state could manage—across to the alley beside the townhouse and into the garden beyond the servant's entrance. He stopped and stood swaying beneath the one lit window in the upstairs of the house.

"Philip," he hissed at the window, which was open just a crack. The act made the world wobble and he had to stop.

After determining that he could not speak simultaneously loud enough to be heard and quiet enough to not draw attention from the neighbors and passers-by, he determined that the direct approach would be better. Holding his tail stiff behind him for balance, he bent over and picked up a pea-sized river stone from the garden and tossed it at the window. It missed entirely, clacking against the brick of the house no louder than his whisper had been.

Alexander fumed, swaying on his feet and bending for another stone. His paw found one, and he hurled it once more, this time connecting. However, he had perhaps underestimated the strength of his throw and the glass cracked in a jagged spiderweb pattern from the point of impact.

"Damn it," he muttered as he wobbled too far and fell backward onto his rear. If he weren't so inebriated, that would hurt. He'd probably feel it tomorrow.

"What the devil," shouted a large silhouette from the now fully-open cracked window above. "Who is it? Who's there?"

"Ph-Philip…" moaned Alexander, all his joints suddenly aching.

The shape gasped, then disappeared quickly back inside. After what felt like three hours and instantaneously all at once Philip was kneeling by the fox's side. The fox's eyes teared up at the sight of his handsome boar kneeling next to him and wrapping the fox in his massive arms.

He wasn't sure what happened after that for a while. Everything turned into something of a dark blur swirling around his head. He felt himself being lifted and carried at one point before darkness completely claimed him.

* * *

The fox woke to Philip watching him from a chair beside the bed, grave concern chiseled into the lines of his young face. Alexander sat up, which he immediately determined was a mistake as the room spun around at least twice before he collapsed back onto the bed to make it stop. It finally did, but still vibrated around the edges a little too much.

"What are you doing here, Alexander?"

"Apparently coming to vandalize your house," the fox said. Somewhere beneath the gin fog in his brain he noted that his speech wasn't slurring as badly as it had been.

"Very funny, fluff," Philip said. He reached out and stroked the fox's ears. Alexander felt the wobbling of the world become more manageable in that fleeting moment of contact.

"But seriously, what are you doing here? You're lucky tonight is father's night at the Metropolitan Club or you could be in a world of trouble. As it is I'm going to have to scent the room to keep him from smelling you."

188

"Needed to see you. I'm an idiot, Philip. A stupid, selfish idiot. And I need to hear that everything is going to be okay."

"Father will come around, Alex, though I think he's not very convinced of the story you told him about Rector Andrews. This will all blow over soon." The boar gave him another pet and a warm smile.

"No… It's not going to blow over unless we make it blow over."

"Of course it is. Rumors come and go and nobody can prove anything, Alex. Have a little faith."

That last remark felt like a spear twisting the fox's guts before finally piercing his beating heart. He sank into the pillow, staring vacantly up at the ceiling. His eyes were unfocused and tears welled up in them.

"Philip… I made a mistake. A horrible one. I thought that if I could just give him what he wanted, that I could make this go away. But it didn't work. He won't let me go now."

There it was. It was out now. Any minute, the boar would toss him unceremoniously out the door into the gathering night.

Alexander felt a huge ham shank of a paw lift his own from the bed. He winced, waiting for the jerk and lift that marked the end of his welcome in Philip's house, not to mention his life. It never came.

The boar held his hand firmly but with the same gentleness he had always displayed in their secret courtship. When Alexander opened his teary eyes again, the expression on his boar had changed, the lines of his face etched with a cold fury. Not one directed at him, but fury on his behalf. The rage of having the one you love hurt and being unable to stop it. Alexander recognized that look. He'd worn it himself, in adolescence, watching his friend, his first kiss and first real love, be dragged away and whipped because he didn't do things the 'right' way. There was the same resolution in the boar's sharply defined features as the fox had worn those many years ago, but something was missing. Absent was the despair, the resignation to the rule of another, stronger and better-connected. Alexander in that moment had no doubt that had Philip been placed in the position he had been with the rector, that Philip would have snapped the mouse in two like the weak little twig that he was.

"This won't stand, Alex. We're going to have to take care of him once and for all," the boar sneered. Alex watched as the boar's snout

189

flared with heavy, angry breathing. He looked every bit as furious as Lord Bolingbroke had when he'd confronted Alexander.

"You can't kill him, if that's what you're thinking. I thought about it, but I'm quite sure that if you do, I'll go to the gallows for it, and probably so will you."

Alexander forced himself to sit up again, this time more slowly, and put his paws on the floor so he could lean forward. The room wasn't shaking now, but he was still well under the influence of the gin. He'd be paying for this tomorrow, he was certain.

"We can't kill him, no, you're right," Philip shook his head, his wiry black mane jostling with the action.

"You said something about people who worked for your father. Is there any chance they could help?"

The boar's expression brightened.

Alexander looked at him quizzically.

"I think I can arrange a meeting with them. You'll have to be the one to go. I can't be seen there right now. I'm too well known, and I think father is having me watched when I leave the house."

"But what—"

"You just do exactly what I say when the time comes. I'll take care of the rest. It'll likely be a few days before I can get you in to see them. Stay strong."

Andrews was mercifully kept preoccupied by other duties for most of the time between Alexander's drunken visit to Philip and when Philip's messenger arrived bearing a sealed letter with specific instructions. He was sending the fox into the depths of Seven Dials, from which many of the upper class did not return, or so popular legend had it. The mouse had summoned him for an interlude only once, and couldn't keep himself erect to finish the deed.

Alexander assembled a disguise as best he could, something that didn't bear so much of his scent, just in case he were to be noticed in the crime-ridden slum. He set out just after dark, hoping that he could avoid being noticed long enough to make it to the address he had been given, and that he would return alive.

* * *

If Whitehall represented the shining city on the hill, then Seven Dials was its fathomless black shadow. Alexander kept his hat pulled low, the collar of his borrowed, worn topcoat turned up. He had opted to forego a walking stick, and so kept his paws shoved into the oversized pockets of the coat to keep from fidgeting.

The scents here would have been enough to make him retch, but he had taken the precaution of dabbing his nose with gin before leaving home. It burned like hellfire at first, but it did the trick of masking the assault upon his olfactory sense. It not only covered up the scents gathering at the gates of his awareness with a fiery battering ram, but also the stench of the gutter that he had smeared onto the back of his topcoat. A dedicated canine nose would pick up on his scent beneath the masking if they could force themselves to sniff through the garbage.

Already a disreputable area in general, the part of Seven Dials in which Alexander now found himself was Sodom itself. The ladies of the evening here were decidedly masculine. As he passed he kept an eye out for police, though he knew better. They didn't come down here unless they came in force, or so the papers claimed. There was nothing here to be redeemed, nothing worth protecting. Anyone who chose to travel or live down here deserved whatever they got simply by association. Whatever Edward Hydes stalked the night through these streets were far worse than even Stevenson's mind could have conceived.

More than once, Alexander felt himself on the verge of bolting when a sneering, rabies-infested indigent stalked by him, or a sailing otter with a bitten off ear eyed him with the lust of a man accustomed to getting what he wanted; The same look he had seen repeatedly on Andrews.

Finally, he came to a ramshackle wooden building that looked as if it had been crammed unceremoniously into a recessed alleyway and forgotten about. The door was painted with a stylized red rabbit's paw. It had been painted in a hurry, as the drips of red paint running down the length of the door indicated. But this is where he would find the one he was looking for.

He delivered the knock, two short and two heavy blows, and waited a respectable distance for acknowledgement. A viewing slit slid open with a *thunk,* a pair of black eyes glinting in the darkness beyond. They stared, expectantly, waiting.

"I am sent by Mr. Goldtusk."

The eyes narrowed, shifting to look for signs of treachery. The slit slammed shut and Alexander heard the clicking of locks and chains. The door creaked open into a dark room that could hardly be called a vestibule but served that function. The smell of burning spices overwhelmed Alexander's nose in spite of the gin. He shuffled inside and the door slammed and locked behind him. With a start, he turned to face the doorkeeper. Whoever he was, he was tall, cloaked head to toe in a black cloak, a mask covering his muzzle.

"What business do you have with us, stranger," the cloaked figure rasped.

"I need a threat removed."

"We are not assassins for hire, boy."

The figure slipped in front of the door, staring at Alexander with those glistening black eyes, unblinking.

"I do not want him killed. Only his reputation."

Another long pause as the figure considered this.

"Who is this threat, and why should we protect you? You are nothing to us."

Alexander swallowed, but forced himself to speak in a measured, confident tone. "Because the threat is not only to me. There is danger to the son of Goldtusk." Alexander pulled a heavy purse from beneath his coat. It contained more money than he had earned in five years as an author. "I have money."

"Money is not the only currency we trade in, boy," the figure hissed, drawing close. Before Alexander realized what had happened, the purse was gone from his hand. "However," the figure cooed, "This is a start. Follow."

The figure glided past Alexander and pulled the heavy drape out of the way revealing a comfortable looking, if cramped, long sitting room. The air smelled heavily of incense and spice here.

"Be seated," commanded the cloaked one.

Alexander obeyed, lowering himself into the indicated wingback.

Two doors, barely three feet apart, along the back wall of the lengthy room opened, and six tall, lean rabbits emerged and filed into a semicircle around the seated fox, keeping a respectable distance.

They all wore sheer silk in rich reds, blues, and greens, and a variety of jewelry and precious metal. Half were male, half female. Their scents were difficult to smell, though the gin had long since worn off, which made his fur stand on end.

The cloaked figure moved to the center of the semicircle, directly opposite the seated fox and pulled the scarf and hood down. Beneath the hood were the long ears and slender face of a jet-black female lapine. She smiled down at him. Her ears were adorned with six or seven gold hoops apiece, glinting in the candlelight.

"I am Ilona. I am the head of this household, and it is I who will make the decision as to whether we will help or not," she said, folding her paws in front of her. "Now, tell me, who is this target," she cooed, all of the gravel and hissing having vanished and leaving a soft velvet musicality in their wake. "And what is the threat to Mr. Goldtusk, exactly?"

Alexander told the story from the beginning, omitting the part about being attacked by Sir Reginald. The rabbits watched with neutral expressions, all save the black one, whose face tightened with concern at each new detail until the fox had finished, and he sat, awaiting an answer as to whether they would help him or damn him to solitude and ruin.

"We will help you. Mr. Goldtusk's son is as dear to us as his father, and we would not see either of them caught up in an irredeemable scandal. Ladies," the black rabbit said, clapping her paws. The female lapines, two brown and one snow white, stood at attention. "Under the circumstances, your services will not be required at present. You may return to your studies."

The females filed out of the room, leaving the three males and Ilona. The black rabbit sat in the chair opposite while the males remained standing, looking straight ahead. Like the females, there were two brown and one white. Unlike the females, their figures were very different. One of the brown lapines was muscular and stocky. He looked powerful and nimble. The second was of what Alexander would consider average build, though he didn't often let his eye fall upon rabbits. The third, the white one, was a few inches taller at the head than the others. His muscles, which were wonderfully framed by the blue silk vest he wore over his bare torso were lean, but well defined enough that the individual lines could be followed even under his fur. His eyes shifted to look at Alexander briefly, before jerking back to their unfocused gaze.

"Rector Andrews is a cunning foe, young fox," Ilona said, gravely. "To fail in defeating him is to invite disaster upon our heads as well as yours and young master Goldtusk." She rose, turning to the three males. "This is a dangerous assignment, and one that cannot be tied back to our house. I will not command you to accept it. If one of you would care to volunteer to help our young vulpine friend, then do so now."

The white rabbit stepped forward immediately. "I will, Lady Ilona."

"Of course *you* would choose this assignment, Devon," Ilona smiled. Alexander looked back and forth between them, wondering what he had missed.

"Now, let us discuss the mission further. You two are dismissed," she said, nodding to the brown males, who turned and silently left the room. "Would you care for tea?"

Alexander graciously accepted the tea, sipping it between answering specific questions about the mouse's habits, his lodgings, and the general area around the church.

"This will require expert timing. There can be no guarantee of success. If we fail, are you prepared to take the consequences upon yourself, if necessary, to protect the one you love?"

The black rabbit's eyes gazed into his own, peering deep. Devon also stared, perhaps even more expectantly that Ilona, if that were possible.

"I am."

"Then let us lay our plans, and may the Trickster guide us."

* * *

The sun dipped low in the sky the following evening as the pair made their way to St. George's church. The young rabbit glided along the pavement silently next to Alexander. He looked light as a feather, almost as if he didn't even need to touch the ground yet did so for amusement's sake. His strides were long and fluid. Alexander was not the sort to be attracted to the effeminate, but were he so inclined this young male would have rated very highly in his esteem indeed.

194

Devon was focused and intense, and did not speak a word as they walked, which suited Alexander just fine. He couldn't talk about what was really on his mind, and his stomach was tied in knots. Anything could go wrong tonight, and if anything did, he was assuredly finished, and likely Philip with him.

The church loomed in the darkness, its multi-hued stained glass windows transmitting the dim glow of lamplight from within. The shadows in the alley leading to the rear entrance concealed the pair as they made their way inside. Alexander couldn't shake the feeling that at any moment the trap would spring. He swallowed, and forced the thoughts down. He pulled the door open and stepped inside. Devon flowed after him, his cloak wrapping around him like liquid shadow.

The lamps were dimmed in the foyer, and completely extinguished in the sanctuary, causing the pair of visitors to cast flickering, sinister shadows along the walls.

"Mister Stewart," murmured the wary voice of the rector, "Whom have you brought with you? I'm afraid I'm very busy this evening."

The mouse stood in the doorway to his office, informally dressed down to his shirtsleeves. His eyes displayed an uncharacteristic dullness. After a moment, the astringent smell of alcohol reached the fox's nose and he realized that the mouse had been drinking, and probably too much from the look of it. His heart did a backflip.

"I have brought this lad who is in need of the same help you have been giving me."

The mouse's grey face twisted, locked in a battle between fury and suspicion. He waved an arm and gestured them into the office, loping in ahead of them. Alexander looked to Devon, whose face was calmly neutral beneath the hood. He nodded once, and followed the mouse into the office. Alexander followed, his heart fluttering.

Andrews closed the door after them, and turned the key in the lock as usual before stalking to his desk, where he stood, eyeing the fox and his cloaked companion each in turn. He did not speak for several long moments.

"So, you have brought another soul, blackened with your sin. Is this your doing, perhaps, Alexander?"

Alexander's lips curled away from his teeth. He started to shout a blasphemy, but Devon stepped deftly between them, throwing his hood back to reveal his slender white ears and sharp features. He kept his head bowed, submissive and contrite, as he spoke.

"My name is Judah, sir" he whispered, "I have lived in Seven Dials for the last few years, ever since my parents died. It's… it's been hard. I've had to do… well, Alexander has told me that I'm not alone. He says you can help."

Andrews eyed the fox with an appraising look. Alexander kept his expression somber, serious, and contrite.

"I thought that you could help him the way you're helping me."

The mouse sneered. "You were a special case, Alexander. I don't have time to take in every stray boy-lover who crosses my doorstep." The mouse leaned in closer, placing his muzzle against the fox's ear and breathed the words, "And bribery will not reduce your penance."

Alexander's heart raced. This had to work.

"Let's get a good look at him."

The rabbit closed his eyes and unfastened the clasp of his cloak, letting it fall to the floor. He was revealed in all his delicious glory. He wore only a pair of tight-fitting pants that hugged the curve of his rump so tightly that the fox could see the divide in his cheeks. It was Alexander's first time getting a look at his body from this angle. The resultant erection threatened to derail everything as he imagined taking the rabbit from behind, perhaps bent over a fence or barrel. The fox shook himself free of that line of thinking. The rabbit was too effeminate for his tastes, really. He preferred the powerful arms and slightly pudgy belly of his boar. Still, the fantasy would have been pleasant, had it not been under such dire circumstances.

He tore his gaze away from the delicious morsel revealed before him and instead focused on rector Andrews's reaction. Exactly as he had hoped, the mouse was leering at his new prey, his mouth agape. When he noticed Alexander looking his way he snapped his jaw shut.

"You know, the Lord must have brought you to me through Alexander. I believe I can help you. Alexander, if you would wait in the next room until I call for you please? Spiritual guidance this specialized must be a private affair between myself, the individual, and, of course, the Lord," the mouse smiled.

"Of course," Alexander said with a polite bow. "May I use the necessary first?"

"Certainly, just don't be long. Judah, please wait here while I retrieve some necessary supplies."

Alexander placed a gentle hand on Devon's shoulder as he passed behind him to reach the side door leading to the bathroom. The mouse left through the opposite door.

As soon as the door clicked shut behind the rector, Alexander began looking frantically around the bathroom. He had been so shaken by what had happened the last time he was in here that he hadn't gotten a good idea of the layout. It was very simple. White and green tile with a washbasin and a clawfoot bathtub, in addition to the toilet and medicine cabinet. He found what he was looking for: a small jar of the scented powder he had used the first time he had had to clean himself here. He slipped that into his pocket and tried the small sliding window along the outside wall. It did not budge, probably was nailed shut.

Damn!

He hurriedly made his way out of the bathroom, and making certain that the rector had not returned, spun and tossed a paw full of perfumed powder into the air and pulled the door shut behind him. He then slipped to the exit door and quietly, but as quickly as he dared, turned the key in the lock, making sure to leave it in the exact position it had been while the lock was engaged.

"Will you be all right, Judah? The rector's guidance can be difficult to endure," Alexander said, loudly enough to carry beyond the closed door, resting a paw on the white rabbit's shoulder. Devon's face bore an expression of concern.

Devon smirked and followed suit. "I will endure anything to be free of my shame, Alexander," he said with a wink. He really was a charming rabbit, Alexander noted with an inward smile. All the more reason to make sure that this whole affair wasn't for nothing.

The creak of the hinge told Alexander that Andrews was returning. No doubt he was listening at the door for any signs of a trap. He reentered the room wearing his canonical vestments and carrying a box, the contents of which Alexander had come to know well.

The fox bowed solemnly to Andrews, and walked past the mouse with no further word, closing the door behind him.

He found himself in a large bedchamber, oak paneling lining the walls and a massive four-poster bed dominating the room. The curtains that hung over the garden-facing window were royal blue with an intertwining brocade pattern. A silver serving tray and its accouterment rested on a bureau. Alexander's rented rooms were well appointed, but this was obscene, especially for a man of the cloth like the rector.

Alexander kept his ears pricked, listening as best he could without putting his head against the thick door, to try and catch what was going on in the next room. He could not make out the conversation clearly, until the mouse's religious fervor caught hold, and the loud prayers began in earnest.

Alexander's paws went clammy. He began shaking uncontrollably, memories of his time in that hell flooding over him and threatening to consume him. He was drowning! He felt the weight of his shame crushing him, pushing him down farther and farther into the depths. Gasping for air, he seized on the image of Philip reaching down into the water, seizing his hand and pulling him upward until he could breathe again.

He'd ended up on the floor, curled around himself and shivering. The cries of religious exaltation from the next room jolted him back to awareness. How much time had passed? The mouse wasn't of great stamina, so if the carnal embrace had begun the fox didn't have much time. He clambered to his feet and ran to the window. He gave the frame an upward tug. It did not open. Panic shot through him. He had to get the window open and get out! He tugged on it again and again but still it didn't budge.

From the other room, he heard "*On your hands and knees for the Lord, sinner!*"

"Jesus," he grumbled, pushing on the window again with as much force as he could safely muster without damaging the glass.

With a groan of protest, the window finally gave way and slid upward until it stopped by the top of the frame with a loud *thunk*. Alexander froze, fur standing on end and tail curled tightly between his legs. He listened for the sound of the door, but could only hear the muffled moaning and preaching that indicated the beginning of the pair's carnal embrace. Alexander put one paw on the windowsill and hoisted himself up, preparing to climb down into the garden beyond when he stopped and looked back at the room. He had time, he hoped.

He hopped down and scurried across the room to an unadorned cedar chest sitting on the rector's nightstand and rifled through it until he found what he was looking for, then quickly restored the contents to their proper order and ran for the window. He climbed to the sill, ready to hop down to freedom, then unscrewed the lid of the scent neutralizing powder and tossed the contents into the air behind him. It wouldn't cover his scent from detailed sniffing, but this wasn't a murder scene. If things went properly he wouldn't need to worry.

As his paws touched the earth of the garden below the window he turned and pulled the window down after him. Just before it closed, his ears pricked to the muffled sound of shouting voices. In a hurry, the fox wiped his pawprints away in the dirt and made for the alley, his pulse thundering in his ears .

When he exited the alley, he forced himself to a brisk walking pace, avoiding his natural urge to run around the block. If he was on time, he'd be on time. If he wasn't, he wasn't. Trying to get there too fast would ruin everything. Everything inside him screamed for him to run, to go and see, but no. He took a leisurely stroll around the block. He came up the sidewalk just in time to see a pair of uniformed policemen chasing after a figure in a black cloak and running straight at him.

"Stop him," one of them, a badger, shouted as he waved his nightstick in the air. The second one, a sleepy-eyed ferret, couldn't shout, as he was too busy blowing his whistle. The cloaked figure's black eyes met Alexander's and gave him an almost imperceptible nod. Alexander reached out and grabbed the figure by the arm. The shape spun and collapsed onto the ground, tangled in his own cloak. The badger policeman staggered to a stop, paws on his knees, breathing heavily. The ferret, in much better shape, trotted to a dignified halt and let the whistle drop from his mouth.

"Ya dinn't haveta run, son," gasped the badger. "We just wanted… to ask ya…question or two."

The ferret looked to Alexander, who had released the figure's arm and stood up, looking very perplexed. "You done good, Mister. We need this one to give us a testimony."

"Uh…here son," said the badger, removing his badge and taking his outer uniform jacket off, "Why don't you wrap this around your waist for now."

The figure had been fully naked under the cloak, white fur now gleaming in the lamplight. Alexander did his best not to look, but he had finally gotten a full idea of the rabbit's physique. Such a lovely creature he was. He sat up and took the officer's uniform jacket, draping it over himself and tying it with the sleeves.

He looked up at the badger and the ferret, then at Alexander, and began to shake and to cry.

"I don't… He made me… it was supposed to help cleanse my sins," the rabbit sobbed. Tears streaked down the fur of his face. It was almost enough to cause Alexander to begin to cry as well.

"We know, it's okay son. We'll keep you out of this as much as possible. You just have to sign a statement for us and we'll take care of him."

The rabbit winced and shied away from the ferret policeman's proffered paw.

"Nobody's gonna hurt you no more, son," said the badger, smiling as much as any badger ever did. He put out his paw, palm up, inviting. The rabbit reached up and took it, and was helped to his feet.

"Thanks again, sir," said the ferret as all three began walking together in the direction of the church. Alexander followed at some distance until they had reached the church. Galen Andrews sat on the steps, surrounded by another two policemen, both large breed dogs, probably mastiffs, as well as a hulking planet of a boar and his much smaller, but equally impressive moon.

Sir Reginald Bolingbroke stood with his massive arms folded across his chest, staring at the rector as if he could burn a hole straight through him. Philip just shook his head repeatedly in disbelief.

"…and caught in the act too! I had my suspicions about ya from the start, Andrews, but I give ya the benefit o' the doubt because yer a clergyman. And this is how ya act?"

"The rabbit tricked me," Andrews screamed, jerking himself to his feet. "This is all a sham! It's a setup by…"

"By who?"

"By *him*!"

The four turned to look at Alexander standing a few paces away from the returning badger, ferret, and rabbit.

"What's going on here? Sir Reginald?"

"And what're you doin' out this way, Alexander, hm," rumbled the boar.

"Well, I was coming down to try and make peace with the rector over those rumors he's been spreading. Let bygones be bygones and all that. What's going on?"

If looks could kill, the mouse's gaze would have put Alexander in an urn full of ashes somewhere in Russia.

The boar looked like he had tasted something incredibly bitter. "It turns out that you weren't lyin' about the good rector's ...ah... proclivities. I came down here because Philip said the rector'd tried to get him to... Well, makes me sick just thinkin' about it, but sure enough we came down with the police to sort the whole mess out and what happened but we caught 'em in the act, makin' that rabbit boy do what he said..."

"Andrews, I told you when I rebuffed you that you couldn't continue like this," said the fox, looking gravely concerned.

The mouse leaped from his seated position with a scream, paws outstretched, and grabbed hold of Alexander's lapels, jerking the fox forward and off balance. Andrews twisted in midair and came down on top of him, driving the wind from his lungs. Alexander felt the mouse's fingers clench around his throat.

The pressure was relieved suddenly when Sir Reginald gripped the mouse by the front of his vestments and lifted him into the air like a rag doll. He planted two punches squarely on the rector's face before tossing him aside on the sidewalk where he landed unconscious. The four police stood aghast. Sir Reginald dusted off his hands and offered one of them to Alexander, pulling the fox to his feet.

"I guess that takes care of that."

* * *

The rector's trial was a swift one. Alexander Stewart took keen pleasure in reading the more sensational articles in the papers. And while he had desperately wanted to avoid being associated with the scandal, his name had become the rallying point around which

201

others brought their own stories of rebuffing the rector's advances to light. In the end, even if the court hadn't found the rector guilty, public opinion would have finished the job.

A side effect of the whole messy affair was that Alexander's books had become some of the best sellers in London.

"It's true what they say," murmured the fox, "Any publicity is good publicity."

He felt the vibrations from the deep contented rumbling in his lover's chest as he chuckled. The fox wrapped his arms around the boar more tightly, burying his nose in Philip's mane and drinking in his scent. Sunlight shone in through the second story window of the fox's bedroom, warming the pair of them.

"I think I'd rather have not gone through that, my love," laughed the boar. "Though I admit that it's nice to have it finished with so we can get back to what matters."

The boar wiggled his plump rear against the fox's sheath. Alexander could already feel his arousal growing again.

"Again? But Philip, we just finished," the fox whined playfully. He ran his paw over the boar's belly.

"We have to make up for lost time, fluff," rumbled Philip, grinding his cleft against Alexander's now fully-exposed, slick shaft..

Alexander grinned and tugged on the boar's shoulder, laying him flat on his back, then leaned in for a kiss. The boar complied, parting his lips to allow the fox better access. Alexander probed the boar's mouth, entwining the boar's thick tongue with his own flatter canid one, caressing and massaging it. He hoisted himself over Philip's thickly muscled legs to plant himself between them, where his turgid member ground against the boar's own growing erection.

Philip whimpered in response. "Please darling," he moaned. "make love to me."

Using one paw to guide himself towards the boar's waiting hole, Alexander pressed his lean frame against the boar's stout roundness, feeling the warmth and vibrations of pleasure from deep within his lover's core. When he could not restrain himself further, he pushed his way inside his lover, already slick with perfumed oil and the seed of their previous embrace. Alexander gasped as he felt the boar's hole grip his member tightly. He began to move inside the boar, whose opening squeezed and milked him.

The pair writhed in mutual ecstasy. Philip's massive thighs gripped the much more slender fox's hips, pulling him more deeply inside. He squeezed his eyes shut, moaning and pleading for more, for the fox to take him harder, faster, to breed him.

Alexander, already weak from the morning's vigorous activities, could not keep at this for long and with a gasp and a long, drawn out, "Ohh God", felt yet another release within Philip's body.

Now spent, the fox rolled off, trying to slip free only to pull Philip with him.

"Ow! Easy fluff! OW!"

"Damn," the fox mumbled, feeling his face and ears flushing with heat.

The boar laughed heartily.

"Nothing to worry about, love. I don't have anywhere to be."

He smiled at Alexander with those goldenrod eyes. Alexander felt his heart melting.

"I however, do," said a soft voice from behind them. The fox yelped and turned, only to see a white rabbit in a cloak over blue silk. He breathed a sigh of relief.

"It's you, Devon. You frightened me out of my wits!"

"What're you doing here," asked Philip, craning his neck to see the figure. Realizing that he had put the pair of them into the most awkward position possible, or apparently out of a simple act of mercy, the rabbit moved into a more convenient field of view. The serious look he bore gave way to an amused smirk.

"I thought it would be a good time to discuss the balance of payment for my part in your little charade with the disgraced clergyman. You're lucky I'm not asking for extra. He was bloody awful. I didn't mind his small stature, mind, but he had no idea what he was doing with it."

Alexander felt the familiar wave of nausea again. As always, he suppressed it. He hoped that one day he would be able to think about what had happened without shame. He noticed that the swelling in his knot had reduced significantly, and slipped free of Philip.

"You couldn't wait until we were dressed," asked Philip in mock annoyance.

Devon grinned. "Not being dressed has never stopped you and I from talking before. By the way, Alexander, you look quite skilled.

I wouldn't mind if you and Philip decided you needed a little exotic spice in your bedchamber on occasion."

The rabbit winked. Alexander stammered for a minute before standing and throwing his robe around himself.

"Ah, right… payment yes… I hope this is what you were after."

He rustled through the top drawer of his dresser, shoving aside undergarments until he found what he was looking for. He pulled out a gold ring, engraved with the holy cross and the symbol of the Church of England.

"What's that," asked Philip, glancing back at Devon, whose eyes were twinkling.

"It's the former rector's signet ring. Useful in the forgery of communications. We've tried to get at one for years with no success. Would've made a few jobs we've done for your father much less convoluted."

"Well, that's that, then," said Alexander, handing over the ring.

"Not quite. There is one other matter that needs attending to before we're square."

The rabbit let the cloak fall to the floor. The pants, which Alexander had thought to be the same blue silk as the first time he had seen the rabbit, were a very fine mesh. He could see everything, including the rabbit's oversized member, standing erect and leaking the tiniest bit of fluid.

The fox looked to Philip, who folded his arms behind his head and grinned.

What a day this was going to be.

For Othello, who continues to push me ahead when I can't find a direction

While the Wind Shook the Barley

by NightEyes DaySpring

It was getting on toward evening when I reached the village of my birth. The train station sat a mile from town, and no one else got off at the stop. I walked down the lane with growing apprehension. It had been years since I had last come home, and the closer I got, the more I wondered if I should have just stayed away.

My red fur stood out against the dusty road, and the expensive suit I wore made me a distinguished looking gentlemen. While I looked the part, I was just a humble fox, even with everything that had happened the last three months. The white fur at my throat no longer bore the stain of coal dust in it, but my paws were still a natural black to remind me of my past.

As I walked into town carrying my suitcase, I felt the pull of eyes on me. My erect ears picked up whispered words like catamite and fairy. I had come to pay my respects, but that didn't matter. They still remembered me for what I had done ten years ago. Only one person commented about my clothes and how well dressed I was.

Of course, there were the lewd ones about me whoring my way through Southampton. Those I knew weren't whispered just for the benefit of the people nearby, but so everyone could hear. I meet their eyes and most of them stopped. A few just grinned. One of the whisperers didn't back down when I looked at him. Instead he stepped away from the door of the local tavern to confront me.

"Funny seeing ya here, Liam," said the lanky red fox. "I didn't think you were evea' going to come back 'ere." He lifted his eyes and met me squarely, definitely. "Finally coming back to pay your dues are ye?"

"Shawn O'Dowd," I nodded. "Funny seeing ya outside of the tavern. Are they out of beer?"

One of Shawn's ears flicked as he walked up close to me. "I'm surprised to see the boys of Southampton haven't whipped that cocky attitude out of ya, or is your cock why they 'aven't?"

I smirked. "You never did seem to mind before."

Shawn snarled and dropped into a fighting stance, but someone rushed up from behind to grab a hold of him.

"Calm down Shawn me boy. Liam hasn't been back in town for five minutes and you're already barking at 'em like a jilted lover," said the badger who held Shawn.

Of course, Shawn was a jilted lover. It had been a long time ago, but Shawn had wanted me to stay in town. He didn't want me to go to England for work. He'd written me a few times after I had lefty, angry about how I'd gone about dissociating myself from Kiltail at his expense. The last I heard, he married a pretty lass, which he showed little interest in except when drunk. His final letter had been the most vitriolic and after that, I had not written him again.

"I think he just needs to sober up a little," I said. It wasn't even dark and the fox reeked of stale alcohol.

The badger patted Shawn on the back and when he didn't calm, he slipped a hand down towards the base of Shawn's tail and pressed. This caused Shawn to relax. The touch was so intimate, that I could tell who was sleeping with the fox now.

"He just needs to get out a bit more. He and the misses are on the rocks again," said the badger as he tried to shoo Shawn off.

I just nodded and watched the two of them walk off. The other person by the tavern door turned his back to me to smoke. The strong smell of Turkish tobacco tickled at my nose.

I looked up. The sign I remembered as a kid was still there, a willow swaying in the breeze, with the name The Sassy Willow written above. I walked up to the door and entered the tavern.

The inside was just like I remembered it. This amazed and depressed me at the same time. So much had changed in the last ten years; I would have thought some of it would be reflected here in Kiltail. So far, the town looked like it did when I left, the paint just more weathered. The inside of the tavern was still dark and smoky from the oil lamps that hung in it. There was also a warm sense to the place that spoke of much better times that had been long ago.

"Good evening," said the barkeep as I walked up. "What brings you to town?" The stoat behind the bar was someone I didn't recognize; a few things had changed. He looked to be in his mid-forties, so there was at least some new blood around here.

"I am looking for the McClearn family. Are t'ey still up at the old farm on the hill?"

"Aye," said the stoat. "That they be."

"Do you have a son? I need someone to run on up and let t'em know Liam McClearn has come back to town to pay his respects."

The bartender put down the rag and glass he'd been polishing. "You're Liam McClearn?"

"Aye." I wagged my tail in slow circles waiting for his response.

He looked me over, with an appreciative eye, noting my tailored coat. "I always envisioned you were more... rough looking then you are," he said finally.

"I spent seven years shoveling coal in a boiler room, friend."

The stoat looked at me surprised. "I didn't think those jobs paid well."

"They don't. They pay enough so you can stay drunk and forget what your life is like."

The stoat eyed me, like I was some type of ghost. "Let me send my son on up. Are you looking for a room for the night?"

"That depends on what comes down the hill. I will though take a good whiskey." I sat down at the bar and put my suitcase down next to my barstool.

"Aye, no problem at all."

* * *

"You lying, cock-swinging son of a bitch!"

I picked myself up off the floor. The stoat hovered behind the bar, unsure of what to do. My father panted hard looming over me.

One of my brothers, Nevan, had him by the scruff of the neck and was trying to yank him back away from me.

"He came 'ere to pay his respects Da. If ye hadn't chased him off, he would 'ave stayed!"

"I ought to chase the both of ya off!"

"Is this how you want us to remember her passing?" Nevan asked.

"Fergal," said the stoat, "there is no need for violence."

"He only came back because she's dead." The old todd shook off his youngest son.

I got up and dusted myself off. My right eye was bruised and starting to swell shut where the old man had given me a good one. "I'm going to say this now so we all understand each other. Ya get one. If you do that again, I am going to haul off and give you one t'at will make mother turn over in her grave."

"You don't have t'e strength you knob jockey," sneered father.

I just growled, hauled off, and punched him in the gut. The old man stumbled back against Nevan. "I shoveled coal for years in a boiler room! Is that not strong enough for you, Da?"

The old man's eyes watered. "I reckon that does toughen you up," he managed to get out.

"Does that make you happy now father?" asked Nevan.

The older fox got his feet back under him and managed to stand straight up. "He is still no son of mine."

"I can catch the next train the morning back to Cork," I growled, crossing my arms

Nevan, gave me an look. "You will do no such thing."

"I will not have him—"

"So help me God, Father, I will punch you myself if that is what it will take to knock sense into you!" yelled Nevan.

The old man was quiet for a moment. "You were all rotten children," he growled. "Fine, but t'ere better not be any trouble upstairs in the night."

Nevan just shook his head. "Come on, 'ets just go home."

The old man walked out of the bar, leaving us both alone with the bartender. I sat back down at the bar and finished my drink in one gulp, letting the whiskey settle my nerves

"Did you have to hit him?" asked Nevan, his ears laid back.

210

I turned in my stool. "Do you think he would 'ave settled down if I didn't?"

Nevan sighed. "He's getting older. He's not got the same endurance he used to have." He leaned against the bar. "At night 'e sits up and pines for Mother."

"When I stood up to shake his hand, he punched me in the face," I grumbled. "At least punching him took some of the fight out of him."

"It hasn't been the same here without you."

I just scowled.

"I've missed you, Mam missed you, and Aithne missed you."

I felt my anger fade away. "Clancy?"

"Not really sure, but he took a job up in the coal mines a year after you left. We see him now and again. I think Father's ranting is why he decided it was time to move on. He did find himself a nice vixen up there."

I sighed. "This all happened ten years ago. Why is he still mad?"

"You're the first born. He wanted you to bring him grandkids. Even though Clancy has two now, he's still not happy."

"Clancy has kids?" I said in surprise.

Nevan shrugged. "Yeah. You miss a lot by not writing letters back home."

"Why did you write me one?"

"I wanted you to know, to maybe see you again, but at least to let you know."

I got up from the barstool and walked over to my brother and hugged him. "Thank you."

"Uh, sure," said the other fox a little embarrassed. "No problem." We broke off and I went over to pick up my suitcase.

"I have to ask," said Nevan, "when did you start wearing tailored suits and jackets. I thought you were working as a stoker."

I picked up the suitcase and swished my tail. "There is a funny story about that."

* * *

POST OFFICE TELEGRAM

RECEIVED FROM CORK IRELAND FOR

CHARLIE BARTHOLOMEW PATTERS
HOTEL ST CROIX BRISTOL ENGLAND

I ARRIVED IN CORK YESTERDAY STOP WILL BE HEADING
UP TO KILTAIL IN THE AFTERNOON BY TRAIN STOP
I AM STILL VERY NERVOUS BUT I NEED TO GET THIS
OVER STOP I WILL SEE YOU BACK IN CORK IN THREE
DAYS STOP GOOD LUCK IN SOUTHAMPTON STOP LIAM

I put down the telegram I had received before embarking and looked out over the railing of the steamer. The coast of Ireland had been there at dawn, just coming into view, and the water glistened in the morning light. The ship appeared to be entering a large bay now.

No one else took breakfast out on deck with me. I wanted to monitor the progress we were making, but the distraction that offered wasn't helping my mood. At least with my gray fur, streaked with red and darker gray, I didn't stand out from a distance. So far, none of the other passengers had come up and tried to talk to me. I wanted to be alone anyway right now.

"Mr. Patters, is there anything you need?" asked the steward who came up to clean up the breakfast dishes. A wolf like me, he had different colorations.

"How soon till we dock?"

The steward looked out over the water. "We're at the mouth of Cork Harbor. It should take about two hours once we pick up the pilot."

"Don't we carry a pilot?"

The steward shook his head. "We'll pick one up though in a few minutes."

I glanced about. "We're in the middle of the bay."

The steward smiled. "Don't worry, we'll pick one up under power. You see that sail out there," he said pointing off toward a small boat.

"Yes."

"That's a pilot boat. Once she pulls alongside, the pilot will transfer over and take us in. Do not worry sir; we'll be in Queenstown on time."

I sighed. "Thank you sir."

The steward cleared off the dishes and left me some tea. I sat alone on the deck watching the ship's progress as she steamed into the bay. On the table I had a copy of yesterday's newspaper folded neatly. The article I had left showing was why I was three days early to Cork. To the casual observer, it would be just an interesting tidbit of gossip, but to me, it was everything.

The article talked about how my father had decided in his closing years of life to leave the bulk of his fortune to my cousin due to "his son's impropriety" and thereby his lack of an heir. That impropriety was currently however dealing with his own family problems.

My response to the old man's tirade was a simple note I had delivered by telegram:

FATHER, STOP I HAVE SEEN THE NEWS AND I HAVE JUST ONE THOUGHT FOR YOU STOP I HOPE YOU CHOKE ON A CRUMPET STOP CHARLIE.

The elder Patters would of course be livid, but I was done with this back and forth arguing. He'd found out when I finally let it slip to him I'd been living with Liam. He did have more fight left in him then I had thought possible. He couldn't recognize my scent, but he still could yell.

It didn't matter anymore though. I might not be a wealthy like him, but I was a successful enough business man to stand on my own. If he wanted to give his money to cousin Ichabod, who would squander it all, let him. My heart wouldn't be swayed.

* * *

The kitchen in the house was small. I watched as Aithne stirred a pot of porridge over the small turf fire. The way she worked reminded me of our mother, and I didn't know how I felt about that.

"Is Father out for the day already?"

She turned to look at me. "Yes. He got up early to tend the animals and then headed into town."

I looked out the door over the fields of barley stretching away from the house. "If he can't stand to be near me, I guess avoiding me is for the best."

Aithne sighed. "Father still loves ya, he just doesn't know how to tell you that."

I pointed at my black eye. "Is punching me in the face how he shows 'is love? Has he hit you or Nevan too?"

She slumped her shoulders forward and put down the ladle she stirred the pot with. She turned to look at me.

"Not anymore. Not since we came of age."

"So the old bugger thinks he can just slap me around? Oh that's rich," I sneered.

"Liam," she spat. "I will not listen to 't'is. Not in our mother's home."

I folded up my arms. "Well I won't impose too long. I can assure you that."

"You're—you're going to leave again?" her ears went flat.

"Did ya think I came home to stay?"

She turned back to the porridge and spooned some out for me. "You should stay a while. We always need help on the farm. Father won't charge you lodgings."

I shook my head. I had taken off the suit and left it to hang. I wore simple laborer's clothes now. I looked the part of a farm hand, but I didn't feel the part. "I can't stay 'ere Aithne. You know that. This isn't my life anymore."

She sat down at the table across for me. "Father will understand if you give him time."

I looked down at the porridge and picked at it in silence. It was simple, just like mother used to make. After a few minutes, I looked back up at her. "How?"

"I don't know how, but I feel he can." She reached out to take his hand.

I squeezed my sister's paw. "I'm catching an ocean liner back to America in less than a week. I don't expect to return again."

"America? Nevan said you were living in Southampton. That's w'ere he sent the letter to."

"The landlady at my last address had my forwarding address. I'm seeing someone Aithne, and we decided England wasn't the place for us. I've been living in New York for the last few months."

She looked away, her ears flat and whiskers drooping. "I didn't know."

214

"As I told Nevan last night after the fight, Charlie is going to be waiting for me in Cork in three days so we can catch a ship back across the ocean."

She was silent then, her body sagging as if the steam had been let out of her. I didn't know what else to say, so I went back to eating the porridge. Together we sat in silence for a while. When I finished I slid the bowl away, and waited for her to speak. Finally, I reached out and patted her hand. She held it, and we stayed this way for a minute until Nevan came into the kitchen. He panted hard.

"Oh good, I found you both," he said out of breath.

We turned to him. Out of the corner of my eye, I could see that Aithne looked upset.

"Yes?" asked Aithne.

"Father had another attack. He fell over in town."

Aithne sighed and got up.

"An attack?" I asked.

"Father has started to have seizures. The doctor told him he needs to cut down on his drinking, but watching Mother pass was hard on him," said Aithne. "We best go and collect him."

"They brought him over to the rectory. Father O'Brien is with him."

"It would be nice if you told me he was having attacks," I grumbled getting up.

"It would be nice if you wrote home occasionally," said Aithne. "You would know."

"It would be nice if Father didn't—"

"Enough!" growled Nevan. "Liam has his life, and we 'ave ours."

Aithne glared at me and then walked to the door to get her coat. Nevan just shook his head at me and walked out. I followed and together, the three of us headed into town.

* * *

"I'm sorry Mr. Patters, but I can't give you a room," said the ermine behind the hotel desk.

"Why not?" I asked taken back. "I have a reservation."

"It would not be appropriate for me to do so."

"Appropriate? What is inappropriate about that? I've stayed here before." I was standing at the front desk in the lobby of one of the large downtown hotels in Cork. I took a coach over from Queenstown and had been looking forward to settling down in my room.

The ermine just shook her head. "There is a place down the road that caters to your kind. You might want to see if they can put you up there."

I blinked. "Excuse me?"

"Down the road there is a pub that caters to men like you. I believe they rent rooms, and you can stay there."

I leaned forward across the desk. "You're telling me you want me to stay at a whore house?"

"Oh no. A brothel is too good for you. It's one of those places frequented by you homosexuals."

My mouth hung agape. I had been to places like that befor; that had been where I had met Liam, but the hotel was refusing my reservation and telling me that was where I belonged?

"Do you know who I am?" I asked.

"Everyone knows who you are. I do read the papers, and I will not have this hotel sullied by someone who has tarnished the great Patters' name. We only rent to respectable guests in our hotel; respectable guests like your cousin." The ermine made a motion to dismiss me; she had no intention of continuing. The conversation was over.

Even though I wanted to reach across the desk and grab the weasel, I stood up and dusted off my suit. "I see." I picked up my suitcase. "I wouldn't want to stay somewhere where the staff had such poor manners anyway."

"Good day Mr. Patters," said the weasel.

I turned around. People stared at me, some whispering to each other. With all the dignity I could bring up, I walked out of the hotel with my tail held high and ears erect.

On the street outside, I paused to gather my bearings. It didn't matter where I went. I had no place to really be right now. Carriages waited outside to take guests anywhere they needed to be, but where would I go? Our trunks were being sent over from Southampton and should be in tomorrow, but they would be at the docks in Queenstown, waiting for me to pick them up for the journey across the Atlantic.

If I checked into a different hotel, I could give a fake name. Any clean room would honestly do. I didn't need to stay at the most lavish hotel in town. A badger walked up to me, dressed smartly in his concierge uniform.

"Monsieur, can I get you a carriage?"

I hesitated. I had no place to be for three days.

"Monsieur?" said the badger straightening up. He was waiting on me to say something.

"Yes please. To the train station." It was someplace anyway I thought.

"Oh of course. Come, we have one waiting."

We walked a short distance to where a Hansom Cab sat waiting.

"James, take this good man to the railway station," said the concierge.

"Aye." I gave the badger a schilling for his trouble.

I got in the cab and it took off with a jolt, the horse's hooves clomping across the cobblestones as we sped away from the hotel. I sat back and watched the city of Cork pass by. I idly hoped Liam was having a better time than I was.

* * *

I stood by the gravestone looking down at it. Aithne stood next to me while the priest, standing a few feet away from us, said a few words. This wasn't the parish priest I remembered growing up, but someone else. The otter wasn't very young either, so he must have come from a different parish. He'd introduced himself as Father O'Brien.

As the priest spoke, I knelt down and touched the cool stone, tracing my paws across it.

"I'm sorry Mam," I whispered. "I'm so sorry I didn't come to see you before you passed."

Aithne put her hand on my shoulder and I bowed my head. I prayed for her, apologizing how I regretted not being able to see her one last time. It had been years since I had prayed, but right now that didn't matter. When the priest finished, he closed the prayer book he had been reading from.

"Amen," said the otter.

"Amen," I said standing up. I didn't know what else I could do, so I turned and started walking back to the rectory next to the church where Father was.

"Your mother was a good woman," said the priest falling in step next to me. "She believed in God and that her children would do right in the world. She rarely missed services."

I looked at the priest and just nodded.

"Aithne, would you go see how Fergal is doing? I would like a few words with your brother."

I stopped and frowned at the priest, but Aithne walked off, leaving us alone in the middle of the cemetery.

"Your mother worried about you Liam. Even as she lay dying, she hoped you were okay. She wanted to see you one last time."

I wasn't sure what I should say. "Aye. I'm sure," was all I could get out.

"God loves all his children, including you. I understand you left home when you were eighteen and haven't been back until now."

"Aye…"

"It saddens me to see a family that can only come together in the face of tragedy."

"My father and I are not on t'e best of speaking terms. I'm not sure ya heard about yesterday's fight in the tavern, but he punched me in t'e face," I said pointing to my black eye.

"I heard," said the priest. "Why is that?"

"T'ere aren't any kits in me future if you know what I mean."

The priest nodded. "I'm afraid in a town this small, rumors like that get around to everyone."

I held out my hands for emphasis. "You think this is just a rumor? You think the fact my father wants to beat the life out of my body for this sin is a joke? You think this is something that I can just wash away with religion, because if I could I would try to. I know though t'at doesn't work."

"No, I don't think this is some type of joke. I see someone before me fighting their own demons and a family struggling to be a family. It is up to the Lord to judge you, not those around you."

218

I grumbled. "And what would you have me do, Father?"

"You should try and make peace with your Da. I know Fergal is a difficult man to get along with, but he will listen to you if you are patient with him."

"Have you told him t'at yourself?"

The otter nodded and smiled. "Of course."

I sighed and started off toward the rectory. The priest followed. "If only it was as easy as you say it is," I said as we walked.

"I don't think it will be easy, but you can make things work."

"I plan to go back to America in a few days. I already have a ticket."

"Nevan and Aithne would like you to stay."

I rolled his eyes as we reached the door of the rectory and entered. "I'm sure, but I don't think that would be wise."

The rectory was a small single story house behind the church. Since Kiltail was a small village, it had once been a farm house that the local parish church had purchased and remolded. The original thatched roof had been replaced and a second wing added for sleeping quarters.

The rectory had a spacious kitchen in the back, through which we entered. Although the building was setup to accommodate up to three priests, Father O'Brien was currently the only priest here. He'd setup his study in the front of the house so he could receive visitors, and on the couch Da was resting, eyes closed, muzzle titled up. Aithne sat across from him.

Father's ears flicked when we walked in but he didn't open his eyes. "Did you pay your respects?" he asked.

I nodded, and when I realized he wasn't looking at me, I spoke. "Yes."

"So that's it then?" The old todd opened his eyes and lowered his muzzle to look at me. He still had strong fierce yellow eyes, but in the light coming through the window, sitting in the rectory, he looked older. Gray had crept into the black of his ears and fore paws. His muzzle was more grizzled then I remembered, and even the white under his throat felt like it had taken on a slight tint.

The changes were subtle, and if you weren't looking carefully, you might think he had dirt in his fur. It was age, and in that moment, he looked frail. He still had strength in his arms, but there was a way he held his head that suggested he no longer had the same spring step he used to.

"Do ya mean am I leaving?" I asked.

"Aye. You have done what you came to do."

I straightened myself up. "Isn't t'at what you want?"

"I never told you ya had to leave," said father. The priest shifted around the room, but didn't say anything.

"You didn't need to tell me, I knew."

Fergal just shook his head. "Aye, so t'at is it then. Back to the sewer for ya, with the rest of ya kind eh?"

I snarled, but Aithne held up her hands. "Father, regardless of what Liam does, he is still your son."

"My son would have known how badly his mother missed hearing from him. My son would have at least had the decency to write. Clancy used to come down once a month to see his old Mam."

"If I'd stayed I'd 've been the laughing stock of the town. 'Oh there goes Liam, the one who swings the wrong way.' Oh t'at would of been a chipper life."

The old McClearn stood up from the couch with an effort. "It isn't just about you Liam. For God's sake, doing that behind the tavern in the middle of a Saturday afternoon? You knew someone might find ya."

"I didn't care at t'at point." I'd had sex more than once behind a tavern, but those taverns were the type of places they expected that. The Sassy Willow was not that kind of tavern, and never had been. I'd known Shawn and I could get caught, but I didn't care. I wanted us to get caught so they could stop guessing and just know.

"Aye, but I've 'ad to listen to stories about my son the pervert for the last ten years. They keep talking about it since there isn't a hell of lot out here to talk about. Didn't that homosexual playwright 'ave a quote about being talked about?"

There was silence for a moment.

"You didn't approve of my penchants," I said finally.

"I still don't, but Clancy has kits now. Things have changed. I haven't been trying to get these two to marry since I need help on the farm."

I growled at him. "I don't want to live with your disapproval around my neck. I've taken enough shit for this, and I'm not doing that anymore. I will not limit myself to being on me knees behind a sleazy tavern because that is we're society thinks I should stay."

The priest coughed. "This is still church property—"

"No, you need to listen to this too. People like me have been forced back into the shadows for a long time, both by the church and society. I can't change who I am and what I like. Lord I tried for a while, but in the end, I knew it would be a lie."

"I came close to killing myself a few times just so I wouldn't have to see the disapproving looks of this great polite society! Stiff upper lip my ass. I had to find the strength inside of myself to be queer."

There was silence in the room; everyone had their eyes on me, even the priest.

I took a deep breath to calm myself down. "When you look out at the vast Atlantic ready to plunge to your death in the cold icy waters because of society, then you can tell me you don't approve."

When no one said anything I walked toward the front door of the rectory.

"I'll be back at the house."

"Peace be to you, Liam" said Father O'Brien as I opened the door. I turned around to look back at the otter.

"And to you too, father," I whispered finally and walked out of the rectory.

* * *

I watched as the little train station came into view and the train rattled to a stop. I didn't know why I had chosen to have the cab driver take me to the train station, but once I was there, I knew I didn't want to stay in Cork. Without knowing of any other place to go, I had bought a ticket for the next train to Kiltail.

It seemed like a smart thing to do, but now it felt stupid. Judging from the size of the station, I wouldn't go unnoticed. Still, if I kept a low profile, I could avoid getting between Liam and his family.

When I got off, I checked at the counter, but the next train wouldn't be till tomorrow in the morning. I then inquired about what type of lodgings there were and where to find them.

"The Sassy Willow has a few rooms, and that's the local tavern. The Broken Bristle is down the street, but it's a smaller pub," said the wolf behind the ticket counter. "The owner has a room he rents out, but the Willow is better."

"Thank you," I said. As I walked up the hill toward the town, I tried to calm my nerves. If anyone asked why I was here, I planned to tell them I was a traveling businessman looking to get a feel for the area. It would keep me out of trouble.

Kiltail was located at the top of the hill, and it wasn't that big. The houses were clustered off the main street, surrounded by farms. I walked into town and found the tavern easily enough. Upon walking inside, heads turned. I panicked mentally until I looked over the clientele. While everyone was clean and neat, no one was wearing a full suit like me.

With eyes following me, I walked over to where a stoat was serving beer.

"The wolf down at the train station says you rent rooms."

The stoat gave him a quick look over. "Sure, but they're kind of basic."

"That's fine, I'm just passing through."

"Let me have my son get the room ready."

I nodded, sat down at the bar, and ordered a whiskey. The stoat fixed the drink for me before he disappeared to fetch his son. Two males, a fox and badger were down on the other end of the bar talking. I ignored them until I realized they were sitting quite close to each other and talking in hushed tones. I titled an ear their way, but couldn't make out any words.

"It will be a few minutes," said the stoat returning. "I want to have it freshened up."

"Thanks." I sipped my whiskey. A red fox came over to the bar and ordered a drink, but I didn't pay him much heed.

"Hey Nevan," called the fox accompanying the badger, "your brother busy out back?"

The fox who had just come in turned toward the other fox. "If I 'ear another word from ya, Shawn, I'm going to put you out on the floor. You of all people should know what he's gone through."

"Or who he's gone through," grinned Shawn. "I'm sure he's got some gutter trash back in Southampton waiting on 'im."

Nevan stood up from the bar. "You're just upset Liam moved on from you. Ten years and you still act like he dumped ye yesterday, even in front of your new play thing."

I jolted when I realized who they were talking about.

"Hey," said the badger. "I'm not a play thing!"

Shawn sneered at the other fox. "Yeah, well at least unlike your brother, I have someone."

"Liam says he has someone," said Nevan, his ears going down.

Shawn laughed. "Yeah, probably some cheap slut."

"Do you people always talk so crassly of people you don't know?" I asked them.

"Whoa, hey mister," said Shawn. "This is personal, and I know you're not from around 'ere. You've got no dog in t'is fight."

"I recognize gutter trash when I see it," I replied.

Shawn got up from his stool and walked up to me.

"You English are all t'e same, always butting your nose in where it doesn't belong. This is an Irish dispute, and not yours."

The stoat had come from around the bar tried to get between me and Shawn.

"Shawn, if you pick any more fights in my bar, I'm kicking you out. I already had one fight last night, I will not have another."

"Let the wolf speak for himself. I know you're no friend of the English," said Shawn pushing back.

I got up from my bar stool and smoothed down my coat and stuck my hand out to Shawn.

"The name is Charlie Bartholomew Patters. You might have heard of me." There went my playing it low key today.

The fox looked a bit stunned and shook my hand. "The Mr. Patters?"

"Yeah. Now your dispute is with a certain Liam McClearn I believe."

"Yeah, wait, how do you know 'im?"

I smiled, flashing all the fang I could muster. "He's my boyfriend."

Shawn's mouth fell open and he didn't say anything else.

* * *

"I really wish you would have told me you were coming," I said sitting on the bed of Charlie's room. The accommodations were pretty sparse, and had the smell of not being used for a while. An oil lamp burned low on one side of the room, casting a dull light through its glass shade. I would have turned it up, but I didn't think it would make the room look better. With how tired he looked, I didn't think Charlie would care. "Also, why the theatrics?"

My brother, leaned against the door watching us. He'd come and fetched me for Charlie after the chatter in the bar had died down.

"I didn't plan it, I just… needed to get out of Cork."

"What's wrong with Cork?" I asked.

"Besides the smell of t'e bay," chimed in Nevan. When we both turned to him, he put his paws up apologetically.

Charlie came and sat down on the bed next to me. The way the mattress sagged with his weight told me the bed wasn't any prize.

"I—I had a problem."

I waited for him to say more, but Charlie got up and went to his suitcase. He pulled out a newspaper which he came and brought back to me. He pointed to an article in it, and I quickly skimmed it.

"Whoa, your father really cut ya off?" I asked after finishing.

Charlie nodded. "Yup. Finally I guess. The hotel also didn't want me staying there."

"Wait, they refused you service because of t'is?"

Charlie sighed. "Yes. I am now a pariah for what is wrong with society."

I put an arm around him. "I'm sorry," was all I could think of saying, my mind racing.

"How can t'ey refuse you service?" asked Nevan.

"Both Liam and I are unclean, and we are not to be served by those who are the gate keepers in society. There is no law that says they have to serve us, so they won't." Charlie squeezed my hand. "But to be frank, I don't care. I don't care about Father and his money, and I don't care about Britannia. I care about Liam."

The wolf leaned forward and pressed his lips against mine and I was surprised by the suddenness of it. I didn't pull away, but held the kiss for a moment. Nevan had looked the other way when I looked at him. I'm not sure how he felt seeing that, but I didn't worry about it then.

"Aye Mr. Patters, but Britannia cares about you," said Nevan after we broke off and he turned to look back at us.

"That, she does, but if I go back to America, she won't bother me."

"Yes, but your fortune?" I asked.

"My father's fortune is his own. I knew this might someday happen, and I've set some money aside and have some of my own business interests. My father can try and ruin me, but I won't let him."

We all lapsed into silence and I sat on the bed with my wolf, holding his paws.

"Are you coming back to the house tonight, Liam?" asked Nevan.

"Let Da be. I'll come back tomorrow to say goodbye, and we'll catch the afternoon train to Cork. From there, we'll go to America." I looked up at my brother. "I hope ya understand."

Nevan frowned. "I will let them know," he said gruffly. He turned and left us alone finally.

"I didn't want to ask in front of your brother, but why do you have a black eye?"

I laughed. "Father and I had a bit of an altercation when I first got into town. He got me good, but I gave him a good one when he didn't want to settle down. It took some of the fight out of 'im."

Charlie blinked. "Is this usual for your family?"

"No, but it's been a long time coming. We don't see eye to eye."

"I can imagine," said Charlie.

"It's not just Father. Nevan and Aithne think I should stay 'ere. They don't want to see me leave again."

Charlie flicked his tail. "I heard what they said about you downstairs. Can they not see that you don't belong here?"

I sighed and propped up my chin with my paws. "It's more complicated than just t'at. A lot of the animosity 'as developed since I left so suddenly and because of the way I left. I meant to burn the bridges when I left."

Charlie slipped an arm around him. "What did you do?"

"I let them catch me blowing Shawn behind the tavern one Saturday afternoon."

The wolf blinked. "Him?" he laughed. "No wonder he hates you."

"Yeah. They've talked about me since then. Kiltail is a small town, so it 'as apparently become part of t'e local lore."

"We'll get through this, Liam. Hopefully when we get back to America, we can settle down someplace."

"I think I am okay. I knew it would be difficult coming back, but I 'ad to pay my respects to Mother."

We lapsed into silence for a while. "It has been a strange last three months," said Charlie finally. "I'm glad you didn't jump, but it seems we're back to small back rooms for where we can be ourselves."

"T'at's how we started, behind a pub in Southampton."

"What is it with you and blowing people behind pubs?" asked Charlie teasingly. "You seem to have a history of doing it."

"With you," I said elbowing him.

"Not just with me."

"Are you jealous of Shawn? We can go behind the Sassy Willow 'ere if you think you're missing out."

"The bed here is good enough for me. I'm hoping my days of meeting men in dark taverns is over, but I don't want to take away from you the things you love."

I grinned and pushed Charlie back against the bed. "Must I show you those things again?"

Charlie grinned and traced his hand across my muzzle, looking up at me with his beautiful yellow eyes. "If you want, but we've just moved from behind the tavern to upstairs."

I reached down and roughly cupped Charlie's crotch. "Oh so this stirring down 'ere isn't because you're into me? Did Nevan try and put the moves on you earlier?"

Charlie smirked. "He is handsome, but I know which McClearn fox I go for," he traced his hand along my chest, "and which one I want to see naked."

"Mm… as if you could tell the difference from a willing muzzle," I said grinning, letting my tongue hang out.

"So I should be trying to get Nevan too?"

"What? No!" I squeezed his paw tight while cupping roughly at his crotch through the fabric, harder this time. "Now you're just being bad."

Charlie squirmed and yelped softly. "Hey now, be gentle."

I slipped down the bed, dragging my muzzle across Charlie's chest. "Ya never complained before."

"If not for me, think of the poor worn bed!" grinned Charlie.

I scoffed. "It was worn before we got 'ere. We are just 'elping break it in more." I slipped Charlie's belt undone and undid the button fastening of his pants and tugged his underwear down. His cock stood out against his dark grey fur.

Charlie growled and tugged at his shirt collar and ascot, loosening them.

"Mm… I'm not complaining."

"Oh good," I said licking my tongue up his shaft. Despite my playfulness, I wasn't sure I was worth him losing an entire fortune for. I had told him we could be more discrete, but he said he didn't care. If he wanted to do this for me, the least I could do for him right now was give him a good distraction.

He had already parted his legs expectantly. I grinned and slowly unbuttoned my shirt and pulled it off making him wait, letting my hot breath wash over his privates.

"Eager tonight are we?" I said gently nosing his shaft, teasing it with my tongue.

He squirmed. "Should I not be?"

I looked up at him, meeting his eyes as he looked down at me, his cock bobbing between us. I licked my lips, letting my tongue curl around one of my fangs. "I don't want you to get bored with me now."

He frowned and tilted his head slightly, letting his ears fall back. "Why would I get bored with you?"

I kept my head low and shifted so I could balance myself on one of my front paws. My tail wagged behind me as I reached up and gently traced the pads of my fingers over his shaft, stopping to rest one on the tip, which I gently teased.

"We've had a very sexual relationship. I don't want ya to feel like that's all t'ere is between us."

The eagerness on his part faded, and I felt him soften just a little. "Are you worried about things?"

"Not exactly," I leaned forward and darted my tongue out to lick his tip. "I just don't want to let things become routine."

He giggled. "Oh you dirty fox, do I need to put you in your place now?"

I winked at him. "Maybe I need to put ya in your place." I titled my muzzle up and grinned.

He blinked and then smirked showing all his fangs. "Oh really now?"

Throughout all of this, I still had my pants on. I reached into my pocket, fished something out. and tossed it onto his chest. I had wrapped it in cloth to keep the metal from clanking. He reached up and unwrapped it, revealing a set of darby style handcuffs.

He looked surprised, but I saw the spark in his eye. "Where did you get this from?"

"A curiosity shop in Cork. They're designed for magicians, but the hidden release mechanism is quite clever."

He picked them up and then looked at me. "You planned this?"

I grinned. "I planned t'is for later. When Nevan said ya were here, I quickly took a bit of initiative and told 'im I would be down in a moment."

His tail thumped against the bed. "I don't know. I've been disowned and now the locals in Ireland are trying to lock me up."

I reached between his legs and stroked his rock hard cock. "Something is into t'e idea."

He gave me a low, rumbling growl. "Do I get to use these on you?"

I smirked. "Next time." I leaned down to give him a quick lick.

"You are such a tease."

I pulled off my pants slowly and then crawled up the bed, letting my fur brush his until I could look him straight in the eye.

"Let me fix that for you then," I said picking up the handcuffs. I continued moving myself forward and up until I reached a sitting position on his chest. I unlocked the cuffs and looped one of them around his wrist, clicking it shut. I then wound the chain around the bars of the metal headboard and reached for his other hand. He shifted under me, and my hardness rubbed against his muzzle. He titled his muzzle away.

"Are you okay?" I asked.

"I'm being accosted by a fox."

I locked his other wrist into the cuff. "Are you complaining?" I reached down to grip my shaft and tease at him with it.

He pulled on the cuffs, and nodded. "Yes."

My ears fell. I thought he would enjoy this. "Let me release you—"

His tongue darted across my cock and I froze.

"Oh now who's teasing!" I growled.

He didn't warrant that with a response and just sucked on the tip. I reached behind to feel his throbbing member, still slick with my saliva and then pushed my own shaft into his muzzle. He grunted in pleasure when I began stroking him.

I had to pause a few times to lick my pads to have enough lubrication, but he had become fully erect and was enjoying it. His knot had swollen fast in my paw. I pushed myself into his muzzle deep, letting him take the whole of my cock.

I yipped when he lightly teased my tip with his teeth, but I had to keep my voice down. I didn't think these walls were soundproof. I also had to make sure I didn't knock the bed against the wall with my thrusts, giving us away.

With a deep moan he came in my paw, surprising me. I wasn't done yet, but I pulled out, letting him rest for a moment.

"Oh god that was intense," he said in a raspy tone.

I gently stroked my shaft, slicked with wolf drool, a bit of his seed on my paw mixed onto it. "I'll finish myself off."

He looked up at me and rattled my cuffs. "If you release me, I can finish what I started."

I shook my head and grinned, instead stroking myself sitting on his chest. "The captive may only watch."

His ears went back and he whined as I stroked my shaft, letting my tail wag. He shifted his weight under me trying to get his muzzle on it, but I kept it away. I was quite close, and when I felt myself on the edge I scooted closer.

"Open your muzzle." I panted.

He obeyed, and I managed to get most of it onto his tongue. A few spots ended up on his chest and the pillow he was braced upon. Finished, I sank back, sitting on his groin, his spent cock rubbing up against my rump.

"Now will you let me up?" he asked rattling the cuffs.

I reached up and carefully unlocked the cuffs using the hidden release. He sagged back onto the bed after he could pull his hands down and rubbed his wrists.

"They chafe a little," he said.

"I'll be more careful putting them on you next time." I rolled off of the bed and surveyed the mess I'd made of him. His pants had spots in the wool and he'd splattered the sheets and his tail. I even found some of his cum under my tail where it had brushed his sticky shaft.

The small washbasin on the side table didn't have enough water for us to clean up with. Hopefully we could get some more unnoticed.

"That was so ungentlemanly what we just did."

I laughed, yipping a little. "We've done worse."

He picked up the cuffs inspecting them. "We'll do something different next time with these," he said teasingly.

Crap, he wanted to get me good with those. I didn't know when we'd get the chance, but a part of me was already excited about the possibility.

"Then don't worry about being a 'gentleman' as they would say. I'm not a lady. I can take it just as well as I can give it."

He looked around the room. "I know, it's just going to take some time to get used to what has happened."

"If I have to, I'll distract you like this every night."

He laughed and leaned up from the bed and I met him with a kiss.

"Ah if only dealing with all of my problems was so simple."

"Dealing with me is." It wasn't, but sometimes I felt like it was.

His eyes twinkled in the lamplight. "I'll remember that the next time you are in one of your moods."

I smiled. We weren't a perfect couple, but at least we were a couple that cared for each other. Why couldn't the world see that?

* * *

WESTERN UNION TELEGRAM
RECEIVED FROM NEW YORK CITY USA FOR
CHARLIE BARTHOLOMEW PATTERS
THE SASSY WILLOW KILTAIL IRELAND

I GOT YOUR TELEGRAM FROM WHEREVER YOU ARE IN
IRELAND STOP I'M AFRAID YOUR FATHER HAS MOVED

TO HAVE YOUR SHARES REVOKED UNDER A CLAUSE IN
THE COMPANIES CHARTER ABOUT BOARD MEMBERS
INCAPACITATED DUE TO INSANITY STOP AT THIS
POINT YOU NEED TO GET A LAWYER STOP I'M SORRY I
CAN'T BE OF MORE HELP STOP CHESTER

I sighed and handed the telegram over to Liam. We were seated at a table in the tavern. I had the morning paper from Cork spread out across the table. The remains of our lunch was pushed to one corner of the table.

"Can your father really do this?" asked Liam.

I shook my head. "No, but it's a ploy to get me into a legal battle with him so he can drain my savings." I flipped back into the paper and pointed at a small article on page seven. "He's also consolidating control over his factories in Birmingham, so he can cut my share out."

Liam looked at the article. "He doesn't waste any time."

"No. He is moving to cut off all of my income."

"So what do we do now?"

I scratched behind my ears. "I can fight him, but he'll bankrupt me before I get anything out of him."

"This completely cuts you off from t'e work you've been doing in New York doesn't it?"

"Basically. I didn't have the paperwork in just my name. This leaves me with the shoe factory in Bristol. He can't get control of that since I invested into that myself against his recommendation. He made sure that was in my name."

Liam nodded.

"It does at least make money now, but it is just a meager income."

"Yes, but isn't t'at enough?"

I looked at Liam and growled in frustration. "Enough?"

"We don't need to be wealthy Charlie."

"Speak for yourself." Father was in the process of cutting me out of my birth-right, and I was angry.

Liam leaned in close. "I will not hear you say that! Look at me, and look around ya. Do you think anyone here is rich enough to own a factory?"

I grumbled. "Being in business is what I learned to do growing up."

"From t'e same people who won't serve you a cup of tea now that they know you won't stick ya prick in a lass!"

My ears fell, and I looked away from Liam. "Aye, from the same people who won't serve me a cup of tea now," I said looking down at the table.

The fox rubbed my back tenderly. "It will be okay."

I sniffed and felt tears begin to well up. "Will it? I don't even have my name now, Liam."

"Charlie, you 'ave me."

I looked up, tears streaking down my face. "And I can't protect you, Liam. I just have myself and a bit of money against... everything society throws at us."

Liam leaned forward to nuzzle me, not caring that we were in public. "It will be enough, I promise."

"But I feel powerless now..."

"I've felt powerless most of me life. That hasn't stopped me."

"No, but you don't understand," I cried.

"No I don't understand, because I never had an inheritance of money to lose, but I understand feeling like everyone else. I understand being poor. I understand being poor much better than you understand it, and I want to point out, you're still not truly poor."

I pulled out a handkerchief to blow my nose with. "I'm sorry, I just can't believe he would do this to me.

"Shh... it's okay. Together, remember?" he took one of my paws.

"Yes, oh god yes."

"Good. Now are we still going back to America?"

I bit my lip. "I don't know."

"This morning, Nevan said I should bring you by to at least meet Father before we left this evening, but Aithne didn't know if t'at would be a good idea."

"From how you've described him, I don't know if meeting him is a worthwhile endeavor. I'm not in the mood now."

"He's coming to terms with me, so I'd like you to come with up to the farm. I don't think it will be so bad now." Liam stood up from the table.

I nodded dully and picked up the paper and the telegrams I'd received this morning. "Let me put these upstairs,"

"I'll be 'ere, waiting."

I nodded. "Thanks."

* * *

The barley swayed in the breeze as we walked up the path toward the house. I wore the simple working clothes I'd worn last night, and Charlie had left his formal wear behind for a simple button up shirt. He almost looked like a working man, except the shirt was impeccably starched, the collar perfect. As a concession to the afternoon sun, Charlie had left the collar open, letting the fur at his throat ruffle.

"So this is where you grew up?" asked Charlie as we approached the stone farmhouse. It was a small house with just three rooms downstairs and an attic upstairs.

"Yeah. It isn't much. The kitchen is the biggest room."

"There were six of you in this little house?" asked Charlie.

"It wasn't so bad. It seemed big enough growing up, although my parents had the only real bedroom. We all had to sleep in the attic."

We reached the front door, and I knocked. Charlie fidgeted with his shirt cuffs. There was some motion, and Aithne opened the door. She looked at us.

"Liam, Mr. Patters," she spoke formally and did a quick curtsy to ruffle her skirts. "Would you come in?"

"Aithne?" asked Charlie

"Yes."

"Call me Charlie, and please don't do that again," he swept his hands down in imitation of her motion. "That feels a bit too formal."

Her eyes sparkled. "He is a bit of a charmer, Liam. Very well. Come in then."

We followed Aithne into the front room of the farmhouse. Nevan was on one side of the room, standing next to a chair. Father sat next to the low fire burning in the fireplace. Nevan nodded his head at us and sat down next to father.

"Sit," said Father pointing to the wooden bench near the fire.

I walked over and sat down. Charlie followed me and I waited for the old man to speak. Aithne closed the door and stood in the back of the room.

"So this is where you ask for my son's hand?" asked the old todd to Charlie.

"I didn't know I should," said Charlie.

"Well if'e is to be your woman, perhaps you should."

"Father," I growled in warning

"I don't know how your kind does this. I'm being honest now," he said holding up his hands.

Charlie cleared his throat. "Perhaps if I tell you we take turns, that might put your mind at ease."

The older fox screwed up his muzzle. "Not particularly."

Charlie just closed his muzzle and looked away, tugging at his loosened collar.

"This is not something easy for me. How does your father feel about it?" he asked Charlie.

Charlie turned to the old fox. "How does he feel? He feels betrayed. He feels vindictive that his only son is not the man he wanted him to be. He just this week disowned me and cut me off, but you know what?" Charlie pointed his finger at Father, "I don't care. I'm upset, but if all he cares about in the world is airs and social standing, he can keep his rotten money."

Fergal sat up straighter. "The English aren't the most compassionate people, if you ask me."

Charlie opened his muzzle and then shut it. He lowered his hand.

"I wouldn't blame your father for feeling that way upon finding out his son is a queer. I felt the same way about mine, and look how he responded to that."

I shifted, but Charlie spoke first. "He's already changed his will and is in the process of cutting me out of business dealing. Is that how you want to treat Liam?"

The old man chuckled. "I've had ten years to think about that. Ten long years. I'm not any younger, and my body hasn't taken kindly to age." The older fox got up and turned to me.

"It wasn't t'e right thing to do, to drive you off. Your mother never forgave me. She understood, but she never forgave. When Clancy had his son, she turned to me and told me I should end this. T'at I needed to write to you and tell you it was okay, t'at you needed to come home. She wanted you to come home, but I didn't do it. Instead I said, 'let 'em rot'. Now look. It was only her death that brought you home." The old fox shuffled toward the cupboard.

"I didn't leave on exactly the best footing."

"No you didn't. I knew you wanted to get caught, to leave me something." He pulled out a bottle from the cupboard and brought it over and to a nearby table. "I think we should at least do a toast to say we're behind all this, so we can move on, and to let you know that I'm sorry. Hopefully the next time you come back to Kiltail it is not to see one of us in the ground."

I got up. "Father...," my voice cracked. This was one of the most profound things he'd ever said to me.

The older fox looked at me. "I'm sorry Liam. I wanted to do right for you, but in the end I didn't. I hope you can forgive me."

I nodded, eyes misting.

"Nevan, fetch the other glasses from the kitchen. Everyone gets a nip. You too, err... what do I call you, because Mr. Patters is out of the question."

"Charlie."

"You too Charlie. For family."

Nevan left the room and came back carrying glasses which he placed next to the bottle. Fergal proceeded to pour out some of the liquid. A sweet smell permeated the room. The whiskey was strong, and once each of the glasses was filled, everyone took a glass, even Aithne.

The elder McClearn held up his glass. "May the hinges of our family never grow rusty!"

"Here, here!" said everyone as we lifted our glasses to our muzzles and drank quickly, letting the whiskey seep into our stomachs. It was a strong whiskey, the kind that's good at keeping the chill out and brought a flush to my face. Fergal set his glass back down on the table.

"So, what will you do now?" asked Aithne as everyone settled in a chair.

I looked at Charlie. "I guess fight with Charlie's father."

Charlie shook his head. "He'd expect me do to that. I won't give him the satisfaction. He can wait for news of a legal challenge for as long as he wants."

"So you're going to walk away?" asked Nevan.

"Kind of I guess. I have a modest shoe factory in Bristol in my name. It will have to do."

"I've always preferred to go bare pawed myself," said the elder fox.

"I can't say I wear footwear a lot myself," said Charlie, wiggling his toes, "but it isn't fashionable to get mud in your foot paws in London. It makes some money, but not a lot. It's what he's left me."

"I've never had much love for the English. I'm not afraid of men like your father, Charlie. I own my land, and if they don't like how we live over here, they can stay over there. The bastards keep coming over here trying to buy up more land, but they never put it good use. Many of the locals in the cities are forced to go without work."

I spoke up. "I don't think now is the time to talk politics."

The older fox shrugged.

"I guess we will go to Bristol. I can take more of an interest in the business and see what I can do with it. It's done fine without my interference though."

Fergal opened him muzzle to say something else when a knock came on the door.

"Who could that be?" Aithne said getting up and getting the door.

Outside stood the son of the inn keeper. The boy was skinny, just hitting his growth spurt and he was breathing heavy.

"Is Mr. Patters 'ere?"

"Yes," said Charlie getting up.

"Here," he said shoving a folded telegram into Charlie's paws when he got close. "This just came in and it is marked as urgent. They said you'd want to see this."

Charlie's hands trembled as he unfolded the letter and started to read.

As he read, his ears started to drop and he sagged. When he finished, he was shaking. "He's… he's taken it all away from me. All of it!"

"Let me see," I said getting up. Charlie handed me the telegram.

POST OFFICE TELEGRAM

RECEIVED FROM SOUTHAMPTON ENGLAND FOR
CHARLIE BARTHOLOMEW PATTERS
KILTAIL IRELAND

I RECEIVED WORD YOU HAVE FOUND OUT ABOUT THE
CHANGES TO OUR BUSINESS IN NEW YORK STOP IT WAS
IMPERATIVE FOR ME TO TAKE ACTION TO PROTECT THE
PATTERS NAME AND BY DOING THIS I CAN RESTORE
THE GLORY IT HAD BEFORE YOU SULLIED IT STOP I
HOPE YOU UNDERSTAND STOP AS PART OF THIS I HAVE
ALSO INVESTIGATED YOUR LITTLE SHOE FACTORY IN
BRISTOL STOP I AM PLEASED TO LET YOU KNOW I HAVE
FOUND A WAY TO TAKE A CONTROLLING INTEREST
IN THE FACTORY STOP YOUR INVESTORS HAVE BEEN
WILLING TO LET ME ASSUME CONTROL SINCE YOU HAVE
BEEN INCAPACITATED STOP YOU WILL BE RECEIVING
£1,000 AS PART OF THE SETTLEMENT BUT YOU WILL
NOT NEED TO WORRY ABOUT THIS VENTURE ANYMORE
STOP PLEASE LET MY LAWYER MR. HANSFORD KNOW
WHERE HE CAN SEND YOU THE PAPERWORK FOR YOUR
DIVESTITURE FROM MY BUSINESS INTERESTS STOP
YOU WILL STILL RECEIVE A SMALL YEARLY SUM FROM
THE FACTORY SINCE I CAN'T REMOVE YOU COMPLETELY
BUT MY LAWYER WILL HANDLE THIS STOP IF YOU EVER
DECIDE TO QUIT THE DEPLORABLE BEHAVIOR LET ME
KNOW AND WE CAN TALK ABOUT WHAT ROLE YOU
MIGHT BE ABLE TO PLAY IN THE PATTERS FAMILY STOP
UNTIL THEN SEYMOUR PATTERS

Reading it, I felt I had been dealt a blow to the stomach. When I finished, the stout's son was still standing in the doorway with Aithne holding it open. I looked at Aithne and shook my head. Charlie had walked over to the bench. He sat with his head on his paws crying.

Aithne reached into her pocket and gave the boy a shilling. "You better go," she said to the boy.

"Yes mam." He ducked out and Aithne closed the door.

"How can he do this?" I asked Charlie after the courier had left.

"I don't know, but the bastard has cut me out of everything. Everything! I have nothing left."

There was silence until I finally said, "You have me Charlie."

Charlie closed his eyes. "I wanted to protect you, and I can't even do that."

I walked over to Charlie and rested my arm on Charlie's shoulder. "We'll get through this."

"What does Liam need protecting from?" asked Nevan.

"The society that sees us as monsters, that looks at who we are and sees only darkness and evil. They don't see us as even people, but things to be cast out, thrown away, and destroyed."

Fergal laughed. It wasn't a joyous laugh but a bitter, sardonic laugh. "That is how the British treat us for being Irish." He got up shaking his head. "There is still farm work to do around here before dark. Are you going back?"

"I have nothing left to go back to," said Charlie.

The older fox turned to me. "Are you leaving then?"

I looked at my brother and sister. "I don't belong here anymore."

"T'en where do you two belong?" he asked us.

I didn't answer and Charlie just stared at the floor.

"Back in Southampton?"

"No," Charlie and I said together.

"Why don't you stay in Kiltail for a bit, until you figure out what you want to do," said Aithne.

"And be gawked at constantly?" I asked her.

"They'll get tired of it. T'e rent at the pub can't be that much, and if you lodge there for a while, you can get a better rate."

Charlie turned to look up at me. Tears stained his fur. He looked lost.

"We best plan for that for the moment." I reached out to trace the underside of the wolf's muzzle.

"Liam, I'm so sorry..."

"Hush," I said to him. "Remember, together right?" We'll figure this out together."

Charlie sighed. "Yes, of course, together."

* * *

I slipped the latch off the trunk and opened the lid. Inside were my clothes. I pulled the shirts off the top. Below, I had left a small carved wooden box. I pulled it out and took it over to the bed and sat down on the worn bed. I pulled it open. The gold cufflinks father had given to me when I had turned eighteen gleamed at me. They were adorned with a monogram on top of them, C. B. P. Next to them a small pouch that contained my pocket watch, which I reached for and took out, looking at the finely polished brass. I ran my pad over the back, feeling the engraving with my name on it.

"Almost every night, you take t'ose things out and look at t'em," said Liam.

I looked up at Liam. I hadn't heard him open the door to our room. "I keep thinking I should sell them," I said. "I need to let go."

Liam walked over and put his hand on my shoulder. "Those are still mementos of your family, of who you are."

"Of who I was. I am just yours now."

The fox rolled his eyes. "No," he said sitting down. "I know these last two weeks have been hard on you, but you can't forget who you are." He reached over to close the box and rested his hands on top of it. "T'is may be all you have left, but a few pounds won't fill that hole in ya heart."

It wasn't the farm work I minded. It was tiring; I wasn't used to it, but I could at least keep up with Fergal. I just didn't have much to keep my mind off what had happened. I had contacted a lawyer in Cork, but he'd told me there wasn't much he could do. Father had sealed everything up nicely. The figured he'd quoted me to pursue the affair was a quarter of what I still had and was unlikely to get me anything in return.

That left me only with Liam, and I could tell he was tiring of my morose attitude and sobbing in the dark after midnight hours, when I thought he might be asleep. It would be so easy to turn my back on him, to go back to the lie I used to live, but I couldn't do that. I knew who I was, I just wished it wasn't so hard to be me. I sniffed. I just need to be strong, and the pain would eventually pass.

Liam took my right paw and held it gently, rubbing the fur and pads gently. "Maybe I can brighten your spirit."

I smiled weakly. The thought of feeling him against me was tempting, but that would just be a brief respite. I was a stranger in a land I didn't belong in. "Thank you hun, but your paws and muzzle can only do so much."

He rolled his eyes and leaned in, his breath and fox musk close to me. I felt a hand slipping down into my groin. "Actually…" I felt a claw tipped finger trace over my sheath through the fabric. "This isn't at all what I was thinking." He pushed me away from himself, and I fell backwards on to the bed, it creaking loudly in protest.

"What?" I yelped.

I felt the paw resting on my hips as he teased me again, through the fabric. "Nope." He pulled it away and got off the bed. "Get dressed," he said pointing at me. I only had an undershirt on with my pants.

I got up and put the box back in the trunk. "Where are we going?" I had been to other pub in town, The Broken Bristle, one night and it wasn't all that different than The Sassy Willow. Going back over there wouldn't improve my mood.

The fox turned and winked at me. "You'll see."

* * *

The night was cool, the late summer air settling in. Harvest time was around the corner, and I could smell the crops in the fields. The ripening barley swayed in the field around the farmhouse, shifting under the light of the moon, a few days from full brightness.

"This isn't what I had in mind of going out," said Charlie behind me. He'd been quiet, but I could tell the spring in his step had faded as he realizing we were going back to the farm.

"Hush," I said walking up to the door and knocking. I could have let myself in, but this was still father's home. Even though we were getting along, I didn't want to push my luck.

The door creaked open, and Fergal peeked his muzzle out.

"Liam?" He looked at Charlie and back to me. "Is there something that can't wait till morning?"

I shook my head. "Nevan and I are going down to the bend in the creek. I'm taking Charlie."

The old todd was quite for a moment. "By the old oak?" He finally asked.

"Aye."

Fergal nodded. "I was wondering why he pulled out the fiddle." He opened the door and retreated back into the room where he had the peat fire burning low to keep the chill out of the house. Charlie followed me in.

"The bend in the creek?" asked Charlie.

"Aye, the bend in t'e creek," said Nevan coming downstairs carrying the case for the fiddle. "Did you want to come Da?"

Fergal looked up from the fire. "Not particularly. I t'ink I prefer the inn at this point if I want a good drink."

"Wait, we are going down to the creek to drink?" asked Charlie

I and Nevan nodded at him.

"It's a waste of good talent," said Aithne coming in from the kitchen. "You could at least play down in the pub if you're going to do that."

"We have a good bottle of Jamison," I said fishing a bottle from the cupboard and holding it up. I hadn't been opened yet. I had bought it for tonight.

Aithne walked over and took the bottle from me. "Is this all ya sailors think about, stiff drinks and stiffies?"

I crossed my arms. "It's how I got through the las' ten years." Charlie coughed uncomfortably behind me, but I just flicked my ears and glared at Aithne.

She rolled her eyes. "My brother t'e unapologetic sodomite."

I laid my ears back as she walked over to where her shawl hung by the door, pulled it off the hook. and picked up a rolled blanket. "Mother wouldn't approve you know," she added.

"Stop teasing your brothers Aithne, and go wit' t'em. Just make sure you all stay out of trouble; try not to fall into the creek either," said Da by the fire putting down a small cup of whatever he was drinking. He picked up a book next to him and went back to reading.

I wagged my tail and smiled as I stepped out the door with a spring in my step. Nevan and Aithne followed me outside, Charlie in tow.

"Is this a tradition in your family, drinking outside at night in the dark?" Charlie asked us.

"Father used to do it when we were young," said Aithne. "Mam used to be mad as 'ell when she'd find out he'd passed out down by the creek. It's been a few years since Da and his friends have headed down to the creek."

"I also cut and left some firewood down t'ere for a nice little bonfire," said Nevan bringing up the rear.

Charlie didn't say anything else, but followed us down the hill, around the field till we reached the creek. I had cleaned up the small fire circle yesterday, and it was ready to go. I laid a few logs with some kindling down by the circle and pulled out the flint and steel I had in my pocket. It took me a few strikes, but I was able to get the kindling going easily.

As soon as the fire started to burn, Nevan put down the fiddle case and pulled out the instrument and its bow.

Aithne spread out the blanket she'd brought and sat down, careful not to get he skirts dirty.

"Did you want to sing Sis?" asked Nevan as he toyed with the violin.

"Later," she said pulling the shawl around herself.

Amongst all of this, Charlie looked on confused. I walked over to him after I finished tending the fire.

"Hey," I said taking one of his paws.

"This isn't what I thought you meant by a night out."

"Nope," I said pulling him over to the fire, "but it's w'at I've got." I leaned in and gave him a kiss.

"It's still going to take some time for me to get used to seeing t'at," whispered Nevan to Aithne. She shrugged and he, pulled the bow across the strings and started to play. It took me a few moments, but I recognized the tune as a "Rocky Road to Dublin," a fast paced tune Nevan had always enjoyed playing.

I smiled, and let myself relax. "If ya going to live here, it's important you learn how to do a good jig," I grinned at him.

"I have never been a great dancer," he said.

Aithane chuckled. "That's why we have t'e whisky."

"Aye!" I said grinning, and he smiled back.

"This might take more than one night," he said playfully.

242

"We've got time," I grinned and pulled him closer to me. He wrapped his arms around me and we swayed, letting our tails sway.

"Get ya paws off me brother, and start dancing," yelled Nevan, "or I won't share any of t'e whisky with you."

I blushed. "Just play Nevan," I said as we separated. "All right, now, the key doing any jig is stepping fast wit' your paws and remember to keep time with the rhythm."

The wind whispered through the field, making the barley sway in the moonlight. "Okay," he said smiling. "Show me, and I'll give it a whirl."

About the Authors

<u>Slip-Wolf</u>

Slip-Wolf is a fledgling scribe borne of the West Colonies, who's gay tellings have brought amusement in expatriate bohemian-clubs and houses of moderate vice from the Hudson's Bay to the shores of New York. His aspirations have thus found him oportunities for creative penmanship with the Sofa-Wolf novel-and-chaise reading-lounge- company of East Minnesota, as well as the Rabbit valley illustrated works and land settlement combine of Nevada territory. Slip-Wolf is honored to bring his latest work to the Fur-Planetarium of scholarly, celestial and Eros studies and prays his fanciful diversions will bring merriment to London and enclaves of the Empire beyond. God save the King.

<u>Whyte Yoté</u>

Whyte Yoté has been writing erotic furry fiction since 1995 when he was probably far too young to be doing such a thing, and he has been seriously pursuing his craft since 2000.

His works have appeared multiple times in Heat magazine, FANG, and ROAR. He also has stories in the anthologies X, The Fortune Teller's Poem, Holidays, Taboo, Will of the Alpha, and Trick or Treat. He has been honored by publication with Sofawolf Press, Furplanet Productions, Bad Dog Books and Rabbit Valley Comics.

Tym Greene

Tym Greene is a writer and artist, particularly of anthro things, and aspires to work in concept art. In the meantime he fulfills his world-building desires with the crafting of fiction.

Apart from a few entry-level courses, he's mostly self-taught and has to thank the pantheon of authors (both classic and otherwise), his editors, and his boyfriend for helping him to be the writer he is today.

Kyell Gold

Kyell Gold is a California writer who is best known for his gay furry fiction, although he has also included historical, supernatural, mystery, science fiction, fantasy, and sports elements in his writing. He has won a dozen Ursa Major Awards and two Rainbow Awards for his novels and short stories. With his husband Kit Silver, he often attends furry, SF, and comic conventions around North America and occasionally abroad. You can find more about him and his work at www.kyellgold.com.

Miriam Curzon

Miriam Curzon is a marbled polecat satyr hybrid alter-ego of the red fox, Camio. He juggles writing furry fiction with academic work. This is his first time published, ever. He resides in a house in New Jersey with his computer programming partner, another fox, where he writes, reads queer theory, and games. Currently, he is preparing for his first academic published article and developing another furry Victorian story into a novel.

Chris "Sparf" Williams

Sparf is a DC area author and actor, which means that he spends a lot of his time wondering where he went wrong. He's an unapologetic furry and has caught a "staff infection" at a few conventions. You can read other works by him in Will of the Alpha from FurPlanet and Trick or Treat 2 from Rabbit Valley.

NightEyes DaySpring

NightEyes DaySpring is a known troublemaker who is rumored to have a penchant for coffee and an interest in dead, ancient civilizations. His stories have appeared in ROAR, FANG, Trick or Treat, and other anthologies. He resides in Florida with his boyfriend. In his spare time, he masquerades as an IT professional.

More information about NightEyes can be found at:

http://www.furaffinity.net/user/nighteyes/

https://www.weasyl.com/~nighteyes

For day-to-day nonsense, follow @wolfwithcoffee on twitter.

About the Editor

Ashe Valisca

This year is Ashe's second year editing the Fang collection. He is a long time furry writer in the community both editing and writing. For the past decade he has worked on the writing track at AnthroCon working to nurture writers in the community attempting to put his English degrees to good use. Known mostly for his quirky teaching style and unorthodox editing style he delights in discovering the hidden potential in new authors.

Always willing to take a risk he specializes in Science Fiction and Fantasy, but will still write more conventional fiction. Ashe is always willing to push the boundaries with his writing willing to bring focus onto the darker parts of human nature—sometimes the good guy has to fail. Art imitates Life and he makes every attempt to make that true.

About the Artist

Mehndi

Ever since she was young Kate Rohn, or Mehndi as she's known in her art, has been fascinated with the world of art and animation. Hardly a day went by that she didn't spend time honing her craft, whether it was quick sketches inspired by everyday life or a complex painting of the family cat. She graduated with a Bachelors Degree in art from Carlow University. These days she spends her time lusting after the next big ink break through while maintaining an active freelance portfolio.

Lightning Source UK Ltd.
Milton Keynes UK
UKHW021025050321
379837UK00015B/1981